THE
KINGMAKER'S
REDEMPTION

HARRY PINKUS

BQB
North Carolina

The Kingmaker's Redemption
©2021 Harry Pinkus. All rights reserved.

Published in the United States by BQB Publishing
(an imprint of Boutique of Quality Books Publishing, Inc.)
www.bqbpublishing.com

Printed in the United States of America

ISBN 978-1-952782-16-9 (p)
ISBN 978-1-952782-17-6 (e)

Library of Congress Control Number: 2021937850

Book design by Robin Krauss, www.bookformatters.com
Cover design by Rebecca Lown, www.rebeccalowndesign.com
First editor: Caleb Guard
Second editor: Allison Itterly

ACKNOWLEDGEMENTS

I can't imagine anyone writing and publishing a novel on their own. So many people have contributed to making mine a reality. First and foremost, I want to thank my wife Jackie and son David for their love and encouragement throughout the process. As in my life, I couldn't have made it this far without them. I also want to acknowledge my Beta Readers: Kathy, Eric, Sue, Linda, and Patrick for their constructive critiques which steered my work in the right direction. Finally, I want to thank Terri and all the staff at BQB Publishing for bringing this project to life. Special thanks to my editors, Allison and Caleb, who taught me so much and guided me so adeptly to the finish line.

I would be remiss if I didn't recognize the influence that our American system of government had on the arc of this story. While flawed in many ways, democracy is ultimately dictated by the will of the people. The individual struggles of our fellow citizens to achieve liberty and justice within that system is the story of America and was the inspiration for this book.

CHAPTER 1

The band was playing "Happy Days Are Here Again" as the newly elected candidate proclaimed victory, smiling to the cheering crowd with both arms raised above his head like a victorious prizefighter. "Seashells and balloons! Seashells and balloons!" Jack said, quoting former basketball coach Al McGuire. Not that he would have been heard over the cheers anyway. These election victory celebrations were opportunities for revelry, not conversation.

Jack McKay had guided another candidate through the morass of a special election campaign and brought him home a winner. On to the state legislature for Brian Gordon. Jack had done the same for Bill Richards, the current assemblyman who had resigned mid-term due to ill health, thus necessitating the special election. The Liberty Party would surely be most appreciative. Jack had again saved the district from the dreaded Opposition, a fact which was underscored by a tap on his shoulder.

"Nice job, Jack," Randall Davies, the local Party chairman, bellowed as he pulled Jack into the hallway. "You've brought in another one."

There was Jack, at a little over six feet tall, handsome, with salt-and-pepper hair, standing toe to toe with Randall, who was at least five inches shorter, balding, with a paunch and an unlit cigar in his hand. The two looked like something straight from central casting for a film noir drama.

"It was particularly difficult this time. Your boy actually had an opponent."

Davies smiled. "Winning the unopposed races are equally

important. Your ability to keep people out of a race is a wonderful byproduct of your many successes."

"And the Party's clout in the area doesn't hurt either," admitted Jack.

"Don't sell yourself short, my boy. Power, money, and expertise are a winning formula. We supply the first two and you bring us home with the third."

"Some would call it an unholy alliance."

"Not at all." Davies smirked. "It's what moves our whole political system. Without influence, resources, and know-how, we'd only have ideas. And ideas are like an automobile—if you don't have gasoline and a driver they go nowhere."

"Wow, Randall. That's deep."

Jack knew full well that Davies's idea of resources and know-how included using any and all means necessary to achieve his objectives.

"So much for political theory," said Davies. "I've got some business to discuss with you. We'd like to engage your firm to run our candidate for Congress. The primary is just a few months off, and we need to get started before the Opposition gets organized."

The Reform Party had long struggled to gain a foothold in Wisconsin, and when the media dubbed them as the "Opposition," the name stuck.

"So, who will you be running?" Jack asked.

"My son, William," Davies said proudly.

His choice was an obvious one. Having his son in Congress would provide the perfect surrogate for Davies to achieve his objectives.

William was currently the head of the County Business Development Commission, an appointment his father had arranged by calling in a couple of markers. It was a visible enough position to get William's name out, and one that allowed him to curry favor with the voters. A few well-placed, revenue-producing programs went a long way.

"Unopposed in the Party primary, I assume," Jack said.

"Yes, and hopefully all the way to Washington," Davies said proudly.

"Randall, I'm sure the Opposition will run someone. They can't let a Congressional seat go unopposed."

"True, but if we pull out all the stops early on, they will only put out a sacrificial lamb. They won't waste a potentially strong candidate on a losing cause. We're shooting for virtually unopposed."

"Sounds like you've got this all figured out. Why do you need me?"

"You're the expert, remember? And why do I have to sell you on this?" Davies smiled. "Here's another guaranteed winner I'm dropping in your lap. A six-figure retainer to ride a shoe-in. Explain to me why you're not, at this very moment, waving a contract in my face."

"I just love it when you get angry," Jack joked. "I'll give it every consideration."

He offered his hand. Davies took it and held it firmly in his enormous mitt. "I will hear from you by the end of next week." It was a statement of fact, not a question.

"You will," Jack assured him.

Davies released Jack's hand and walked briskly away.

As Jack left the hall, he took a moment to reflect. He was a very skilled PR man. His specialization in getting candidates elected was unmatched, but had he turned into a puppet for the Liberty Party? He had worked for Reform Party candidates from time to time, but when the Liberty Party called, he always answered and ultimately delivered. The Liberty Party dominated the political landscape in southeast Wisconsin, gaining so much overwhelming influence that they had become known simply as "the Party," and Jack had played a major role in that. Was it something to be proud of or just a way to make a living? Either way, he had most assuredly made a fine living.

His PR firm now had sixteen associates with clients ranging from major consumer products companies to candidates for the school board. In Lakeville, if you wanted to promote your product or your candidacy, you contracted with McKay & Associates.

While the firm was well respected in all areas, Jack specialized in politics. He was most skilled in getting hired to promote a candidate. His reputation was such that just his being retained was often enough to keep the opposing candidates at home. Capitalizing on a "hire me or I'll find someone to run against you and make sure that they kick your ass" modus operandi, he intimidated numerous unopposed candidates into paying him to do nothing except to keep them unopposed. He rationalized that they got elected so they received fair value.

It did not, however, do much for his self-esteem, which was already waning. The cynical nature of the job was obviously taking a toll.

Jack hurried to his car in the crowded Marriott parking lot. It was a typical cool autumn night. This time of year, the brisk breeze off Lake Michigan was a sure sign that the seasons were changing. So, too, was his life.

The twenty-minute drive home gave him enough time to collect himself for the uncomfortable encounter that awaited him. It would be nothing unusual. A cool greeting from his wife Sandy, followed by a warm, adoring hug from his daughter Maya. It reminded him strangely of a hot fudge sundae, cold and hot all at once. That was his home life, a hot fudge sundae.

He was sleeping in the guest bedroom these days. Sandy was, as always, a warm and loving mom who took great pains to keep their home life as close to normal as possible. When Maya was around, Sandy was civil to Jack but showed no signs of affection toward him. Maya knew something was up but didn't seem to be overly fazed by it. Six-year-olds were very perceptive, but Jack was convinced that her interpretation of what was going on was that Mommy and Daddy were mad at each other over some grown-up issue and that it would pass. Sandy was not about to let it pass.

Their house was one of those nouveau Tudors. It was enormous, almost six thousand square feet, and made to look like a seventeenth-century country estate in the Cotswolds. He parked the Lexus in the three-car garage and entered his castle.

"Maya, it's time for bed," Sandy ordered after Jack received his welcome-home hug from his gleeful daughter.

"Daddy just got here. Five more minutes, please!" Maya pleaded, pulling on her pigtails. She was small but nonetheless formidable when pleading her case.

"Daddy will tuck you in and that will be your five minutes." Sandy had negotiated this before and was, like with this round, most often victorious.

Jack, the master dealmaker, was merely a bystander in these negotiations.

"Okay," Maya conceded as she headed off to get ready for bed.

Jack turned to Sandy and told her, "You're great at that." He meant it.

"If only I had that kind of influence with you," Sandy bemoaned. Her bright green eyes showed both anger and sadness.

"Listen, I have always respected your wishes," Jack said as he stood. Even his seven-inch height advantage was no match for Sandy's intensity.

"Let's not have that discussion right now. It will only escalate, and we need to get Maya to bed. Tonight's a school night, and it's already an hour after her bedtime."

"Fine, I'll put her to bed and then we can put the boxing gloves on," Jack said,

Sandy said nothing, but the tears in her eyes spoke volumes. Brokenness that had no tool for fixing. Where there was once a bright burning flame, he saw only a single ember, kept aglow for their daughter's sake.

As ordered, Maya had gone to her stuffed-animal-filled room and was lying in bed when Jack entered. "Daddy, tell me a story," she begged. Funny how all kids invoked that line to buy a few more minutes before lights out.

"Not tonight," Jack responded. "It's already way past your bedtime. I'll owe you an extra one tomorrow."

"All right, two stories tomorrow. Good, long ones with monsters and a princess and a turtle who's really a handsome prince."

"I thought it was supposed to be a frog who's really a prince."

"I like turtles better."

"You also like to stall. Good night, little lady."

"Good night, Daddy."

Sitting on the edge of Maya's bed, he kissed her, and then hugged her a little tighter than usual. Turning out the light, he closed the door and returned to the living room knowing that he had to go a few rounds with Sandy before he could rest.

"She's in bed now. Let the games begin," Jack kidded as he sat down in his usual spot, the leather armchair across from Sandy's position on the couch.

Sandy kept a straight face. "It's sad that you think this is in some way funny. Our marriage is ending. Our daughter will be devastated, and you see it as some kind of game."

"What do you want from me? I'm only trying to be civil. A little humor makes it easier for me to deal with all this."

"I didn't see it as humor so much as trivializing our sorry state of affairs."

"At least affairs aren't part of our problem."

"As far as I know," she said sarcastically as she poured herself a glass of Merlot.

"Now who's being pejorative," he shot back.

"Okay. Let civility reign."

"Sandy, I still love you and want a chance to try to save our marriage."

"I know you do, but your version of love and mine are not in sync. I need to be the center of your universe along with Maya, of course. Your career consumes you to the point where there is almost nothing left for her and me. It would be unfair for me to ask you to change, even if I thought it possible. Which I don't."

"So, I get no chance to prove you wrong?" Jack poured himself a drink.

"No. I want out and expect you to go through with the collaborative divorce meeting on Monday. If we do this thing cooperatively, we can save a lot of pain for all of us, especially Maya."

"Okay. But can I ask you one question?"

She nodded.

"Do you still love me?"

"I still love the memory of the man I married. Unfortunately, that man is long gone."

This was feeling more and more like a prizefight, Jack thought. Lefts, rights, rounds won and lost. He decided it was time to throw in the towel.

"Fine. Monday then. I have a late dinner meeting tomorrow, but I'll be home first to spend some quality time with Maya."

"Good. I'm going to bed."

Jack flipped on the TV and turned to the news. There was the victorious Brian Gordon with his hands thrust above his head like a football referee signaling a made field goal.

The newscaster reported, "The Liberty Party has retained the District Forty-Two seat in the state legislature. This win allows them to maintain their legislative majority." Jack drifted off to sleep knowing that he had had a successful day on at least one front.

CHAPTER 2

Jack awoke to the sound of the garage door closing. It was Sandy driving off to take Maya to school. Somehow during the night he had made his way from the living room to the bed in the sparsely decorated guest room. He showered and dressed in the bathroom he shared with Maya, then headed to the kitchen where he wolfed down a bowl of Cheerios and headed off to the office.

The morning commute was routine until he encountered a dump truck full of gravel that was peppering the cars behind it. He was very protective of his new Lexus and imagined the flying gravel creating a galaxy of scratches on the hood and windshield of his $60,000 automobile. Jack popped the accelerator and flew around the truck. The exhilarating rush of horsepower did much more to wake him up than the triple latte he'd picked up at the Starbucks drive-through. The sheriff's deputy had clocked him going eighty-five in a fifty-five-mile-per-hour zone.

"I was trying to pass a gravel truck that was spewing its load all over the freeway," Jack said.

"You passed him like he was standing still," the deputy responded. "I had you at eighty-five miles an hour."

"Sorry, I was just trying to save the paint job."

"It's my job to save lives. Your driver's license and registration, please."

Jack handed them over and watched in the rearview mirror as the deputy made his way back to his cruiser to run the plates and driver's information through the on-board computer. He returned a few moments later.

"Your record is clean, Mr. McKay. I'm letting you off with a warning. Next time try to stay within the speed limit when taking evasive action. By the way, the sheriff says hi."

Jack realized that his good fortune was due in large part to having run the sheriff's campaign. The sheriff must have overheard the deputy calling in the incident and ordered the warning. Thankfully, he hadn't run the opponent's campaign.

The offices of McKay & Associates were housed in a converted warehouse building on Bay Street on the downtown side of the harbor. The building had been home to the Greenfield Grain Company for nearly one hundred years. The company folded in the early sixties and the building stayed mainly vacant until 1975 when the area became the focus of the early gentrification movement. With over two hundred thousand square feet, it was the largest vacant building in the harbor area with a lake view. Its proximity to downtown made it perfect for conversion to loft offices and condos. Jack's firm had acquired a twenty-five hundred square foot space in 1995, two years after establishment of the firm.

McKay & Associates grew steadily in the nineties, and when the architectural firm next door closed in 1998, they expanded into that space, giving them a little over five thousand square feet. The offices were an open concept with exposed beams, painted pipes, and shiny industrial ductwork. The majority of the staff occupied high-tech cubicles arranged in pods. The key executives each had private offices with lake views. The two conference rooms were furnished in typical boardroom fashion: large, polished wood table with swivel chairs.

When Jack walked through the door that morning, he received a standing ovation from the staff. This was customary on the morning after a successful election outcome. It was a little awkward on those occasions when they represented several candidates running for various offices in the same election as invariably some won and some lost. But the unwritten rule was that the staff stood and applauded if anybody won.

"Well done, Jack," congratulated Peter Evans, the firm's managing partner. Peter was Jack's right-hand man, almost from the beginning. Jack elevated him to partner after five years, allowing him to buy a minority stake over time using a portion of his annual bonus.

"Thanks, Peter, but it was a team effort as always."

"Spoken like a twenty-game winner at an awards dinner."

"Clichés are the lifeblood of PR, you know that."

"Just calling them as I see 'em," Peter said, carrying on the gag.

"So, what do we have going today?" Jack asked, returning to business.

"The Consolidated Foods people have decided to go with a regional firm and are ready to meet. They want a full capabilities presentation. It's down to us and two other firms, one from Milwaukee and one from Chicago."

"The meat of the sandwich again.'" Jack alluded to the geographical irony. Lakeville was right between the two on the map and was often considered an unsophisticated buffer zone, as it was half the size of Milwaukee and about a tenth the size of Chicago.

Getting the analogy, Peter responded. "The meat's the best part." Jack hoped so. Landing the contract for opening six grocery stores would be huge. The grand opening events alone would generate over $100,000 worth of billable hours. And they had the home court advantage. No firm knew Lakeville the way McKay & Associates did. But knowing the market and the ability to reach it were not the same. They needed to impress upon the client that they really knew their stuff and had as much firepower as the big city boys.

"Their key execs are coming in from their Atlanta headquarters to lay out their plans for entering the market and to review our capabilities. A typical meet-and-greet. They've scheduled us in for eleven on Monday morning," Peter said.

"Crap!" Jack exclaimed. "I've got a commitment on Monday that's going to be almost impossible to break."

"We have to make that meeting," Peter huffed. "Their people will only be in town on Monday. It's then or not at all. I can handle it if you're busy."

"No, I'll be there. This is too important to miss. Sandy's going to have a fit." Jack had to be there. Peter was extremely capable, but Jack was the personality. No one could sell the services of McKay & Associates like McKay himself.

"Your meeting is with Sandy? Sorry to pry, but what's so important."

"We're getting a divorce," Jack said, slumping into his private office.

"I'm very sorry," Peter responded.

Jack knew it was no surprise. The rumors had been circulating for months. He closed the office door. His office was modern, like the rest of the company's except for the antique mahogany desk that had once belonged to his father. It was in terrific shape with just the right amount of wear to show it had been well used. Jack sat down at the desk and stared out the window at the harbor. All he heard was his assistant Donna rustling papers at her desk outside his office. Donna had long been the company cheerleader and den mother. She had joined the firm at the very beginning. At the outset she was the entire clerical staff. Her job grew as the company grew, eventually overseeing all of the office administrative functions. Jack made her his executive assistant, which allowed her to step back and enjoy some time off, something she seldom did.

His mood had turned sour. All of the exhilaration of the election victory ovation and making the finals of the Consolidated Foods deal was gone. How was he going to explain the need to change the meeting to Sandy? He told her he would make the session without fail. It would only serve as further evidence of his "business over family" attitude. He was certainly guilty of that most often, but this was a case of poor timing, not a conscious decision on his part.

The collaborative divorce session could be rescheduled without harm, he thought. The meeting in Chicago could not. The question was how to explain it to Sandy in a way that would not instigate another major battle. Ever the PR man, he would explain diplomatically that the circumstances, not his endeavors, created the scheduling conflict. He would clear his calendar to accommodate any mutually agreeable rescheduled date. In fact, this new contract, if won, stood to increase his net worth and therefore her share of their community property.

Gathering all of his arguments, he called Sandy on her cell phone. He knew full well she was going to be angry no matter how well he positioned the dilemma.

"Hi," he said when she answered. "I've got a problem that I need to discuss with you."

"We have lots of problems that need discussion. That's why we've hired divorce attorneys," she shot back.

"Funny that you should bring that up—"

"You're not canceling for Monday, are you?" she interrupted.

"Well, yes," Jack said rather sheepishly.

"Unbelievable. It took you less than a day to break your pledge. This really pisses me off. So, what's your well-concocted excuse?" Her voice rose several octaves.

"The well-concocted excuse, as you call it, is very real. Consolidated Foods has set a meeting in Chicago for Monday. If we don't attend, we're out of the running for a huge contract."

"Send Peter," she countered.

"I can't. We need all hands on deck for this one. My name is on the door, remember? My presence is required."

"Your presence is required at our meeting too," Sandy reminded him.

"Listen, I will clear my calendar for any alternate day or time. Cut me a little slack on this, please. I *will* make this up to you." Jack pleaded, angrily tossing his notepad on the desk.

"I *will* see what I can do," she said, mocking him. "As far as making it up to me, I'll just add it to the long list of 'make goods' you owe me. Expect to pay off on all of your markers as we come up with a settlement. Jack, there is a price for everything, and your turn at the checkout counter is coming." Sandy's tone was extremely edgy, almost ominous.

Jack breathed a small sigh of relief. He knew his day of reckoning was coming, but he had apparently averted the issue for the moment. He now had to collect himself so he would be able to proceed with the Consolidated Foods meeting. Peter would be relieved.

Jack's assistant buzzed the intercom. "Jack, Lindsay Revelle is holding on line three for you."

"Thanks, Donna," he answered. Curious as to what the call could possibly be about, he paused for a few seconds and then pressed the line-three button. "This is Jack McKay."

A deep, warm voice on the other end said, "Mr. McKay, this is Lindsay Revelle. You probably don't know who I am, but I'm considering a run for Congress and I'd like to talk to you about it."

"First, I do know who you are, and second, call me Jack."

"Well, Jack. Will you take a meeting with me when I tell you that I am going to run against the Liberty Party candidate? Oh, and please call me Lindsay."

"Lindsay, we have represented many candidates from the Reform Party."

"The word on the street is that William Davies will be the candidate for the Party. I assumed your close working relationship with his father and the Party would preclude you from representing anyone else."

"It wouldn't, and if you assumed I wasn't available, why are you calling?" Jack was somewhat puzzled.

"I was hoping you hadn't committed to a candidate yet and that you had an open mind."

"I haven't and I do," Jack assured him.

"Good. A meeting then?"

"Sure. When would you like to get together?"

"How does Monday sound?"

Jack laughed out loud.

"Did I say something funny, Jack?" Revelle said quizzically.

"No, Lindsay, not at all. It's just that Monday's schedule has been a collection of conflicts for me all day. How about lunch on Wednesday?"

"Lunch is fine with me, but do you want to be seen in public with me? Your Party friends might get uncomfortable."

"You seem a lot more concerned about my relationship with the Party than I am. Besides, I could be meeting with you to talk you out of running against their guy or just seeking campaign advice from a Rhodes Scholar in political science."

"You don't need any advice from me on campaigning. That's why I want to meet with you. I'm the one seeking counsel."

"Wednesday lunch it is," he said.

They made plans to meet at Kathryn's, a delicious soul food restaurant. Jack was still pondering the phone call. Would he actually run a candidate with ideas who held real promise as a public servant? Randall Davies would string him up by his balls.

Jack returned to his desk and moved on to his emails, which were mostly the usual newsletters, press releases, and spam. A press release from the County Business Development Commission caught his eye. PetroMark Oil, a large oil and gas company, was looking for a location for a Great Lakes depot where tankers would off-load fuel that would ultimately be distributed to their Midwest gas stations. Lakeville was a potential site. McKay & Associates had represented PetroMark when they entered the market five years ago, and now they were considering working on William Davies's campaign. The same William Davies who, for the last three years, chaired the County Business Development Commission.

He and Peter should stay on top of this one. PetroMark might need a little PR assistance, given the environmentally sensitive area of the harbor. Under the circumstances, young William would need to be guided through a potential political disaster if the PetroMark project encountered substantive local opposition and he was on the wrong side of public opinion.

"Peter, can you join me for a minute?" Jack squawked into the intercom.

"Be right in," Peter replied.

Jack started in before Peter had made it all of the way through the doorway. "Did you see the tidbit on PetroMark looking for a depot site?"

"Yes. And I spoke with Rick Cartwright about it yesterday. He said they would like to work with us and we're going to chat again tomorrow."

"I suppose you didn't feel this was worthy of mentioning." Jack was visibly irritated and gave Peter a most disapproving stare.

"I was saving it for the staff briefing at ten. We always review these sorts of things at the briefing. It only happened yesterday after you left, and I've seen you for all of five minutes this morning. I'm not hiding anything, if that's what the look is supposed to imply."

"It's just that big, new opportunities are the things that we live for. They are the 'breaking down the doors to deliver the news' kind of occasions," Jack said in his most professorial tone. "Particularly when they're tied into a political candidate that we've been asked to represent."

"You mean William Davies is in on this?"

"Here. Look at this." Jack showed Peter the press release email.

"Hmmm. Could be a conflict for us. What's your take?"

"It's an ethical dilemma for sure. Legally it may or may not be a problem. Regardless, if we take on Davies's campaign, we should recommend that he recuse himself from the PetroMark project negotiations. "

"If?" Peter said in disbelief.

"Yes, *if*. We may want to go with the underdog candidate on this one."

"Who's the candidate?"

"Lindsay Revelle."

"Lindsay Revelle? He can't win."

"We have backed a few long shots in the past."

Peter was turning red. "Not like this one. Win or lose, the Party will blackball us until the twenty-second century. We'd be out of the political campaign business, and since the majority of our corporate clientele are affiliated with the Party, we'd be committing professional hara-kiri. And furthermore, if Lindsay Revelle opposes the PetroMark project, we lose on all counts. How can this be good for the firm?"

"As you said, we'll discuss it at the staff meeting," Jack said dismissively.

Peter left without a word. Jack envisioned steam whistling from Peter's ears.

Could I really align myself with Lindsay Revelle? Jack pondered. Revelle certainly had all the right stuff: education, physical presence, progressive politics, and strong ties to the community. Even a reputation as a star basketball player. He rolled all of it around in his mind. Was it something he might really enjoy and reinvigorate his passion for politics or merely some quixotic attempt to save his self-esteem? One thing was certain. It would surely be a return to the roots of his political upbringing.

Growing up in a working-class home, in the Milwaukee south side neighborhood of Bay View, he adopted the belief early on that a well-organized group representing the common man could use the political process to compete with big money interests on legislative issues.

His father, Raymond, had been a foreman and union representative at Bucyrus-Erie, the company that manufactured giant industrial cranes in nearby Cudahy. Jack's father instilled a strong work ethic in him early on. Jack had many chores, and he cut lawns and shoveled snow for spending money. It often seemed like his father was his foreman too. Actually, his father wanted a better life for Jack and recognized his ability, if not the drive in him. He used to say, "Jack, you need to go out on a limb sometimes, that's where the fruit is."

His father also introduced Jack to Sir Arthur Conan Doyle's Sherlock Holmes. Together, they watched all the old movies with Basil Rathbone and Nigel Bruce. Jack read all the original short stories and books. He was particularly influenced by Sherlock's oft-repeated saying, "You see, but you do not observe." He took it to heart. Attention to details helped him in school, on the basketball court, and in business.

His father's union involvement in those days gave Jack insights into their political power. Candidates got nowhere without their support. How times had changed. Union members had become much more independent, seldom voting as a bloc. They had also gotten much more conservative, coming curiously close in ideology to the big money interests they once opposed. It occurred to Jack that the African American and Hispanic political groups had the potential to wield political clout in much the same way as the unions once did. It was a detail that weighed heavily, and it reminded him of his father.

His intercom buzzed with another incoming call from Donna. "The staff is waiting for you in the large conference room for the briefing," she reminded him.

"I'm on the way."

When Jack walked into the crowded conference room, Peter was passing out copies of the County Business Development Commission's press release on the PetroMark project to the six-person team seated around the large wood conference table with a pile of file folders and a laptop in front of each team member. Jack took a seat, grabbing coffee and a sweet roll on the way.

Peter began the briefing. "As you all know, we have represented PetroMark in the past. I spoke with Rick Cartwright, their executive VP, and they'd like us to represent them on this. We would be working directly with Don Buckley, their VP of marketing. Jack and I feel there may be a conflict if we choose to represent William Davies for Congress. His commission is negotiating with PetroMark for the land, tax concessions, etc. Thoughts?"

"Is there a legal conflict for Davies?" Carol Meyers asked. She was the head of McKay's Marketing Communications Department and effectively number three in the organization.

"I don't think so," interjected Jack.

"Then why would it be a problem for us?" Carol asked.

"It's not that it would be a problem for us," Jack responded. "It's because it could be a problem for both of the clients by creating the appearance of collusion. We would be the connection between them. With us being tied to both, they in turn would be tied to each other. That perception would damage both of their causes. Not exactly the positive PR they would be looking for from us."

"I see your point. Which client do we choose?" Carol asked.

"Jack has another variable to throw into the hopper," Peter interjected somewhat sarcastically.

Jack laid out the details and implications of Lindsay Revelle's call. When he finished his scenario, he could tell not everyone was sold.

"So," he said in admission, "we have quite a maze to traverse."

Peter was the first to respond. "It seems to me the best option is just to sign on with PetroMark and sit out the campaign. They can be a lucrative, long-term client whereas the candidates could be a once and done deal. Even if they win and continue to use us in the future, it still doesn't match what PetroMark can mean to us."

The heads around the table were bobbing up and down in agreement, except for Jack's.

Peter looked at Jack quizzically. "You don't agree?"

"It's definitely the safest approach," Jack asserted. "I'd like to have my meeting with Lindsay Revelle before we decide. If he doesn't present some compelling reason for us to run his campaign, I'll go along with the group. The more I think about it, the less I want to work with Davies. This situation gives us the perfect out with PetroMark being a long-standing client."

If Jack knew anything about Peter, he knew his business associate was squaring him up, deep down preparing for battle should Jack try to impose his own will on the firm.

CHAPTER 3

As promised, Jack hurried home from work to spend time with Maya. As he drove, Jack reflected on how he and Sandy had met nine years earlier when Jack was doing the PR for an event to commemorate a new wing at the art museum. Sandra Freeman, "call me Sandy," was the assistant to the managing director of the museum. They had worked together planning the event and took an immediate liking to one another.

She was smart, funny, and very attractive. Jack had long been a bachelor and was not easily infatuated. In Sandy, however, he found that certain someone who totally captivated him. She, too, was taken in. He was tall, dark, and handsome, not to mention accomplished. The romance moved quickly. They were living together within a few weeks and married less than a year later. Now they were adversaries in a crumbling marriage.

Jack arrived as Maya was finishing her favorite meal, macaroni and cheese. Sandy nodded hello and vacated the kitchen quickly when he arrived.

"Daddy, want some mac and cheese? Mommy made lots."

"No thanks, honey. I have a dinner meeting later." Jack grabbed a Pabst Blue Ribbon from the refrigerator instead.

"I thought we were going to have a story night and everything." Maya pouted.

"We are. My meeting doesn't start until after your bedtime."

"You work too much." Maya sounded very much like her mother.

Jack couldn't disagree. "You're right. But I'm home now so let's have some fun."

"It's story time," she squealed as they adjourned to her bedroom.

Jack spent the next hour and a half by Maya's bed telling her stories. Some he read, some he made up. They all had happy endings, which, like all fathers, he wanted Maya's life story to have. He promised her silently he would do everything he possibly could so his little princess lived happily ever after.

After tucking her in and telling her the story of the turtle who became a handsome prince, he turned out the light and headed to the garage. On the way out, he encountered Sandy in the kitchen cleaning up.

"I'm really sorry about Monday. I know it will be a hassle rescheduling. It was unintentional, I assure you," he said in his most conciliatory manner.

"I've reset it for Wednesday at two. I trust you can make it."

"I have a twelve-thirty lunch date. It will be tight, but I can make it work."

"See that you do."

Jack resisted the temptation to respond. It would only end in rancor and cause him to be late for his dinner meeting. He left saying nothing further.

―――――――――

Jack accepted for the first time that his marriage was actually over. He had hoped somehow, someway he could save it. His feelings for her hadn't gone away but Sandy was so bitter and full of blame directed at Jack, and there would be nothing he could do to stop it. It was time to move on, and no one would be a better sounding board than his dinner companion, Mickey Martin.

Mickey had been the first big-name client of Jack's firm. In fact, he was Jack's first client period. Jack moved to Lakeville from Milwaukee in 1992 after a four-year stint with Blackburn & Benjamin. B&B was the premier PR agency in Milwaukee and probably the entire Midwest. Jack had always wanted to be involved in the political campaign side of the firm but was stymied by his boss, Norman Dudley, who ran that department and didn't care for Jack at all. Jack was the young up-and-comer, and Norman Dudley was old school. They clashed at every intersection. Jack knew if politics were to be in his immediate future, it would not be at B&B.

Jack's big break came when Mickey called and announced he was running for Circuit Court Judge in Lakeville and wanted him to run the campaign. Jack jumped at the chance and bolted from B&B to open McKay & Associates.

Mickey was an old family friend, having met Jack's father when Mickey defended some of the union workers involved in a highly publicized picket-line scuffle during a labor dispute. In those days, Mickey was ever the people's champion, always rising up to protect the oppressed and unfairly accused. He relished being the underdog in a case. His reputation grew after winning numerous high-profile cases against enormous odds. He was a larger-than-life character, sort of a combination of Rocky Balboa and Robin Hood.

As esteemed as he was as a defense attorney, it was as a circuit court judge where Mickey did his best and most important work. He was known throughout the county as the most fair and impartial arbiter of justice in the court system. It was rare to find a judge so universally praised by both defense and prosecuting attorneys.

In his first election campaign, Mickey had fierce competition from the Party. Jack was masterful in exploiting Mickey's reputation as the people's champion fighting against the big political machine. Ironically, that campaign ultimately brought the Party to Jack's doorstep, retainer in hand. Jack's first and possibly greatest political accomplishment was getting Mickey elected to the bench in 1993. Fifteen years later, Mickey would be standing on the other side of the same bench.

Easing the Lexus onto the freeway, Jack dialed Mickey's number on his cell phone.

Mickey answered quickly, "Jack, how are you?"

"How did you know it was me?"

"The powers of deductive reasoning, my dear Watson," Mickey said in a poor imitation. "I was expecting your call. I seldom get any others except solicitations, so it was a good guess. Anyway, I had my housekeeper program special rings for certain callers. Amazing devices these new phones. Even a blind man like me can have caller ID."

Mickey teased about modern technology even though he'd had one for years.

"What would you like to eat? I can bring something in, or we can go out," Jack offered.

"Let's go to Scarfido's. I'd love a pizza and some garlic bread."

"Sounds great. I'll be there in fifteen minutes."

Mickey was legally blind, the result of a horrific car accident seven years ago on Valentine's Day. He was an alcoholic, and that night he was driving home drunk from a romantic evening out with his wife, Dolores. Mickey had lost control of the car and drove into a ditch, flipping his Oldsmobile over four times. Dolores was thrown from the car and killed. Mickey suffered multiple broken bones and head trauma, rendering him almost completely blind. He endured a long, painful recovery in the hospital followed by an equally painful court battle on felony charges for drunk driving and manslaughter. Most of all, he suffered the painful loss of his wife and family.

Dolores had been the center of his universe for more than thirty years. She shared his life in every way. On that fateful night, he'd not only lost the love of his life, but he'd lost the love of his daughter, Roberta. Bobbie, as she was called, could not forgive him and subsequently moved to Madison. They had not spoken since.

His life was shattered. His wife was dead, his daughter was

estranged, his career and eyesight were gone, and he only had himself and his alcoholism to blame. After a successful plea bargain, Mickey did thirty-nine months for involuntary manslaughter in a minimum-security facility in Allenton. It was there where he started to put his life back together. After overcoming the physical effects of withdrawal, he attended Alcoholics Anonymous meetings to work on his sobriety and emotional scars. His salvation was the only way to acknowledge Dolores's sacrifice. Mickey studied the disease and wrote articles on alcoholism treatment and worked to draft legislation to fund programs that assisted the afflicted and their families. He had found a new purpose for his life.

When Jack drove up in front of Mickey's, His Honor was sitting on the porch in one of his unusual costumes enjoying the beautiful fall evening. Mickey had always been the Antichrist of sartorial splendor, but after he lost thirty pounds in prison and stopped drinking, his appearance got downright silly. Mickey hated to spend money, particularly on clothes, so he refused to buy anything new that fit his current physique. So, there he was, all of five-six, looking like a fourteen-year-old boy going to a junior high school dance wearing his father's blue blazer. A green- and white-striped shirt over madras plaid pants completed the comical ensemble.

"It's nice to see you, Mickey. Dressed to the nines as always," Jack opined.

"I wish I could return the compliment," Mickey joked. Mickey's blindness wasn't total. He lived in a visual fog, only able to make out vague shapes and varying degrees of light. He saw just enough to allow him to live on his own. Fiercely independent, he took great pride in navigating without assistance.

"You see a whole lot more than you let on. I wish I had your powers of observation."

"And my good looks," Mickey playfully added.

"Enough with the amusing pleasantries. Let's get going. I'm

hungry and I have some serious stuff to discuss with you." Jack took Mickey's arm.

"My counsel comes at significant cost," said Mickey.

"So I'm buying dinner again?"

"Yes. My pension from prison is meager," Mickey lamented tongue-in-cheek.

"Are you kidding me? You still have your confirmation money. I'm only buying dinner because I feel sorry for you, you cantankerous, old sot."

"Insults. You expect me to be an enjoyable dinner companion and to give you the benefit of my infinite wisdom and you insult me. I should turn around and go back in the house."

"You won't."

"Why?"

"Because you're hungry and I'm buying. Besides, you know I love you."

"I do, but I still won't sleep with you."

It was good to know the playful repartee had never been lost.

On the way to Scarfido's Pizza, Jack laid out the firm's dilemma with PetroMark and Davies. Then he rounded out the story with the call from Lindsay Revelle.

"Well," Mickey said, pausing for emphasis, "Peter's solution is certainly the easiest and most prudent. You can probably get off the hook with the Party citing your ongoing representation with PetroMark. Randall Davies will most likely hit the ceiling, but you'd be able to move on without burning that bridge. That is, if you don't sign on with Revelle."

"Agreed."

"But you seem intrigued with Revelle. Is it that you feel an affinity toward him because you were both jocks who turned out to have more to offer than a sweet fifteen-foot jump shot?"

"First of all, I rode the pines for four years in Madison. I'd hardly call myself a jock. Lindsay Revelle is a Rhodes Scholar. A well-respected man of ideas. The fact he averaged over twenty points per game in college and was known as 'Ring the Bell Revelle' has nothing to do with it."

"Spoken like a true PR man. Are you sure he hasn't hired you already?"

Without answering, Jack pulled into a parking space in front of the restaurant and took Mickey inside. Scarfido's was a Lakeville classic. It opened in 1953 and hadn't been updated since. Top-notch thin-crust pizza had made them the local favorite among those who preferred the wafer-thin, crisp variety to the deep-dish Chicago style. The crowded bar area still smelled of cigarette smoke from the past. The feisty waitresses scurried about the dining room serving pizza and drinks to hungry patrons seated at tables and booths covered in plastic tablecloths.

They made their way to their customary corner table in the back of the dining room. The waitress knew they didn't need menus. Mickey agreed to share their usual, a large cheese and sausage along with an order of garlic bread, but with one caveat. "I'll share, but no pepperoni." Getting down to the business at hand, Mickey put both hands on the table and leaned towards Jack.

Listen. The real question is whether or not you're willing to risk your livelihood for what you believe in. And frankly, you're not even sure what you believe in since you haven't yet met with Revelle. You must be expecting a Revelle-ation," he quipped.

Jack smiled. "Your puns are getting worse in your old age. It's not that all of a sudden. If I've gotten religion, it's because I need a change from doing what's expected or easy. I want to enjoy the challenge which can only come when the outcome is in doubt."

"Sounds like religion to me."

"Come on, Mickey. I'm talking about changing my life here."

"Why the sudden revelation? Sorry, I mean new direction for

your life. Is there something more going on here you haven't shared with me?" Mickey said

"Well, there is one small thing. Sandy wants a divorce," Jack replied sarcastically.

"Small thing, hmm. I'd hate for you to omit any big things."

"That's it for now. What's your advice?"

"Stay away from the pepperoni. It'll talk back to you all night. The last time I had the pepperoni, I drank an entire bottle of Maalox."

"Mickey!" Jack growled, wanting Mickey to get back to the subject at hand.

"OK. I'm giving no marriage counseling, but it certainly complicates matters. You're going to have to seek advice on that subject elsewhere. I will, however, be watching out for Maya's wellbeing. I take that responsibility of being a Godfather very seriously. As far as your career is concerned, you obviously need to meet with Revelle and decide if he is the man you think he is. If in fact he is, you owe your associates an in-depth explanation of your position and together you need to decide what's best for all concerned. They have a tremendous stake in all of this, particularly Peter. The long-term implications for the firm are enormous."

"You're right on all counts.

They laughed and made small talk for the balance of the evening. Mickey never let on, but Jack could feel the worry in his voice. The road ahead was going to be rough. Some very deep potholes were approaching at breakneck speed.

CHAPTER 4

Deputy District Attorney Faye Villarreal had moved quickly up the ranks at the DA's office displaying a formidable combination of dogged determination and skill. Her rapid rise in the department was unusual for a woman, almost unheard of for a woman of color. Unlike the other disadvantaged Latinas she grew up with, Faye had been able to graduate from college and get a law degree. Her parents worked multiple jobs to provide the financial wherewithal for Faye to achieve her goals. Thankfully, her father had lived long enough to see her graduate.

She was sitting at her desk working on a motion for a reckless endangerment case when her phone rang. It was her boss, District Attorney Ted Erickson.

"Faye, can you join me for a quick meeting in my office?"

"Sure, be right in." Faye headed down the hall, her boot heels making a rapid clicking sound that echoed off the marble walls as she briskly made her way to Ted's office.

The DA's office was teaming with activity. Friday mornings were always busy as everyone tried to get out on time for the weekend. It was a large department, over forty lawyers and staffers. As the county seat, they handled the caseload for sixteen separate municipalities. Faye stepped into the room and took a deep breath. The DA was seated behind his desk, with Detective Jake Mallory from the police department, and two men whom she didn't know all seated in a half-circle around it.

"Faye, I'd like you to meet Special Agents David Harris and

Roger Obregon from the State Department of Justice," the DA said.

"Nice to meet you both." She shook hands with each of the men standing at the table.

The DA closed the door and motioned to David Harris, who was obviously the senior official of the two agents, to begin.

Everyone but Harris sat down. He straightened his tie before speaking. It was a typical government official's "now let's get down to business" gesture. "Our department is launching a major offensive against both the possession of and the distribution of child pornography. You would be astounded at the number of people engaged in child porn—the ones who entice and rape young children, the ones who produce the material for profit and, probably the saddest of all, the poor slobs who create the market with their insatiable hunger for pornographic material.

"This initiative has been given a top priority by the attorney general with the full support of the governor's office. Even though we almost never convene a Grand Jury in Wisconsin, we feel using them under these circumstances demonstrates to everyone just how seriously we're viewing these offenses and the resources we're applying to bring the offenders to justice.

"The task force we've created is focusing on several communities in the state where we suspect this activity is taking place. Lakeville is one of those. It will be our job to conduct the investigation and supply local authorities, like your office, with the evidence needed for warrants, arrests, and convictions."

As he finished, Harris motioned to Erickson that the floor was his.

"We will make this effort a priority for our community." Erickson added, speaking for the police chief as well. "You will have the full cooperation and participation of all forms of law enforcement."

"Thank you," replied Harris appreciatively. "We will be conducting this investigation on the ground in Lakeville's schools, businesses, and on its streets. With the help of federal authorities, we will be checking for violations using the mail and, of course, the Internet."

Erickson turned to Faye. "Deputy Villarreal, you will be the liaison to the task force from our office. Detective Mallory will do the same for the police department. You will devote as much time and resources as possible in support of this operation and work in concert on any cases in our jurisdiction. The two of you will be responsible for keeping the DOJ and me up to speed." Faye was exhilarated to be at the center of this investigation.

"We'll be in touch once we get things rolling," said Harris. "I know you will be instrumental in making this effort pay off."

After they all exchanged business cards, the DA opened the door and dismissed the group. He motioned to Faye to remain.

"This is going to be high-profile stuff, Faye. It's an election year, and everyone from the governor on down will be watching. Whatever happens, we will do this by the book. I don't want anyone to be railroaded or let off the hook just to make the politicians happy. These are very serious crimes in my eyes, and people who prey on children, particularly sex offenders, will incur the full fury of this department."

"Understood." Faye held back a smile. She had been singled out by her boss for a weighty assignment.

"Good. Keep me posted on any developments."

"Will do."

Faye headed back to her desk barely able to keep her composure. While the subject was a most serious one, she had waited a long time to be able to strut her stuff. She was determined to show the DA he had made the right choice. As she arrived at her desk, the phone rang. It was her mother.

"How ya doin', hun?" Her mother, Alice, often spoke in contractions and fragmented sentences.

"Great, Mom. Just got a nice assignment from the boss."

"When'ya gonna be home?"

"About six, I think. Anything wrong?"

"Nope," she said, "I'll see you soon." Then she hung up.

Faye couldn't wait to go home to see her daughter, Abby. She was grateful that her mother could watch Abby every day after she got home from kindergarten. She had thought working her way through law school was tough, but having a young child, a demanding job, and no significant other was definitely tougher. Having Alice's help on weekdays was a godsend.

"What's up for the weekend?" Jill asked as she walked into Faye's office. She had been working as Faye's assistant for the past year and a half and they had already developed a nice rapport, although Jill occasionally forgot about the line between business and personal interaction.

"Quiet night at home tonight with Abby and then we're hosting a play date with her friends tomorrow afternoon."

"Good for you," Jill said. "By the way, what was going on in the DA's office? Looked like something very important." She was always one to probe.

"The door was closed for a reason," Faye scolded gently.

"OK. I'll go back to my cubicle and make up something for the gossip hounds at the water cooler," she teased.

"You'd do that anyway. Seriously, it's a confidential matter like so many other confidential matters that end up in this department. And you'll know more when it becomes a case. You'll be in it up to your elbows. For now, that's the story."

"You're not mad about my asking, are you?"

"Not if you drop it," warned Faye.

"Got it."

Faye really liked Jill, but sometimes she needed a stop sign. Happily, Jill realized enough was enough.

The motion Faye had started on before the meeting was completed on time, as were the other items on her Friday to-do list. She left at five-thirty for what promised to be a relaxing weekend, knowing full well as soon as the justice guys got started, her free time would vanish.

CHAPTER 5

Jack and Maya arrived at the Pancake House a little after eight. As part of their weekly ritual, Maya ordered the buttermilk pancakes. Jack wasn't sure whether she liked the pancakes on merit or merely as a conveyance for the maple syrup she smothered them in. Sandy wouldn't approve of all of the sugar, but Jack didn't mind spoiling her every now and then. Since he'd been watching his cholesterol, Jack had an egg white omelet and dry whole grain toast.

"Where are we going after pancakes?" Maya inquired.

"The laundry is next. Then to the grocery and finally the hardware store," he replied.

"Oh," Maya sighed.

"You sound disappointed."

"We're not going to any kid places."

"Where would you like to go?"

"The zoo," she shouted.

"Sweetheart, it's too cold for the zoo. How about the toy store?" Jack was employing the old parental argument avoider, saying no by offering an alternative.

"OK, but I get to buy something. Right?"

The master negotiator had just been bested by a six-year-old. "Yes, you do."

They finished breakfast, scrubbed the stickiness off Maya's hands, and headed off to the laundry. Jack dropped off and picked up shirts, suits, and ties each week. He never subscribed, at all, to business casual. The thought of "blue jean" Fridays made him cringe. It was also why Mickey's getups drove him nuts.

After picking up a few groceries, they headed to the hardware store.

"What are we doing here?" Maya asked.

"Getting a few things for Mickey. I promised him I would do a couple of repairs at his place this afternoon."

"Can I go?" she requested.

"No, you and Mommy have plans."

"I want to go to Mickey's," she implored. Maya loved Mickey. Jack's parents had passed away before she was born, and Sandy's were retired in the Milwaukee suburb of Shorewood, so Mickey was her local doting grandpa. She also loved Molly, Mickey's adorable Golden Retriever.

"Sorry, honey," said Jack. "We can go next time."

"Soon?"

"Yes, Maya, soon."

They paid for the hardware and off to the toy store they went. Jack was overwhelmed by the mega-store stocked with toys, board games, radio-controlled cars, bikes, furniture, everything a child could imagine. Two dolls, a coloring book, and Disney DVD later, they headed back home. They'd had a wonderful morning full of father and daughter togetherness. It was so hard for Jack to contain the guilt he felt knowing the pain he and Sandy would soon be inflicting on this lovely little girl.

Jack dropped Maya off at home and proceeded to Mickey's place. The door was unlocked, so he went into the hallway where he was greeted by Molly. As always, she spun in circles on the floor in front of him, squealing with delight.

"Some watchdog you've got here," he yelled.

"She knows you, remember," Mickey responded from the kitchen. "You hungry?"

"No, I had a big breakfast out with Maya," Jack called out as he headed into the kitchen.

Mickey made his way into the kitchen through a well-organized furniture arrangement designed to eliminate as many obstacles for him as possible. The kitchen had been arranged so Mickey would always know exactly where everything was. He had to amend the various room configurations from time to time after bumping into the same pieces of furniture multiple times.

After a brief coughing spell, Mickey responded, "Good, there wasn't enough for two anyway. Sit with me while I eat." Years of hard drinking and heavy smoking had taken a toll on Mickey even though he'd quit both while in prison.

Jack sat on one of the high stools at the counter and watched Mickey finish preparations on a Dagwood sandwich. Two thick slices of French bread slathered in mayonnaise and topped with turkey, ham, cheese, lettuce, and tomato.

"There's enough on there to feed all three of us and have left-overs," Jack scolded.

"Must be my eyesight," Mickey mused.

"Well, I got the hinge and the caulk. What are my assignments?"

"Keep me company while I eat, and I'll return the favor while you work."

"Seems fair."

"I've given a lot of thought to your dilemma," said Mickey. "Surprisingly, I still recommend listening to Peter. Your professional life will be much less complicated. Goodness knows what's in store for you in this divorce. I'm not usually one to back away from a confrontation, and I certainly believe in fighting for what you believe in, but Christ man, you can only fight battles on so many fronts."

"With all due respect, how do you know what I can handle?" Jack's eyes narrowed, showing his displeasure at being scolded.

"Handling it and doing what's best are not mutually exclusive. Seems to me you're going to need the income to underwrite the divorce. Kissing off the PetroMark revenue and the Davies' retainer for what Revelle can afford to pay is foolish." Mickey was dutifully fulfilling his role as mentor.

Jack's tone shifted from annoyed to sarcastic. "I thought you were the champion of the underdog and the common man. Lindsay Revelle should have you writing speeches and twisting the arms of every political contact you have."

"I intend to do just that. It's just your involvement I'm against. This will not be good for you, Jack."

"We'll see," Jack said, wanting to change the subject. "Which door needs the new hinge?"

"The one between the library and the living room." Mickey had said his piece and they both decided to let the subject rest, at least for the moment.

Jack loved Mickey's house. It was almost a century old and very warm and inviting. The high ceilings were set off by intricate crown moldings. Each room had architectural details of some kind: built-in cabinets, beams, or bay windows with window seats. The house even had three fireplaces.

The neighborhood was also charming. It was a long-standing residential area called Point Ridge. It was situated on a bluff just above downtown. People in the neighborhood walked to the nearby shops, restaurants, and movie theaters, and often stopped along the way to chat with neighbors. No wonder Dolores and Mickey had lived here forever, and, thankfully, Mickey was still able to continue living there given his limitations. His neighbors were a constant source of friendship and support.

Jack fixed the door hinge in the oak-lined library and recaulked the bathtub adjacent to Mickey's bedroom. All in all, the repairs took about an hour. After cleaning up, he found Mickey napping in front of the TV in the den. Looking around the room, Jack realized, once he moved out Mickey really needed someone to take care of him on a regular basis. Unfortunately, Molly could only provide companionship. Knowing full well this would be an uphill battle, he decided to table that discussion for another time and sat down on the chair near the fireplace. When he turned the TV off, Mickey awoke.

"Finished?"

"Yep. Nothing to it. And thanks for keeping me company."

"What do I owe you?"

"I'll put it on your tab."

"I have a tab?"

"Yes, and it's quite a tidy sum."

"Don't tell me. I'd probably have to declare bankruptcy."

"Sure, you will," Jack teased. "Anyway, let's change the subject. Have you heard anything from Bobbie?"

Jack knew this was going to be painful, but he felt that if he didn't inquire it would seem like he didn't care. Besides, if Mickey eventually needed care, she would need to be involved.

"Nothing, I'm afraid. We haven't spoken since the accident. I've called her office and cell phone dozens of times over the years and she won't take my calls. Her home number is unlisted."

"What about a letter?"

"Tried that. Came back unopened. I understand why she's mad, but I thought we could at least fight about it. This silent treatment is the ultimate punishment. The thing is, she gets nothing positive out of it. I would do absolutely anything to get her back, but I don't know what to do."

"Keep trying. I know she'll come around eventually." Jack realized his advice must have sounded trite.

"Some PR guy you are. The best suggestion you have for swaying an opinion is 'keep trying.' I know she'll come around eventually.

It's been almost seven years since her mother died. How long do I have to wait for a wound to heal?" They'd had this conversation many times before.

Mickey was almost pleading to Bobbie as if she were there. He was also pleading with Jack to help. This was not new. Mickey had often lamented the same thing to Jack.

Jack got up from his chair and sat down on the couch next to Mickey. He put his hand on Mickey's shoulder and said in his most comforting voice, "Unfortunately, as we've discussed before, you have to wait until she's ready, and apparently she's not there yet. Have you recently tried to contact any of her friends or former associates in the public defender's office?"

"Yes, she's even shut them off. I guess she decided long ago that she needed a clean break. No more Lakeville, no more public defenders, no more old friends, and no more Mickey." He was sounding more and more dejected as the discussion went on.

"Do you have any information on how her private practice is going?"

"Miles Darien had a case with her a couple of months ago. She seemed fine to him. That was all. You know Miles, don't you?"

"He's your private investigator, isn't he?"

"Yes."

"Actually I met him at one of your parties. He was quite flamboyant for a PI, I thought. Nice though. What's his story?"

"Let's see. PhD in forensic science, gay, Jewish, former left-wing radical, ex-police crime lab guy, just your typical Lakeville, Wisconsin, resident."

"Quite a résumé. How'd he end up here and in a crime lab?"

"Well, he was hired on a consultancy by the police department. It was for a year to augment the department while they sought a permanent hire. He met a guy and decided to stay in town when the consultancy was up."

"Why didn't he take the permanent position?"

"Let's just say his background and lifestyle did not sit well with some of his associates. He became a PI so he could make a living using his skills and stay near the guy. Turns out he loves PI work and doesn't miss the lab, or the guy, at all."

"A fairytale ending you, might say."

Mickey frowned. "Not very PC of you, Jack."

"C'mon, Mickey, lighten up. It was just too good a straight line to pass up."

"I know. I'm just pissed that you beat me to the punch . . . line."

"Must I continually endure these terrible puns?" Jack shouted, awakening Molly from her nap in the corner.

"Yes," Mickey demanded.

Molly came over to see what the commotion was all about. She nuzzled her nose between the two men, looking for one of them to pay attention to her. Mickey rubbed her nose and sent her back to her place in the corner. She obeyed but halfway there she looked back to see if he'd changed his mind.

"Too bad kids aren't more like dogs," Mickey said. "You know that unconditional-love thing. If Bobbie were more like Molly, we'd have been back together a long time ago." Sadness trailed off in his voice.

Jack decided it would be best to conclude his visit. This discussion was going nowhere but downhill. He excused himself by saying he had promised to be home when Maya arrived. He knew Mickey would never ask him to stay instead of being home with Maya, particularly given his laments about Bobbie.

Jack gave Molly's head a good rub and headed home.

CHAPTER 6

On Monday morning, Jack gave himself about an hour to tie things up before heading to Chicago for the Consolidated Foods meeting. He'd found Peter and the other four McKay & Associates staff members of the presentation team in the conference room polishing up their discussion points.

He was greeted with a "morning, Jack" in unison.

"Hello, everyone. Are we about ready?"

"The presentation's ready. How about the presenter?" Peter said, only half kidding.

Jack sat at Peter's laptop and clicked through the slides of the pitch presentation. Finishing, he said, "Good to go. Nice work. Just the right mix of grounded down-home expertise and cosmopolitan savvy. Who's riding with whom?"

"Jack and I have some stuff to go over. You four ride together," Peter insisted.

Everyone agreed and adjourned to respond to a few emails before departing. When Jack got back to his desk, he had a note to call Sandy.

She answered on the first ring. "I think you have a problem. You left your laptop at home. Don't you need it for your meeting?"

"Thankfully no. Our presentation is on Peter's. I really appreciate your concern. Does this mean—"

"No," she cut him off. "Being concerned doesn't mean I'm having second thoughts." She paused, then said, "Jack, no matter what, I want you to be successful and happy."

"How very altruistic of you." As soon as he said it, he knew it was a huge mistake.

"Fuck you," Sandy said, and she hung up.

Jack thought about calling her back to apologize, but knew he'd be better off letting her cool down. A drawn-out argument wouldn't help matters. He had to focus on the upcoming meeting.

The McKay & Associates caravan left the office on schedule to Chicago for their meeting with Consolidated Foods. As soon as Jack's Lexus cleared the on ramp, Peter started in.

"Jack, I'm uncomfortable with the direction our relationship is taking," he said.

"How so?"

Peter's eyes were fixed on the road ahead, but Jack could feel them staring intently at him nonetheless. "Even before you promoted me to be your partner, we consulted on everything. Lately, you have become distant. It's as if you are a sole practitioner. The partnership we have, and the teamwork of the organization, cannot survive without everyone on the same page."

"You sound like Sandy."

"I suppose I do."

"Are you suggesting a professional divorce?"

"No. We just need to get back on track. For our firm to survive, we need to make some changes."

"What did you have in mind?" Jack said warily.

"I propose that we create a steering committee. It would decide which contracts we pursue, which candidates we represent, et cetera."

"And who would you appoint to this committee?" Jack said as he changed lanes to pass a minivan.

"You, me, Tom and Carol," Peter suggested, clearly very prepared. These were the obvious choices since they were the other senior staff members in the firm.

"Won't work," Jack said tersely.

"Why not?" shot back Peter.

"No tiebreaker. Any problem-solving group must be an odd number. Otherwise you're prone to stalemates."

"Well then, I do have a candidate for the fifth." Peter was apparently prepared for this as well.

"Who?"

"Mickey Martin."

Jack clenched his hands on the steering wheel. Peter had made the perfect choice. Someone Jack would have to approve, and someone who would go out of his way not to show favoritism to Jack's position in a dispute.

"Sounds like a plan," Jack conceded reluctantly. He knew Peter was right; he just didn't like getting outmaneuvered.

"Thank you, Jack. I feel a whole lot better."

The conversation moved on to sports and world politics. Jack knew Peter was smart enough not to press his luck by bringing up Lindsay Revelle. He'd leave that discussion until another time and, if need be, to the newly appointed steering committee.

They all arrived in Chicago about thirty minutes early. They parked in a parking garage on Lake Street and walked to Consolidated's regional headquarters on Wacker Drive. They stopped at a coffee stand in the lobby and had one last blast of caffeine before heading into battle.

They ascended to the fiftieth floor where Arlene Metcalf, Consolidated's Communication Director who had flown in from Atlanta for the meeting, greeted them.

"Welcome, McKay & Associates. We're glad to have you here. Follow me, we'll get you set up in the boardroom."

They followed her into the boardroom, and it was breathtaking. The enormous forty-by-forty room was anchored by a conference table that seated twenty-four comfortably. Above the table was a stained-glass skylight that cast a multicolor hue on the room. The walls were inhabited by numerous pictures of past executives that reminded Jack of the paintings he had seen of the Founding Fathers in the National Portrait Gallery.

The McKay crew unpacked their computers and laid out their materials. Arlene excused herself and then returned a short time later with the selection committee in tow.

The presentation went extremely well. The capabilities material Peter and his staff had prepared was right on target. Jack's delivery was somehow totally focused on the task at hand. He came off with charm, wit, and professionalism. He had a keen sense of drama, and sales presentations were his forum for articulating it.

When he was a child, Jack thought he wanted to be an actor. His mother even paid for acting lessons, but he was never any good. He learned the lines and understood the motivation, but he played every character as "Jack." Jack could only be Jack. Not good for an actor, but properly executed, great for a pitchman. Add to that the poise he acquired competing on the basketball court, and the expertise he had acquired during his career, and he was a force to be reckoned with. The boardroom was Jack's stage and he played the part of PR impresario to an Academy Award level.

They all left the meeting feeling they had a great chance to win the business. Peter praised Jack all the way back in the car. It fell on deaf ears, however. Jack was fixated on the stupid remark he had made to Sandy that morning.

Sandy was making dinner with able assistance from Maya when Jack got home.

"Daddy!" Maya shouted. Jack gave her a big hug and kiss, lifting her from her perch on a stool by the sink.

Jack nodded to Sandy, who merely shrugged. He hoped Maya hadn't noticed their cold greeting. He was wrong.

"Kiss Mommy, too," Maya implored.

"Mommy's busy," Jack explained, hoping to deflect Maya's request.

It appeared that Sandy had decided this was not the time to bring Maya into her battle with Jack, so she walked over to him and they exchanged polite pecks on the cheek. Maya was satisfied and rushed off to her room.

"I should have never made that snide remark this morning," Jack said, hat in hand. "It was wrong, and I apologize."

Sandy turned away from him. "You know something, Jack, I've stopped caring what you say. I guess when you stop loving someone you can deflect their cutting remarks more easily. It merely strengthens my resolve to end this marriage and move on," she said with both anger and sadness in her voice.

"What are we going to do about Maya?"

"If you mean custody, that will be decided in the divorce proceedings."

"Custody is an issue of course, but I am much more concerned with how we deal with her emotional well-being. This situation will be devastating for her. We need to find a way to provide her some sort of a soft landing."

"I'm not sure how we do that," Sandy said, losing the edge in her voice. "Maybe we need some counseling on what to do."

"We can go that route if you think it would help. I suspect they will simply tell us to explain to her that it's not about our love for her but rather about the fact the two of us don't love each other anymore."

They each heard a faint whimper. Maya was standing in the doorway to the kitchen with tears streaming down her cheeks. They had found a way to tell her but without the soft landing they had intended.

Later that night, Jack tried without success to sleep. The guest room was darker and lonelier than it had ever been. He rationalized that Maya would have to find out sooner or later and there was probably no good way for that to happen. Still, he knew he had caused her great pain. Nothing was worse for a parent than the feeling that they have hurt their child. He had failed her, and it made him feel totally empty and alone. It made him understand what Mickey had gone through with Bobbie and why he so much wanted to fix his relationship with her. Jack swore that he would make things right again for Maya even though he had no idea how he would do it.

CHAPTER 7

Wednesday started as a bright and sunny autumn day. Jack could only hope his outlook would remain as bright and sunny given what was on his agenda.

That morning at the office was routine, consisting mostly of returning phone calls and emails. The exception was an impromptu heart-to-heart talk with Peter about PetroMark, William Davies, Lindsay Revelle, et al.

"Got a minute?" Peter asked, poking his head through Jack's office doorway.

"Sure, what's up?"

Jack knew the answer. Peter was going to push hard for Jack's commitment to drop the idea of representing Revelle. He was likely going to offer dropping William Davies as a potential client as a concession. Peter wanted the PetroMark business badly and his logic was difficult to dismiss. Jack motioned for him to come in and have a seat.

Peter sat down, crossed his legs, cleared his throat, and started in. "Jack, I know this is covering old ground, but I really feel staying out of the congressional race is the only way for us to go. Supporting either candidate will potentially harm the firm and supporting Revelle in particular would be devastating."

"Why would representing Revelle be any more devastating than representing Davies?"

"We could represent Davies if he was willing to abstain from the PetroMark negotiations with the county. If we represent Revelle, we'll lose the Party forever."

"But not PetroMark," Jack pointed out.

"And I believe PetroMark, too."

"Why?"

"Apparently, Lindsay Revelle is a proponent of utilizing the lakefront and the harbor area for recreation. Remember, that side of the bay is populated by working class and minority families. The location is perfect for a 'People's Park' delivered by the 'People's Candidate.' I'm sure he will fight tooth and nail against any commercial development, especially a PetroMark depot."

Jack felt blindsided. "How do you know this? This is news to me."

"Ever heard of the Water's Edge Trust?" said Peter.

"No." Jack suspected he would not care for Peter's explanation.

"Well it's an organization formed solely to lobby for recreational use of the remaining open waterfront land in Lakeville. It's headed by Robin Revelle, the wife of guess who?"

"How come I have never heard of them?" Jack said.

Peter shrugged. "I hadn't either until I started researching potential opposition to the PetroMark project. It seems Lindsay Revelle's wife Robin recently founded this group to oppose a condo project that was to go before the planning commission. The developers ran out of backing before it went anywhere, so her group didn't get much exposure. Angela Burgess sits on the planning commission; I called her to see which way the wind was blowing on the potential of PetroMark applying to build. She was giving me an overview on probable proponents and opponents and the Water's Edge Trust came up."

"So you're assuming Robin Revelle's group and, by default Lindsay Revelle, will oppose PetroMark's project?"

"Absolutely!" Peter had made his point.

"I appreciate your concerns, Peter. I'm having lunch with Revelle today. If it doesn't go amazingly well, you'll get no argument from me." What Jack didn't say was that he was expecting Lindsay Revelle to make a compelling case, so Peter still might not get the decision he was looking for.

Peter shifted into full pitch mode. "Jack, I know you'll do what's best for the firm. It's just that PetroMark will be a real feather in our cap. And a long-term one at that. I feel strongly that we will get additional business from them beyond the local assignments. They're making a big push in the Midwest region with an objective of over three hundred new stations in the next five years. That's a lot of announcements, press conferences, and special events. The stars are aligned for us on this. We have a great relationship with Rick Cartwright, and we have performed admirably for them in the past."

"I understand the implications, Peter. Let's see what happens at lunch."

Peter continued to pitch. "Can we meet on this today after your lunch? I'm really anxious to resolve this issue."

Thankfully, Jack had a legitimate excuse that would buy him more time to consider. "I have the rescheduled meeting with Sandy and the divorce attorneys right after my lunch. It will probably run for the balance of the afternoon. Believe me, you won't want to try to have a rational discussion with me following that encounter."

"First thing tomorrow then?"

Jack was getting annoyed. "Peter, are you on some kind of timetable for this that I'm not aware of? You're pushing awfully hard for closure. I think it's too important a decision to rush into."

"The 'timetable,' as you call it is not entirely mine. This situation is weighing heavily on me, sure, but I promised Rick Cartwright a prompt response and it makes no sense to give him a yes and then have him fire us over Lindsay Revelle. We need to get back to him before he considers another firm and you said yourself, we also need to give Randall Davies a yea or nay by week's end."

Jack had to concede. Peter was only looking out for the firm and deserved every consideration.

"I understand. We'll talk again tomorrow."

Jack and Peter had developed a rapport over the years. Each said what was on his mind, and then the two of them would thrash out any disagreements behind closed doors. After they inevitably arrived at a compromise, they would then present a unified front to the other members of the firm. It would be unfair not to resolve this quickly and in the same manner.

Peter left Jack's office without saying another word.

Jack stood up, coffee cup in hand, and stared out the window. Lakeville Harbor was spread out before him. The site where PetroMark planned to build was directly across the bay. He imagined what the PetroMark depot would do to the view. Not just the view out of his window but the landscape of downtown Lakeville as well. He also wondered what electing Lindsay Revelle, an African American, would do for the political landscape of the entire district. Whether Jack liked it or not, he was going to be an architect, instrumental in the design of one of those landscapes.

Kathryn's Restaurant was within walking distance of Jack's office. Since the meeting with the divorce attorneys was only a couple of blocks further, he took the occasion to enjoy some fresh air and sunshine by walking to his two appointments.

Downtown Lakeville had enjoyed a healthy renaissance during the 1990's-fueled primarily by the convention business. The Lakeville City Council had wisely supported the construction of a small but modern convention center completed in 1997. They reasoned correctly that with Milwaukee's Mitchell Field and Chicago's O'Hare Airport each only forty miles away, Lakeville's proximity would make it a most desirable convention location, easily accessible from anywhere.

Jack's firm had represented the convention bureau since it was formed. The bureau managed the city's convention business and, due in large part to their guidance, the convention center was booked almost every week since it opened. Lakeville's niche was small trade shows and association meetings needing space for two thousand attendees or less.

The weekly influx of conventioneers flocked to Lakeville's downtown establishments, which fueled continuing downtown growth. Empty historic brick buildings adorned with soiled gargoyles and cracked concrete pillars, which had once been home to "five-and-dimes", dress shops, and cobblers were now renovated and filled with upscale restaurants, clubs, and unisex day spas. The Carriage House and Harbor Plaza hotels were thriving as convention destinations. Jack couldn't help but feel a real sense of pride knowing the significant role McKay & Associates had played in the downtown's revitalization.

Kathryn's was a long-established soul food restaurant that had risen from very humble beginnings. Their first location was small and located in a primarily African American neighborhood on Lakeville's south side. Great food and hard work had paid off handsomely for Kathryn and her family. Now situated in the heart of downtown, it seated over two hundred patrons and catered to a most interesting and eclectic clientele. Factory workers could be seen sitting at the table next to his or her company's CEO, each enjoying plates of fried chicken and black-eyed peas.

He arrived at Kathryn's five minutes early and was pleased to find Lindsay Revelle already seated and waiting for him. Jack extended his hand.

"Hello, Lindsay, I'm Jack McKay."

"It's nice to meet you face to face. I appreciate your agreeing to have lunch," Lindsay said, rising to shake hands. He was six-four and very athletic looking. The only thing that looked scholarly was his receding hairline. Although only three inches taller than Jack, he seemed much larger.

Jack took a seat across from Lindsay so he could look him in the eyes when they spoke. Observe him rather than just see him. His love of everything Sherlock Holmes made him a big believer in finding body-language clues. He subscribed to the concept that the eyes were the mirrors of the soul.

"I would never pass up the opportunity for a good lunch at Kathryn's and to talk politics with a Rhodes Scholar," Jack said, putting his napkin in his lap.

Lindsay leaned in toward Jack, as if to confide in him. "I understand your appreciation for Kathryn's but frankly most of the poly-sci folks from Oxford are pretty dry. Besides, we both know the classroom and real life are two different worlds. You can't gain any real experience in a classroom."

"A friend of mine says, 'Experience is what you get when you don't get what you want.'" Jack often quoted Mickey, who generally was quoting someone else in the first place. Mickey would say, "At my age there isn't much original thought going on in my head, just the uncanny ability to recall something apropos."

"Your friend may be right," said Lindsay, "but with this run for Congress, I'm not looking to gain experience. I want to win this job. I want it very much."

"Unfortunately, so does William Davies," Jack reminded him. "And he has the resources of the Party and the backing of their legions of loyal followers and donors."

Before Lindsay could respond, the waitress arrived. She was one of Kathryn's daughters, Marie.

"Hi, Marie," Lindsay said.

"Hey, cuz, nice to see you," she responded. "Nice to see you too, Mr. McKay. What would you guys like for lunch?"

Lindsay ordered barbequed pork shoulder with mashed potatoes and gravy, and Jack ordered the fried catfish with boiled potatoes and green beans.

"So, are you actually related to Marie?" Jack inquired.

"Kathryn is my aunt, my father's sister."

"I see, well your aunt has sure been successful."

"She's one of the few," said Lindsay. "Unfortunately, most Black businesses in this country fall short of their potential or fail altogether because the African American community hasn't learned the lessons of economic history." He was going full speed now. "Most of the world's oppressed cultures have survived and ultimately prospered on one basic principal: support your own businesses first. Keep the money flowing in a circle within your community and then expand into the mainstream. That's the type of change I want to effect."

Jack's table position delivered the desired results. He saw genuine passion and sincerity in the warm, brown eyes looking back at him.

"I understand, but why a national office? It seems to me this issue needs to be addressed at a grassroots level."

"Funding, Jack, funding. Any far-reaching, meaningful program is funded at the federal level. I want to be instrumental in improving things all over the country. If I'm successful, Lakeville will benefit, but not on an insular basis."

"A laudable objective," Jack admitted. "But you're talking about representing a broad-based local constituency with numerous pressing concerns. Improving the economic status of minority businesses is too narrow of a focus to get elected by a divergent voter base and, quite frankly, not enough substance to deserve the office."

Lindsay straightened up in his chair. His face took on a much more serious tone. "Believe me, I have much more I want to accomplish, particularly as it relates to real healthcare reform and proper funding for public education. These issues affect every American and must be dealt with now."

Lindsay was sounding very much like a candidate.

Their conversation was interrupted by the arrival of lunch. As they took time to enjoy a few bites, Jack was struck by just how far Lindsay Revelle had come and who he had become. There was no question in Jack's mind that this man had poise, intellect, commitment, and personality, everything you would want in a candidate and elected official. He had used his basketball abilities as a ticket to become a scholar and now he wanted to use his academic talents to better his world. Jack realized backing this man was going to complicate his life even more. He had been with Lindsay Revelle for less than an hour and he was already convinced that he wanted to help him get elected. Jack hoped the campaign would also be an opportunity for him to recapture some his self-esteem.

Lindsay broke the food-induced silence. "You know I once saw you play basketball when you were in high school?"

"Saw me? You were the basketball star," Jack responded modestly.

"Stop it, Jack, you were the star of your high school team, and then you played college ball."

"When did you see me play?"

"When I was in junior high my dad took me. We saw you in the regional qualifying for the state tournament. You guys were playing Rufus King."

"We lost that one in overtime when I missed a last-second shot. Thanks for reminding me. I may not be able to finish my lunch," Jack kidded.

"What I remember is after the buzzer sounded and you lost the game, I remember everyone on your team, including the coach, had their heads down wallowing in their disappointment . . . everyone but you. You walked over to the King players alone, smiled, and offered your hand in congratulations. That was truly inspirational for me. It was one of those little life lessons that stick with you forever. Frankly, it's why I called you. I figured with your professional achievements, connections, and that kind of integrity, you were the only one who could fight this fight with me." He smiled. The way he said it showed just how genuine his admiration for Jack was.

"Lindsay, I'm truly flattered. But there are some things going on in my life right now that may prevent me from even considering your offer. Also, a lot of water has flowed over the dam since those high school days. I may not be quite the man you think I am."

"Jack, we all have our blemishes, but when inspired, our character and ability will generally rise to the top. Please consider my offer. I think that together we have a legitimate chance to win this thing."

"What's your game plan?"

Lindsay chuckled. "You show me yours and I'll show you mine. Tell me you're in and I give you full disclosure."

"I guess you did learn a thing or two about real-life politics since Oxford. Give me a few days to sort things out and I'll get back to you on your offer. Either way, I really enjoyed our lunch."

"Hopefully it's the first of many, Jack."

As he walked out of Kathryn's, Jack was struck by the bright sunlight. He was also equally struck by the bright light that was Lindsay Revelle. People often said truly qualified individuals didn't run for office because of the toll it took on their personal lives and the difficulty they would have in effecting meaningful change. Lindsay was one of those truly qualified and committed individuals the likes of which were seldom seen in American politics, let alone in a Lakeville congressional race. Lindsay Revelle was someone who was willing to risk the intrusion into his personal life because he felt he had to try to initiate change. Possible election strategies consumed Jack's thoughts. He knew there was almost no way he could take Lindsay up on his offer, but he still couldn't stop conjuring up ideas to get him elected. While the dilemma he faced loomed large, he was exhilarated by the thought of leading a truly meaningful campaign fight.

CHAPTER 8

The meeting was at the office of Watkins & Relford, Sandy's divorce attorneys. Jack was represented by Steven Clark, an old friend and top-notch family law practitioner.

When Steven had last met with Jack a week prior they had agreed on a collaborative divorce. Jack and Sandy would agree to work out a settlement outside of court that covered the division of their property as well as their respective responsibilities as Maya's parents. It motivated the lawyers and kept the court from intervening.

Given Sandy's state of mind, Jack was skeptical this process would work for them. He hoped Sandy would be more likely to reach an agreement quickly and amicably now that Maya knew what was going on.

Steven was waiting for him in the hallway outside of Watkins & Relford. He greeted Jack and they went in together. The receptionist ushered them down a long corridor into a conference room that looked as if Currier and Ives had decorated it. They sat down at the early American conference table on very uncomfortable chairs. The only thing that appeared to be from the current century was a speakerphone that sat in the middle of the table like a modern centerpiece.

The door opened and in came Sandy and her attorney, Anthony Watkins. Soon after, Susan Light, the jointly retained financial specialist, joined the conference. Jack was sure he had spent a thousand dollars just getting through the introductions.

Anthony Watkins convened the proceedings. "OK, let's get

underway. It is my understanding both Mr. and Mrs. McKay have been briefed on the collaborative divorce procedures. Steven and I have agreed on contract language for the agreement to proceed with the collaborative process. We have prepared copies for all parties to sign. Susan, please help me out and hand the documents in front of you to Steven for his approval and signature and for signature by his client."

Steven read over the documents to ensure they were as advertised. He passed them to Jack to sign, which he did. The paperwork made its way around the table and all the parties signed. Then came the one aspect Jack and Sandy fully agreed on, assigning a mental health professional to assist Maya with the trauma.

Next came the fun part. Susan Light started in on the division of property. "I will need the following information from Mr. McKay: the mortgage documents on the McKay residence, a listing of all securities, all bank statements including joint and individual accounts, tax returns for the last five years, a listing of all liabilities, an independent valuation of Mr. McKay's equity in McKay & Associates, and a schedule of all personal property including all vehicles."

Jack saw Sandy snicker when she said "vehicles" because they both knew it meant all vehicles, including his motorcycle.

Jack cringed at the thought of having to buy back from Sandy a share of any of those things he already owned. He understood the concept of community property, but when it became his reality, it made him furious. To pay her for half of his Harley when she had hated the idea of it from day one struck him as totally absurd.

"I will also need all records pertaining to Mrs. McKay's work history to determine her earning potential," Susan added.

Before Jack could start an argument over the motorcycle, Steven interjected, "We assume the cost of the equity valuation will be split between the parties."

"Fine," replied Watkins. "Now on to the matter of custody of the child, Maya."

Jack spoke for the first time. "There is nothing to discuss here. Joint custody with some equal time provision is what it will be."

Steven stepped in again before anyone could respond. "Jack's position is clear: he wants to continue to share his parental responsibilities and to enjoy the opportunity to be a significant part of his daughter's life. I'm sure Mrs. McKay understands that and will agree to a fair schedule for all concerned."

"Are you sure you'll be able to find the time with your busy daily work schedule and full dance card of evening meetings?" Sandy shot back, leering in Jack's direction.

"OK, everyone, let's keep our respective cools," Watkins said. "Steven, why don't you and Mr. McKay put together a proposal for shared custody and submit it to us with the rest of the documentation. Then all the cards will be on the table."

"Assuming Mrs. McKay supplies a listing of all of her personal property, bank accounts, trusts, etc., that will be fine," Steven offered.

"Good. This has been a most productive meeting," Watkins said more cheerily than the conditions warranted.

They discussed dates for submissions and the next meeting. While those discussions were taking place, Jack stared out of the window, not noticing Sandy, who was wiping away a tear.

Once all of the calendars had been synchronized, Jack and Steven left the office together. They agreed to go over the disclosure items on the phone. Steven would fax Jack some forms to fill out, which would help organize the information. As they exited the elevator, Steven had one more bit of counsel.

"One more thing, Jack. They are going to request that you move out, most likely at the next meeting. They can't force you to leave, but I suggest you make some arrangements before the issue becomes contentious."

"Why do I—"

"Because you do, Jack. That's how it's done. Sandy and Maya need a place to spend their days as well as their nights. Unless you plan to quit your job to see to Maya's daily needs, this is the way it will end up. It's really Maya who gets the house. Sandy's merely the one staying with her."

"This just keeps getting better and better."

They parted company as they walked out of the building.

The beautiful sunny day had suddenly turned into a black and cold evening, both literally and figuratively. As Jack headed back to his office to get his car, his cell phone rang. It was Randall Davies, and he was not happy.

"How are you, Randall?" Jack said, attempting to be cordial.

"Truth be known, I'm a little pissed at you. I haven't heard from you regarding William's campaign, and then I hear you're hanging out with Lindsay Revelle." Randall's voice became a growl.

Word traveled fast in a small city, especially with Randall Davies's connections. Jack felt equally agitated.

"Sorry you're pissed, Randall, but I don't see why. By our agreement, I have until the end of the week to let you know about Williams' campaign. As it relates to Mr. Revelle, you can't expect me to make an informed decision on the campaign without sizing up the opposition.

"Well then, as long as I have you on the phone and now that you've sized up the opposition, where do we stand?"

It was the full-court press. Jack had to push back as hard as he could to buy time.

"Randall, decisions like these are made with the input of key members of my firm, not by me alone. Since you're watching my every move, you know I have not been back to the office since lunch, so no such consultation could have taken place."

"I see. Well, it seems to me from your tone that you're leaning away from us on this one."

"Not necessarily. Listen, Randall, I just left a meeting with three attorneys and my soon-to-be ex-wife. We're initiating divorce proceedings. You caught me at the worst possible moment. I will meet with my folks and get back to you by the end of business tomorrow. OK?"

"Thanks, Jack. I can live with that. Sorry about the divorce, by the way. I've been through three of them and they're murder. Call me tomorrow before six. I need to move on this."

"I'll call you tomorrow. Good night, Randall." Jack hung up sensing tomorrow's festivities would most certainly make today's proceedings look uneventful.

Driving home, Jack's mind was racing as he reflected on the day. The confrontation with Peter, the revelation with Lindsay, the divorce. He decided some music would help drown out his guilt and unhappiness. He hit the radio button and on came the Band's "The Shape I'm In." He laughed, as it was a fitting anthem to his day and, for that matter, his life.

Jack parked his car in the garage and entered the house through the kitchen. He was startled to see Sandy sitting on a bar stool at the kitchen counter perusing a family photo album and drinking a glass of wine.

"You're up late," he said.

"Just having a party," she said snidely. "This is my kind of fun, sitting in the kitchen in my robe guzzling Merlot and remembering how nice my life used to be."

Jack noticed an empty bottle by the sink and a half-empty one next to her glass. He also noticed she had been crying. Their once-happy life as portrayed in the album had disintegrated into anger and sadness. He knew that he was largely responsible. Indeed, the memories hurt.

"Mind if I join you?" he asked.

"The wine is half yours, help yourself."

"Sandy, it's late, can we stop trading barbs for the evening? This will be a whole lot less uncomfortable if we at least try to be civil," Jack implored.

"You're right," she said flatly. "Being angry all of the time is tiresome. I wasn't very nice today. Sorry."

"I completely understand. It's actually easier to be mad. It gives you the adrenaline rush needed to continue on with the fight when you just feel like running away."

"You feel that way too?"

"Sure. But tonight, I'd rather take the gloves off and just relax." Jack sighed.

"Good idea." Sandy actually smiled. Then she got up to pour him a glass of wine. As she passed him, it became apparent she was only wearing the robe. Jack caught a glimpse of her breasts as she set the glass down in front of him. He wondered if she noticed him noticing. She had.

"It's nice to know I can still attract your attention," she said in a most seductive tone.

"Sandy, since we met, you've been the only woman who has. My work may have come between us, but—" She placed her hand over his mouth, cutting him off. Then she kissed him and opened the belt on her robe, inviting him in.

"Is this a good idea?" he whispered.

"No, but let's do it anyway." The wine and the memories were potent aphrodisiacs.

Jack lifted her onto the bar stool, her back resting on the counter. She took off his tie as they kissed. The rest of his clothes followed quickly. Jack had almost forgotten how wonderful it felt to caress her. She shivered as he moved slowly down her chest, nibbling on her breasts and gently rubbing her stomach. As he knelt in front of her, she pulled his head between her legs. They both responded feverishly to the stimulation. He then stood and joined with her. They made love as if he was going off to war and they might never see each other again. She moaned with ecstasy as he climaxed. It was a signal their truce was ending.

They shared one last kiss and then went off to their respective beds where they both cried themselves to sleep.

CHAPTER 9

It always took Jack awhile to get oriented when awakening in the guest room. Navigating Maya's little girl stuff in their shared bathroom didn't help. It wouldn't be for long, however. His moving out was inevitable.

Today, he wanted to escape the house before Sandy got up. The thought of seeing her after the events of the night before was too difficult to even imagine. It was pain better postponed. He did, however, long to see Maya, so he snuck into her room.

"Hi, Daddy, is it morning?" she said, both surprised and disoriented by the darkness in the room.

"Not quite, sweetheart. I have an early meeting and didn't want to leave without giving you a kiss." Jack leaned over and gave Maya a big hug and kiss.

"Daddy, I don't want you and Mommy to get a divorce," she implored.

"Maya, do you know what a divorce is?"

"It's when people stop being married and don't live together anymore."

"That's true. But you need to know, even though Mommy and I won't be married anymore, we both love you and always will."

"But where will I live?"

"You will live here with Mommy."

"Where will you live?"

"I'm working on that. It will be somewhere close by where you and I can be together."

"I thought you said I was going to live with Mommy." Maya was finding the scenario confusing.

"You will live with Mommy but be with me a lot."

"Will you have a dog there?"

"I don't think so. I'm gone all day and it wouldn't be fair to leave a dog alone. Maya, we will talk more later. I have to go now. I love you."

"I love you too, Daddy."

"Go back to sleep now. I'll see you later."

"Okay," Maya solemnly replied as she turned over and went back to sleep.

Jack quietly closed Maya's door and walked down the hallway through the kitchen to the garage. As he backed out of the driveway, he saw the light on in the master bedroom and Sandy's silhouette against the drapes.

Jack was actually relieved after his conversation with Maya. The situation was out in the open, and he and Sandy could stop discussing it in code. He hoped Maya could be spared from the unpleasantries that were sure to come.

Now on to the day's next drama, he thought, as he pulled into the Olympus Café, a twenty-four-hour Greek diner near his office. Fortification would be needed for the battles ahead. He loved this place because whatever he had a taste for was available. From chop suey to spaghetti and meatballs, they had it. Today, he opted for a Greek omelet with spinach, gyro meat, and feta cheese with sides of hash browns and thick Greek toast.

After ordering, Jack began to lay out his challenges for the day. First, he needed to find a way to keep peace in the firm and still represent Lindsay Revelle. Then he needed to figure how to tell Randall Davies that he was opting out of William Davies's run for Congress without getting his legs broken. By the time he had finished his food and three cups of coffee, he had a plan.

Even though he had stopped for the breakfast planning session, Jack was the first to arrive at the office. He made himself a pot of decaf, as he was already over his caffeine limit, and then made notes of the plan he had devised. This was the technique he almost always used when making a presentation. He seldom referred to the notes but writing them down solidified the concepts in his mind.

Peter arrived around eight, greeting Jack as he passed his office. "Good morning. Looks like we'll see the sun again today."

"I hope so," said Jack. "Can we meet at ten to discuss the matters at hand?"

Peter nodded. " I'll move the staff meeting to ten."

Jack headed into his office and closed the door. He was actually ready, but he wanted to postpone the discussion to make sure he was completely comfortable with his approach. He wanted to call Mickey first to sound him out about his concept and to ask him for shelter.

Mickey answered on the first ring. "Hello, Jack."

"Hi, Mickey. I see you also have my office number programmed into your caller ID. Listen, I need to talk to you about a couple of things. Do you have time now?"

After a brief coughing spell, Mickey said, "Sure. Do those things include a rundown on your meetings yesterday?"

"Yes. In fact, the meetings yesterday precipitated my call. As you might have guessed, Lindsay Revelle was everything I expected and then some. As you might also have guessed, the divorce meeting was everything I expected and worse. Just another day in the life, so to speak."

"Details. I want details."

"Let me start at the beginning of my day."

Jack filled Mickey in on his meetings with Peter regarding PetroMark and Lindsay Revelle and that he needed to make some choices regarding the direction the firm would take. He went on to give him the play by play on the divorce meeting and his phone conversation with Randall Davies. He decided not to discuss what transpired last night with Sandy when he got home.

"It seems you're about to be homeless and unemployed," said Mickey. "Well, you've come to the right place. You can move in here with me. I'd love the company. There is even a room for Maya, when you have placement. As far as the firm goes, I must confess to having been previously informed of your predicament by Peter."

"He called you to see if you'd serve on the steering committee, didn't he?" Jack was obviously irritated about the subterfuge. "Of course he did. You wouldn't respect him if he hadn't covered all the bases before recommending it, would you?"

"You're right. But you know how I hate being outflanked."

"Listen, you chose Peter as your partner because he was smart, aggressive, and wily. Don't be critical of those traits when you're challenged by them. So what is your plan?"

Jack filled him in on how he was going to turn down Davies, accept the PetroMark business, and still work for Lindsay Revelle.

"You're walking a tightrope without a net, Jack. You must orchestrate every detail to a *t*. Your plan can work if everything falls into place. A word of caution: everything seldom falls into place." Mickey's voice was, in no uncertain terms, sounding an alarm.

"Thanks for the sage advice. I'll let you know when I will be moving in." Jack hung up, comforted in knowing that he had at least secured a roof over his head. He was about to take several huge risks with his plan. Mickey had voiced his concerns but hadn't tried to talk him out of it. Jack figured, in a roundabout way, he had gotten the advice he had been looking for.

Peter came into Jack's office, notebook in hand, promptly at ten. He sat down and Jack, who had been staring out the window, turned and got immediately to the matters at hand.

"First of all, I want you to know I do not want to represent

William Davies. I feel strongly that we need to get off that merry-go-round. I understand saying no on this one will likely end our relationship with the Party, and it may be difficult to maintain our political practice without the Party, but I can't stomach their action anymore." Jack's remorse for his past affiliations with Randall Davies and his shady organization was palpable.

"I hadn't thought about it in those terms," said Peter. "I did think we could bow out gracefully, but you're probably right. If we thumb our nose at William Davies's campaign, we'd be PR firm non grata at the Party headquarters. Actually, I'm OK with it assuming we go ahead with our representation of PetroMark."

Jack was surprised and pleased with Peter's response. "Here's how I'd like to approach it," he continued. "We go forward with PetroMark and we advise Lindsay Revelle."

"How can we possibly do that?" Peter interrupted. His agreement had turned to confusion.

"We just do."

"What if Revelle comes out in opposition to PetroMark directly or indirectly by supporting the Water's Edge Trust? We'd be back to square one."

"Not necessarily," Jack said. "Since the planning commission won't begin to consider any proposals until after the primary, Revelle will not need to oppose the project before he is nominated. If it is approved and he chooses to oppose it, we will formally resign as his election consultants."

"That's fine with me, but is it fair to him?"

"Yes, because I will let him know it's a condition of our retainer."

"Won't you be leaving him out on a limb or forcing him into an untenable position? He would have to choose between getting our help, which he would need to get elected, or staying true to his wife and their shared beliefs."

Jack noticed that both their voices had risen to argument level.

"I have that covered. We will prepare a complete election strategy before the primary. It will recite chapter and verse each element and timeline for the campaign. It will provide our successor, if one is required, with a step-by-step roadmap to getting Lindsay Revelle elected."

"But, Jack, who else but you could orchestrate the strategy?"

"No one has to. I will advise the campaign on an unofficial, unpaid basis. I will do it on my own time and totally behind the scenes, communicating with Lindsay Revelle only. The successor firm would merely follow his instructions."

Peter stood and paced the room.

"Risky, Jack, very risky. What if it plays out that Revelle opposes PetroMark, then we 'resign' from the campaign, and PetroMark finds out we faked our resignation? We'd be finished with them and, with our integrity impugned, totally ruined as a firm. I am not willing to take that chance."

Jack sat down calmly his in chair and looked up at Peter, who had temporarily stopped pacing. "I have a remedy for that as well—A plan B, if you will. Let's say the worst happens, I will cop to having consulted with the campaign on the sly without your knowledge, and I will resign from the firm giving you total control. PetroMark would be satisfied and the firm would move forward in your capable hands."

Peter stopped pacing. "But you'd be playing Russian roulette with your professional life. Is Lindsay Revelle worth that type of gamble?"

Jack sighed. "Peter," he said a softer tone, "I don't expect you to fully understand this, but I am looking for some form of redemption here. I have made too many compromises in my life. It's cost me dearly, both with my family and my self-esteem." Jack felt the resolve in his own voice. "I have an opportunity to at least get my self-esteem back, and I will not back down. Can I count on your support, or do we need to convene the steering committee?"

"That won't be necessary, Jack. You deserve the opportunity to set things right for yourself. And besides, if your plan A works, everybody wins."

"And if plan B works, you win."

"I would not look at it as a win if you left the firm. We would be diminished in so many ways." Peter sounded appropriately hurt.

"I didn't say you would rejoice; it is just that you and the firm would go on and be able to flourish. That would be very important to me."

"Thanks, Jack. Do what you think is right. Let me know what you need from me."

"Thank you, Peter. I am really glad you're OK with this."

Jack genuinely cared for Peter and was extremely pleased with the way this played out. What he didn't know was which plan Peter really favored.

Jack wanted to call Lindsay Revelle immediately after meeting with Peter. He was so exhilarated by his decision and Peter's acceptance of it he could hardly contain himself. Before he could place the call, Donna rang him on the intercom.

"Sandy is here."

"I'll be right out." Jack had no idea what this was about. Sandy almost never came to the office and under the circumstances it was even more unusual.

Jack opened his door, "Hi, c'mon in."

Sandy walked past Jack without saying a word and sat down. She was very upset.

"Jack, I'm furious with you." Her eyes were aglow with anger.

"About last night," he guessed.

She stood up and put her hands on her hips. "No, I'm mad

at myself for that. It's this morning we need to talk about, and I wanted to speak to you where Maya couldn't hear. She's overheard enough already."

Jack was puzzled. "What's made you so upset? Is it that I left without speaking to you?"

"No, it's what you said to Maya. You discussed our divorce and what was going to happen without me being there. You were trying to be the good guy at my expense." She glared at him.

"Hold on a minute. I went to her room to see her before I left for work. I missed saying good night last night, and I wanted to spend a moment with her before leaving this morning. Our little talk consisted of me answering her questions in the best way I could. I did not try to undermine you in any way." Jack's tone was significantly softer as he tried to diffuse the situation.

"Well you did. You could have come and gotten me. I was home." Sandy started to pace.

"You're right. It just didn't occur to me," Jack said, truly remorseful about his oversight.

"From now on any discussions with Maya about what's going on need to take place with both of us present," she demanded.

"That's not practical. We are both going to be alone with her from time to time, and we can't shut her down when she wants information."

"Well then, you at least have to tell me right away about any such discussions. I felt like it was a sneak attack." Sandy stopped pacing as her anger had begun to soften.

"I'm really sorry I didn't tell you about it. I do agree, we must keep each other up to speed on our conversations with Maya. Please understand, I was not trying to do or say anything at your expense."

"OK, I accept your explanation. Let's please stay unified on this point at least. And let's make a point to consult with Maya's child specialist to be sure we handle this correctly for her."

"Fine with me. And by the way, about last night—"

"Let's just add last night to our album of memories, shall we? It was a nice farewell."

Jack noticed her eyes had turned from fierce to melancholy as she got up to leave.

After catching his breath and refreshing himself with a bottle of mineral water, Jack picked up the phone and called Randall Davies. He just wanted to get it over with.

"Hello, Jack," Davies answered. "You're early, it's not even close to six yet."

"I didn't want to keep you in suspense any longer, Randall. We've . . . decided to accept the opportunity to represent Lindsay Revelle in the congressional campaign." Jack almost stuttered as he uttered the words. As the consummate professional, he was seldom uncomfortable in these situations, but it was different when you were burning a bridge and, for Jack, this was the Golden Gate.

Randall's agitation was approaching a fever pitch. "Well, we expected that you were going to pull a stunt like this. You know this means that you're through with the Party and we now consider you the enemy. This is one war I will personally enjoy, you ungrateful son of a bitch."

"I understand how you feel and look forward to kicking your ass in the campaign. Goodbye, Randall."

Jack hung up before Randall Davies could say anything else. His heart was pounding, and the sweat was pouring from his forehead. Even though Randall Davies would be ruthless in his retaliation, it had been a long time since he had felt so good.

It was time to call Lindsay Revelle. His fingers were shaking so badly it took him two tries to get the number right.

The phone rang four times. Jack was hoping to speak to Lindsay directly. This was not something he wanted to leave on voice mail. He wanted to hear Lindsay's reaction to the news. Luckily, Lindsay answered before the fifth ring.

"Lindsay, this is Jack McKay. How are you?"

"Fine, Jack. What's up?"

"Are you available on Monday for a meeting to discuss campaign strategy?" Jack was playing with him a little.

"Jack, are you showing me yours?" Lindsay said hopefully.

"You bet I am," Jack gleefully responded.

"Where and when?" Lindsay was doing everything he could to sound businesslike, but the cracks in his voice betrayed him.

"My office about nine a.m. Does that work?"

"It does. Jack, I am very happy you're on board, and believe me I know you're paying a heavy price for this." Lindsay sounded genuinely appreciative and understanding of the consequences Jack would suffer for turning his back on the Party.

"I am totally at peace with this and so should you be. See you on Monday morning."

"Thanks, Jack. See you on Monday then."

When the call ended, Jack was smiling from ear to ear. Now he had to figure out how in the world he was going to win.

CHAPTER 10

The weekend days were becoming the most difficult time for the McKay's. They didn't know how to act around one another when they were together at the house. Sandy would take Maya to the store. Jack would take her to breakfast and the cleaners. There were no family outings. Jack would play with Maya, and then Sandy would play with Maya. There were no family games except divorcing parents hide-and-seek. Jack and Sandy would avoid each other, and Maya would try to find them and get them together.

"Sandy, this is so ridiculous," Jack pleaded. "Poor Maya doesn't know how to act around us anymore. We've got to figure something out so she is not uncomfortable in her own house."

"The solution is simple. You move out, then she will have the undivided attention of the one she is with and we won't be playing tag with her emotions. Have you found anything yet?"

"I'm considering moving in with Mickey temporarily. His place is big enough, so Maya can have her own room as well."

"Why not just find an apartment or condo, something more permanent? Moving twice seems silly."

"Because I don't know what type of accommodations I want longer term. There is so much turmoil in my life right now, I would just like something temporary until I get things sorted out."

"I guess that sounds reasonable. How soon will you be moving?" Sandy pressed.

"Within two weeks. By the way I need a small favor. I'd like to leave some things here. I don't want to overwhelm Mickey with all of my stuff."

"You can leave a reasonable amount here for a short while, but I don't want this place to become your off-site warehouse."

There was no doubt she was allowing a small concession to hasten his departure.

"A couple of months be OK?"

"Sure. By the way, a package came for you yesterday. It's in the garage."

"Must be the trunk for my motorcycle. I'll see if Maya wants to help me out with the installation."

"Jack, I'd like to go out tonight with a couple of women friends. Can you watch Maya?"

She had granted Jack his favor, and the two of them together in the same house would only be uncomfortable. He was actually relishing the opportunity to spend time with Maya and to have a night in his own home without combat.

"Sure, no problem."

Jack and Maya retreated to the garage to work on the Harley. She was ecstatic to be tabbed as his assistant mechanic. The garage was attached and heated, which made it quite comfortable, even in the dead of winter. Jack loved working there. He had every tool imaginable, even though these days he kept his mechanical challenges to a minimum, with tasks like oil changes and attaching new accessories like the storage trunk he had just received. It was the only place on earth where one could ever find Jack in torn jeans and a soiled T-shirt.

In his youth, Jack had really been into working on cars and motorcycles. He had a part-time job in an auto parts store where he learned all about the components of a vehicle and what it took to fix them. At seventeen, he bought an old Chevy and rebuilt its failing systems in his parents' garage. His friends often brought their malfunctioning cars and motorcycles over to Jack's house for his expert analysis and free repair assistance. Cars and basketball consumed his high school years.

Once Jack graduated from college, this all changed. He decided such endeavors were the stuff of hobbies, not professions. His aspiration for money and stature had relegated his passions to pastimes, his overalls to secluded Saturday afternoons, and his high-top sneakers to the back of the closet.

His Harley was a Softail model, a bike that was fun to ride around town and substantial enough for over-the-road cruising. All black and chrome with a small logo on the fuel tank, it was very "stock" looking without a lot of the customizing most Harley owners indulged in. If Ralph Lauren had designed a Harley, this would be it. Even Jack's riding outfit was understated: a black leather jacket devoid of frills, studs, and event patches topped off with a solid black helmet. On the road, he resembled Darth Vader on wheels.

He bolted on the new trunk with Maya's capable assistance. She held the wrench for him while he adjusted the bracket by hand and fetched water for him when he got thirsty. He purposely made a half hour job into a two-hour job.

He savored the afternoon in the garage and the evening that followed. Chinese carry-out from Wei Lu's for dinner followed by several challenging games of Chutes and Ladders, and a bedtime story ending with a giant kiss and hug before lights out. Had he appreciated days like this more in the past, Jack realized the demise of his marriage and the pain they all were feeling might have been avoided.

Before turning in early, Jack prepared for his Sunday football ritual by watching a cable sports program detailing all of the pre-game hype for Sunday's Packers game. He was sound asleep but awoke briefly when Sandy came home. He pretended to still be sleeping. He noticed she was staggering slightly from too much to drink and her clothes were slightly out of kilter.

Sunday was very quiet. In the morning, Jack and Maya shared some scrambled eggs and watched cartoons while Sandy slept in. The afternoon was equally uneventful. Jack cheered for the Packers, Maya played with her toys, and Sandy read the newspaper through bloodshot eyes.

CHAPTER 11

Peter loved arriving at the office early particularly when no one else had. He was always very focused on the job at hand and did his best work in solitude. Peter's private line rang at 7:45 on Monday morning. "This is Peter Evans," Peter said, picking up the receiver.

"Peter, this is Arlene Metcalf from Consolidated. How are you?"

"Very well thanks and you?" Peter hoped her early morning call meant he would be feeling even better.

"I'm fine and glad to find you in early. With the time difference, I wasn't sure you would be there. Listen, Peter, I have a meeting in a half an hour, and I'd like to go over a few things with you first."

"Fire away." Peter couldn't help but be encouraged.

"I am going to recommend McKay & Associates be appointed as agency of record for the project we met on in Chicago, but before I do, I need to ask you a question which may seem to be from left field."

"Go ahead. Under the circumstances I will gladly answer if I can." He could hardly contain himself.

"Good, I want to know if your firm plans to continue representing PetroMark."

"Arlene, it would be unethical of me to discuss our relationship with another client with you." Peter was feeling most uncomfortable. He wanted to cooperate, but professional ethics would not permit such a disclosure.

"Even if Rick Cartwright and Don Buckley were on board with it?"

"I don't understand," he said.

"You see, we are negotiating to include PetroMark stations in the parking lots of our new Lakeville stores. We feel there are real synergies with providing extra services at our stand-alone locations. We don't want to get into the gasoline business, and it makes sense for PetroMark to open more Lakeville outlets now that they are planning a major distribution depot in Lakeville. It's the proverbial win-win situation. The PetroMark folks think very highly of you guys, and I'm sure you can see the value to all concerned if we shared the same PR firm."

"It makes a lot of sense," Peter said as calmly as possible, knowing full well this was the big deal of the day. A little disclosure at this point wouldn't hurt. "We haven't formally accepted their offer, but I feel comfortable in telling you that I fully support the concept you've laid out. Getting an approval from Jack should be only a formality."

"Good, then I will go to my meeting and make my recommendation contingent on your acceptance of both retainers."

"Arlene, thank you so much for including us in your plans."

"You're welcome, and don't forget to thank Rick and Don. They're the ones who put you over the top." She hung up.

Peter was on cloud nine. This was a dream assignment. Two enormous clients, paying two enormous retainers, all in one fell swoop. There was no way he would consider anything but an affirmative stamp of approval from his partner as he walked over to Jack's office. Surprisingly, Jack was on board immediately.

"Sounds great, Peter. This will provide tons of work and revenue for the firm."

Peter told him about Arlene's call. "I would have had you join in on the call, but I didn't know you were here. I didn't see your car when I came in."

"I have Sandy's minivan this morning."

"What's the occasion?"

"Seems the latch that reclines the back seat broke last night when Sandy was out. I could have fixed it myself, but it's under warranty so I'll let the pros at the dealer work on it. Anyway, I am genuinely excited about the Consolidated contract. You really did a masterful job pulling it all together."

Peter was startled at Jack's immediate approval. He had expected something of a struggle. "Thanks, but the two clients working in concert was just dumb luck."

"Hey, if we weren't good and hadn't been pitching both companies, no dumb luck could have made this happen. You put us in position to get lucky, which takes all the skill in the world. I'm really proud of you." And he was.

"We did this together." Peter was somewhat embarrassed by Jack's effusive compliment.

"Shall we sing 'Kumbaya'?" Jack teased.

"That won't be necessary, and hopefully resigning Lindsay Revelle's campaign won't be necessary either," Peter said, reminding Jack of his promise.

"I hope so too. Speaking of Lindsay Revelle, he will be here at nine. Can you stop in for minute and introduce yourself?"

"Glad to," Peter replied.

Jack had the sense that Peter was masking his true feelings in the meeting. He knew Peter thought they would be much better off without Revelle's campaign but had no alternative but to play along. It was apparent to Jack that while he'd gotten his way, the subject was far from settled.

Promptly at nine, Donna rang the intercom to let Jack know his appointment had arrived. Jack went out to the reception area to greet Lindsay Revelle. He was surprised to see Lindsay was not alone. A woman was with him. She had an engaging smile, but Jack could also see, by the way she carried herself, she was formidable in her own right.

"Hi, Jack. Let me introduce you to my wife, Robin."

"Nice to meet you, Robin," Jack said, extending his hand.

Robin smiled as she accepted the handshake. Jack led them down the hall to his office. As they walked, he was struck by how perfect they looked together. She was also tall, five foot ten inches he guessed, and drop-dead gorgeous. He heard she was smart, having given up a tenured professorship when they moved back to Lakeville to enter politics, he as a candidate, she as an activist.

"So, you're the kingmaker," Robin said as they took their seats.

"I'm not really fond of that characterization. It is the voters who elect their 'kings,' not me."

"Jack, I just met you and I've managed to insult you right out of the box. I only meant it as a compliment and as wishful thinking. No offense was meant."

"None taken, really. It's just by taking on Lindsay's campaign I hope to right a few wrongs. You see, my affiliation with the Liberty Party over the years has not always been something I'm particularly proud of. Even though our tactics have been legitimate, I've helped a lot of candidates get elected who probably didn't deserve the office they ended up with, not to mention what they ultimately did after they were elected. I believe Lindsay deserves the office he seeks, and the people of Lakeville deserve him serving them in that office."

Lindsay nodded and smiled. "Robin and I are very excited to have you on board. What are the next steps?"

Jack clasped his hands together. "Have you formed a committee to elect? Have you begun getting nomination petitions signed? Have you made sure you meet all residency requirements? Do you have an election fund started? Who do you have endorsements from? What colors do you want to use on your posters, buttons, and bumper stickers? What's your slogan? What events are you scheduled to speak at? What community events do you plan to drop in on? Have you hired bodyguards?" Jack rattled off like shots from a machine gun.

Lindsay laughed. "I guess the next steps are too numerous to mention."

"They are too numerous for you to worry about. You worry about one thing only at this point: What issues are you planning to run on? I'll get started on the rest. You stick to the message; I'll stick to the details."

Just then, Peter knocked on the door and came in.

"Robin and Lindsay Revelle, this is my partner Peter Evans."

Lindsay held out his hand, "Nice to meet you Peter."

"Yes, nice to meet you," Robin echoed.

"We are very excited to be working with you." Peter's feigned enthusiasm was obvious to Jack as he shook hands all around. Then the intercom rang.

"Jack, Sandy's on the line. She says it's urgent."

Irritated, Jack picked up the phone. "What's up?"

"We . . . we were almost killed." Sandy's voice was quivering.

"You and Maya? What happened? You're OK?" Jack was panicked. The others in the room were transfixed on him, their eyes staring at him. He looked away and motioned to Peter to invite the Revelles into the hallway to give him some privacy.

"We're okay. I'm shaken up, but she's fine."

"Shaken up? Are you hurt?" Jack said, trying not to sound as panicked as he was.

"No, just kind of in shock I guess."

"What happened?" Jack repeated.

"We had just gotten on the freeway and this car came out of nowhere. The car must have been going ninety miles an hour and cut into my lane. The other car hit the front of our car and we spun around several times. It happened in slow motion just like you hear about—slow motion but then over in an instant. Thank God we ended up facing the right direction. The car skidded off the road into a ditch, and I was able to get it together enough to steer into a snowbank. It was under the overpass. We almost hit the concrete."

"And you both are really all right?" Jack needed reassuring.

"Yes, we'll be fine. Maya was in the back seat strapped in. She didn't even know what was going on. I actually think she enjoyed the spinning."

"Where are you? I'll come and get you." Jack was already up and starting for the door.

"The tow truck is already here. The deputy said he will drive us to the Lexus dealer."

"I'll meet you there and take you home."

"Thanks. My knees are knocking so bad, I don't think I could drive home." Sandy hung up. Jack turned to his partners.

"Listen, everybody, my wife and daughter were in a car accident. They're fine, but I have to pick them up at the car dealer. Peter, can you arrange for a convenient time to reconvene?" Jack said as he hustled out the door.

"No problem, Jack," Peter said as Jack disappeared down the stairs.

When Jack arrived at Lee Motors, he could see the Lexus hanging lifeless, like a side of beef, from the hook of a tow truck. He parked and went inside. Sandy and Maya, looking frazzled, were talking with the owner of the dealership, Phil Lee.

Phil saw Jack first. "Hi there, Jack. Looks like we've got the whole family here now."

Jack grabbed Maya and lifted her up for a kiss. He gave Sandy a concerned smile, which she took in appreciatively. "How's everybody doing?" he asked.

"I'm good, Daddy. Mommy's much better now too." She gave

him a hasty play-by-play. "We were driving, and a car hit us, and we spun around and around and landed in the snow. A tow truck came and picked up our car and then we got to ride in a police car."

"Sounds like quite an adventure," Jack answered. "Sandy, are you really OK?"

"Yes. Much better, thanks," she said, obviously relieved but still visibly shaken.

"Would you like me to take you home now?"

"I am really much better now. I can drive home, but how will you get back to work if I take the minivan?"

Phil interrupted, "I'll fix him up with a ride. I'm sure the insurance will cover it, and if not, Jack will just have to do some pro bono work on my wife's charity walk for the arts."

"Go ahead then, take Maya home. I'll check on you later," Jack conceded. "I'll stay and barter with Phil."

"Thanks," Sandy said as she took the keys in one hand and Maya in the other.

"Bye, Daddy."

"Bye, sweetheart."

Phil told Jack to have his insurance man call the dealership's body shop to make arrangements for the estimate and repairs. He then gave Jack the keys to a loaner. Jack hopped into the car and headed back to the office. On the way, he gave Mickey a call and filled him in on the events of the last hour.

"You sure were lucky," said Mickey, surprised and relieved. "We could have lost both of them."

"I know." Jack sighed.

There was a rather long pause. Jack thought he might have lost the connection, but then Mickey spoke.

"You may not like this Jack, but I think there's a chance this wasn't an accident at all. You have really pissed off some powerful and vengeful folks. By telling Randall Davies to shove his six-figure retainer up his ass, you may have angered the gods. I wouldn't put it past him to order a hit on you."

"Don't you think you're being a little overdramatic, Mr. Holmes?" Jack was only half kidding.

"You can only call me Holmes when I use the accent. Seriously, these guys play for keeps. If you think about it, this will accomplish a lot for the Party. Your death exacts the ultimate revenge, as well as puts William Davies campaign back on the fast track. It also saves them a ton of dough by not having to hire someone to fight it out with you on the campaign trail. No way would Lindsay Revelle win without you. They'd figure to coast across the finish line."

"I know these guys can be ruthless, but murder?" It didn't seem probable to Jack.

"This would not be the first time. There have been many other dirty dealings over the years. Remember Bruce Tiernan, the Opposition candidate for mayor? His death during the '88 campaign was rather suspicious."

"Fell down his basement steps, didn't he?"

"The coroner in those days was George Wahl, one of the Party's boys. Many of us suspected Bruce was dead long before his erstwhile trip down the stairs and old George doctored the evidence to make it look accidental. In those days, violence and blackmail were everyday Party methods of swinging elections. You know that. Actually, Jack, you have saved a lot of people a lot of pain by getting Party candidates elected the old-fashioned way, with votes."

"I was just another form of hired gun. Nobody died, a small consolation considering some of the lowlifes we put into office. Anyway, what now?"

"For you, it's business as usual. Let me get Miles on the case. The authorities will do nothing for you on this. With no one hurt and likely no witnesses or good description of the other vehicle, they have nothing to go on and little motivation given the minor nature of the infraction. So we're on our own. If anyone can find a trail on this one, it's Miles," Mickey said.

From the way Mickey was talking Jack knew he could smell a conspiracy a mile away. As for himself, he just didn't know if he believed that someone had tried to run him off the road. But he did detect a foul odor coming from this. "Go for it," he finally said. "Let me know if Miles needs anything from me or Sandy."

CHAPTER 12

Jack was on the road early and lost in thought when his cell phone rang.

"I hope I didn't catch you in the shower." It was Mickey.

"I don't usually take my cell phone into the shower. Actually, I'm on my way to the Milwaukee Airport. I have meetings in Atlanta this afternoon and tomorrow. You're up awfully early for a man of leisure. What's on your mind?"

"Well, I have news about the car accident. Miles did a little checking and came up with a lead. It seems that a car did in fact try to run your Lexus off the road."

Jack gasped. "What?"

Mickey continued, "It seems one of the employees at the meat market across from the entrance to your subdivision saw a car hanging out in their parking lot on Monday morning. He remembered it was big, a dark color, and had tinted windows. He got to work around eight thirty and the car was parked there. The next time he checked, maybe an hour later, it was gone, so the timeframe matches. Miles also checked out your car. The dent on your lovely pearl-white Lexus was adorned with black paint from the car that ran it off the road. Listen, Jack, I have an even stronger feeling than before that this was not an accident. We must get to the bottom of it before anyone is actually harmed."

"Are Sandy and Maya in danger?" Jack's heart pounded. For the first time, he let himself believe this actually could have been an attempted hit.

"If something sinister is going on they will be much more careful to make sure it's directed at you personally. Harming your family doesn't accomplish their mission. And after the accident with the car, it will be very hard to make anything else seem like an unrelated incident." Mickey was clearly trying to be reassuring, but Jack was not totally buying his reasoning. If they could have mistaken them for him once, why couldn't it happen again?

"What do we do next?" Jack's voice exposed his fear.

"I'd like for Miles to see if Sandy can corroborate."

"How will he do it and not spook her?"

"That's easy. He will say he is with the insurance company and simply getting a statement about the incident, which obviously will include a description of the other car. If she remembers anything, he'll get it from her."

"And if she remembers a dark-colored car with tinted windows?"

"I'm working on that."

"Work quickly," Jack urged.

"That's why a man of leisure such as myself is up at this ungodly hour of the morning."

"Thanks, Mickey. I can't begin to tell you how much I appreciate your help."

"Don't worry about it. I'm merely accumulating meal credits," Mickey said in the most light-hearted tone he could conjure.

On the plane ride to Atlanta, Jack's thoughts went around the horn between Mickey's call, the upcoming meetings in Atlanta, his pending divorce, and Lindsay Revelle's election strategies. He decided to outline the campaign on his legal pad, needing to adjust his mood, or the meetings in Atlanta would certainly be jeopardized. Planning the campaign was the most likely antidote for his uneasiness.

He looked over at Peter, who was seated across the aisle, fully absorbed in the research on Consolidated Foods the staff had prepared. Before they boarded, Peter had shared with Jack how PetroMark was connected to this project. *Focus,* Jack thought. He went back to planning, crossing out entries and scribbling notes in the margin of his notepad.

Peter peeked over. "You know, Jack, if you did your writing on a laptop, you'd have a much easier time editing your work."

"Once in a while I enjoy doing things the old-fashioned way. Besides, this way I don't have to drag all that stuff with me. Between the laptop, the power supply, and all of the cords it's a royal pain."

"Yes, but how will you check email on the road?"

"I'll use my cell phone, your machine, or the room Web-TV hookup if they have one. Anyone who really needs me in an emergency can call me on my cell. We've all become too connected these days. I, for one, am rebelling."

Jack enjoyed lashing out at modern technology. It was a harmless outlet for his anxiety. Peter decided the discussion had run its course and returned his attention to the research file.

The flight took just over two hours and was on time. They grabbed their overnight bags and briefcases from the overhead as they deplaned. After heading down the steepest and most crowded escalator imaginable, they jumped on the tram headed for the main terminal where they caught a cab and proceeded downtown to the meeting.

Jack and Peter walked into Consolidated's building a little before two p.m. They passed through security and took the elevator to the thirty-third floor. The reception area was a shrine to the growth of the company over the past eighty years. It featured maps showing the national landscape of stores along with pictures depicting the evolution of store interiors and the accompanying technology.

They were greeted by Arlene, who took them back to her office for an informal briefing on the agenda for their visit.

"Gentlemen, I'd like to begin with a short overview of Consolidated Foods' history, followed by a meeting with our marketing staff, who will lay out our launch plan for the six Lakeville area stores. That should take us to the end of the day. You can then go across to the Westin, check in to your rooms, and freshen up for dinner. Our president, Bill Henry, will be joining us this evening. He's very bright and engaging. Tomorrow morning we'd like to devote to ironing out the details of the working agreement between our companies."

"Sounds great, Arlene. Before we begin though, I'd like to thank you for honoring our firm with your business. Peter and I couldn't be happier and look forward to a long, mutually beneficial relationship." Jack was on stage once again.

Arlene graciously accepted his thank you and started in with the background on Consolidated. It was a great American success story. One store became two became twenty and so on, all built on the premise of high-quality products, low prices, and superior service. It struck Jack as odd why more companies didn't adopt these three simple principles for success. Most companies and their MBAs overlooked or at least undervalued this obvious formula for success when developing their business models.

They were then joined by four staffers who laid out, in painstaking detail, the mechanics of the store-opening plan. At 4:15, they adjourned. Jack and Peter went across the street to their hotel with a couple of hours free to check email and relax before meeting with the Consolidated folks for cocktails. When Jack got to his room, he called home.

It was Maya who answered. "Hi, Daddy, where are you?"

"I'm in Atlanta on business. How was your day?"

"It was real good. I just got home from Jenny's house. Mommy's sleeping."

"Sleeping? It's not even dinnertime. Is she feeling all right?"

"Jenny's mom dropped me off and Mommy let me in. She said she was tired and was going to take a little nap. It's okay. I'm watching TV and she said she would take me to McDonald's when she gets up."

"Have a great evening, Maya. Tell Mommy I'll try her later," Jack said, masking his concern.

It was not like Sandy to nap. Jack wondered if she was ill or if she was so frightened by the accident that she was using the nap to escape her fears. Given their strained relationship, she was not likely to open up to him. Regardless, he would call later hoping to get an explanation.

The view from the Sun Dial Lounge was spectacular. The lounge sat atop the Westin Peachtree Plaza on the seventy-third floor and overlooked Atlanta in all directions. Peter and Jack got there before the others and reviewed the day's meetings over martinis.

"Doesn't it strike you as odd that they're making such a big deal over six stores?" Jack asked. "Even giving us the red-carpet treatment, with the CEO and all, is somewhat over the top given the size of their company and the relatively small size of this deal."

"The thought had crossed my mind. I have a theory. It's not the size of this deal that's important. Getting into bed with PetroMark is the key. If this premise is successful, they'll clone it all over the country. This alliance will allow them to take market share from all of the major grocery chains, big box stores, and gas station operators. They are looking for the pot of gold at the end of the rainbow."

"If this all works out as you describe, we're in on the ground floor, so to speak." Jack chuckled, realizing how silly his statement sounded given their current extremely lofty perch.

"It's what I was alluding to the other day," said Peter, practically salivating." This deal could move us into national prominence. It could make us rich."

"I wouldn't spend it quite yet, my friend, but I do agree this could be a huge opportunity for the firm. Hey, here comes the entourage. Smile nice for the clients."

Jack shifted into high gear. "Good evening, everyone. What can I get you?"

The entourage included Arlene, the four staffers from the afternoon session, and Drew Tucker, Vice President of Marketing, whom they had met briefly when he stopped by Arlene's office during their meeting. Bill Henry had not yet arrived. They all ordered drinks and began the getting-to-know-you ritual, which consisted of "how many kids," "where'd you go to college," "who'd you work for before this," "do you know so and so," and "who is going to win the Super Bowl" type of questions. Jack emceed the proceedings. After two drinks and a half hour of storytelling and odds making, they were as thick as thieves.

Arlene received a call from Bill Henry. He would meet up with the group at dinner. They adjourned and headed across Peachtree Street to a private dining room at the Ritz-Carlton's Atlanta Grill.

Bill Henry walked into the room after the group was seated at the dining table. Jack got the feeling that if Bill Henry had been of the New England aristocracy instead of the Southern variety, they would have mistaken him for a Kennedy. He had the relaxed demeanor of old wealth coupled with a steely-eyed resolve to do big things. His body language screamed "CEO of a Fortune 500 company."

Mr. Henry made his way around the table greeting each member of the group, finishing with Jack. "Nice to meet you, Jack," he said in a most sincere and friendly way.

"Nice to meet you as well, Bill. We are very pleased to be here with you and your team."

"Speaking of team, are you a Packers fan, Jack?"

"Yes, unabashedly so," he confessed.

"Me too. I went to Texas Tech with Donny Anderson. I was a couple of years behind him. We helped each other both on the gridiron and off."

"So you showed him how to be an All-American running back?" Jack joked, hoping Mr. Henry had a sense of humor.

"No, I showed him how to be an All-American with the girls," Mr. Henry deadpanned, proving much to Jack's delight and relief that he did.

Jack smiled. "What did he help you with?"

"He helped me up off the ground after he ran over me," Mr. Henry said. "It caused me to redirect my efforts into academic pursuits."

"It seems to have worked out well for the both of you," Jack said.

"It sure did. Let me change gears here for a moment. We are excited to have you guys on board. I'm sure you've sensed there is more going on here than the six stores in Wisconsin. If all goes well, this little pilot program will be replicated all over the country. Our friends at PetroMark are with the concept one hundred percent, and you guys can go along for the ride. We'll need a complete commitment that you will prioritize this project within your firm. We want your undivided attention."

"Bill, we are prepared to do what it takes," Peter chimed in.

"Peter's right, Bill." Jack went for the solid "quid pro quo" pitch. "Assuming our contract reflects the type of commitment you're asking for, you will be our number one priority."

"Understood," Mr. Henry said. "You will be handsomely compensated for your work. And our investment will be handsomely rewarded. Everybody wins. Now let's eat."

Bill Henry was through with business for the evening. He had delivered his message and gotten the proper response. They could all now relax and enjoy their steaks and martinis.

They finished eating after ten. The Consolidated folks headed home having done their duty. Jack and Peter walked happily back to their hotel to turn in. It was time for Jack to call Sandy to make sure she was all right.

Sandy answered and sounded somewhat startled. "Uh, hello."

"Hi, I wanted to see if you were OK. Maya answered earlier and said you were napping."

"I was. I had a headache." Her tone showed she was angered at being questioned.

"Are you feeling better?"

"Yes. Anything else?" she snapped.

"Not really. I'm glad you're better."

"Thanks. Good night then." She hung up.

Jack sensed something more was going on than a headache, but there was no way to deal with it from a thousand miles away.

CHAPTER 13

Jack was up early and watched the sun rise over Atlanta from his room on the sixty-fourth floor of the hotel. He wanted to get an early start at organizing his campaign strategy notes as the balance of his day was going to be consumed with hammering out an agreement with Consolidated Foods.

After Jack finished outlining all of the logistical aspects of the campaign—from the announcement of Lindsay's candidacy to the location of his election night victory celebration—he sat down to do the hard work of establishing the philosophical thrust of the campaign. He came up with three basic concepts, which would become the motivation behind every move the campaign would make.

1. The first concept: This campaign was about enriching people's lives in a real way—education, healthcare, public safety, and providing for the elderly.

2. The second concept: To win the election, the constituency of this campaign must be broad based and appeal to multiple ethnic groups, economic strata, and causes while not straying from its stated goals.

3. The third concept: They must demonize the Party at every turn.

As if on cue, the phone rang as Jack finished the last concept. It was Peter.

"Good morning. I trust I didn't wake you." Peter was particularly cheery.

"No, I've been up for hours."

"I have some additional good news," Peter said. "I received a contract proposal by email from PetroMark on the depot project. They will give us a retainer for a minimum of one hundred hours per month for thirty months. Jack, it's twenty grand a month or more, guaranteed. With the deal we're going to make today with Consolidated, it could easily double."

Jack could almost see Peter beaming on the other end of the phone. For him, securing a contract was just like winning an election, only better. You received a job for a specified period of time based on your expertise. You understood the job ahead and how much you would be paid. But for Peter, winning a contract every few days for a new project was far better than for an election every few years.

"That's really terrific. We should come to Atlanta more often. How do you see us billing PetroMark for their participation in the Consolidated project? Is it part of the depot retainer or separate?" Jack asked.

"The email I received from Don Buckley covered that. Consolidated will contract with us and bill PetroMark back for their share."

"Couldn't be simpler. I like it. Since all of this solidifies our revenue stream for the foreseeable future, breakfast is on me," Jack said. "I'll meet you in the coffee shop in twenty minutes."

"Sounds like a plan," Peter said.

Like most mornings, Faye Villarreal was hustling to get into the office before the daily briefing started. Just another hazard of single motherhood. She made it, but just barely, tossing her coat on her chair as she dashed off to the conference room.

The briefing was rather ordinary: assignment reviews, complaints about caseload, and understaffing. The meeting ended at nine thirty.

District Attorney Ted Erickson dismissed the staff but asked Faye to stay.

"The guys from the attorney general's office called. They've gotten their assets in place and will now begin the investigative stage of the initiative. We should expect to have a case or two pop up in the next thirty days."

"Boy oh boy, they've gotten their act together fast."

"It's really quite easy when you get a priority green light from the governor on down. I need you to alert the enforcement people that something will be coming down soon."

"I'll call Jake Malory this morning and update him. Is there anything else I need to do?"

"Read everything you can find on child pornography case law. Send me copies of all the significant cases you find. This is going to get a lot of attention. We need to do our best work in these trials. The public will be up in arms if we fail to convict, not to mention the reaction we will get from our elected officials. The governor and attorney general will be particularly unforgiving," Ted warned.

Faye felt the pressure as well as the excitement this opportunity presented for her. She knew she was up to the task. "I get it. Rest assured we will be ready," she said. The conviction in Faye's voice made Ted smile.

"Yes, we will," Ted said.

Jack and Peter walked into Consolidated's building in lockstep. Buoyed by the contract proposal they received from PetroMark, they entered this meeting knowing that, by the end of the day, they will have solidified the financial wellbeing of their firm for years to come.

"Good morning, gentlemen," greeted Arlene. "I trust you slept well and are ready to do battle over an agreement." She smiled.

"We are ready, but it appears we're outnumbered," Jack said as he looked around the crowded conference table. It included the entire group from the previous evening's dinner, sans Bill Henry, as well as two new faces.

Arlene introduced Blanche Fischer and Warren Duncan, attorneys from their legal department.

Everyone shook hands and sat down. Over the next hour and a half, they discussed the role McKay & Associates would play in opening the new stores. They agreed to a fee schedule, which included hourly rates, minimum hours per month to be guaranteed by a retainer, expense reimbursement, etc. Then came the legal points of the contract. Consolidated proposed their language for a non-disclosure section within the contract which called for complete mutual confidentiality, as well as clauses outlining termination provisions with and without cause. And finally, a rider which encompassed the PetroMark participation in the project. It was all very straightforward and in keeping with similar agreements McKay & Associates had worked under in the past.

"These proposals are acceptable to us in concept," Jack said in closing. "The final language will need to be hammered out with our legal counsel, but I'd say we have a deal. Thank you so much for the confidence you've shown in us. We will commit all of the necessary resources to ensure the success of your project."

There were handshakes all around and, assuming the lawyers were in accord, they agreed to reconvene next week by conference call to get the project underway. Jack gave Peter a little elbow nudge as they packed up to leave. They had gotten everything they could possibly expect and then some.

The ride back to Hartsfield-Jackson Airport was quick as there was little midday traffic. Jack and Peter used the time to check their office voicemails and give a few instructions via email to staff members on various projects. Once on the plane, Jack's thoughts drifted toward what was going on with Sandy and how he would approach her about it. Their strained relationship and pending divorce would make it very difficult to get any cooperation from Sandy, but his concern for Maya's happiness and safety was foremost. Jack would have to be at his diplomatic best if he was going to get to the bottom of it.

When they arrived at Mitchell Field, Jack and Peter parted ways, As soon as Jack hopped into his car and exited the parking lot, he called Mickey.

"Did Miles get any information from Sandy about the accident?" he asked eagerly.

"Yes," Mickey answered. "He got a good corroboration on the car. Sandy confirmed the dark color and the tinted windows." He paused for a moment. "She also confirmed something else."

Jack swallowed a lump in his throat. "What's that?"

"It appears she had been drinking before Miles got there. Being the top-notch detective that he is, Miles checked your recycling bin in the driveway on his way out to his car. It was filled almost to the top with empty Merlot bottles. Unless you've emptied some of those yourself, I'd say she has a severe drinking problem."

"Just dandy," Jack said sarcastically. "That explains her being asleep in the middle of the afternoon when Maya got home." He sighed. "I'm not sure how to handle this. I want to help Sandy, and I must protect Maya. Any ideas?"

"Talk to Steven Clark. There may be a way bring it to light through the collaborative divorce process."

"I don't understand."

"If Sandy is confronted with losing custody or other privileges as a result of a drinking problem, she will be more likely to seek help."

"If I don't confront her about it now, Maya could be in danger."

"True. But take it from a very experienced alcoholic: she won't stop just because you tell her to. She could be very contrite and promise not to drink when she's responsible for Maya and the next thing you know she's drunk at the school picnic. You don't have the power to make her stop, even if you were on the best of terms. Given your strained relationship, you have virtually no chance."

So I just wait for it to come out in the divorce discussions? I can't stand idly by."

"Call Steven. And call me later and let me know what he says."

Jack agreed. He called Steven and left a voice mail. He arrived home shortly after being extremely apprehensive about what he would find there.

He came into the house through the kitchen. He fully expected to find an open wine bottle on the counter. Much to his relief, there was none. He would avoid a confrontation on the drinking issue at least for tonight.

Maya and Sandy were in the family room. Sandy was on the computer and Maya was watching *Finding Nemo* for the forty-seventh time.

"Good afternoon, ladies," Jack said in a light-hearted tone.

"Daddy!" Maya squealed as she ran to him.

He gave her a giant hug. He got an indifferent nod from Sandy who was engrossed with the computer.

"Did anything exciting happen while I was gone?" Jack asked.

"Nope," answered Maya, as he had hoped.

Sandy looked up from the computer for a moment. "A guy came by from the insurance company. Asked a few basic questions about my recollection of the accident," she said matter-of-factly.

"Anything on the approval of the claim for repairs?" Jack was carrying out his part in the charade.

"Nothing."

Miles had obviously done his job to perfection. Sandy suspected nothing. Jack hoped it would turn out there was nothing for her to be suspicious about and that Miles would be the last any of them would hear about Mickey's murder-for-hire theory. He wasn't particularly confident that would be the case.

CHAPTER 14

Jack headed off to work excited about the day. With two huge new contacts in tow, the morning briefing would be uplifting for everyone. There would be new assignments for staff members, additional hires to contemplate, outside resources to alert, press releases to write, and most importantly, that special vibrancy that comes from competitive business. He had the instant excitement of being chosen over his competitors and savoring the spoils of victory. He couldn't help thinking this process was just like being asked to go to the Sadie Hawkins dance by the most popular girl in school.

When he got to his office, Jack sat down to outline his thoughts from the meeting at Consolidated. They had covered some contract concerns for the firm's attorneys and an initial project overview to be covered at the staff meeting. His notes regarding Lindsay Revelle's campaign were much more extensive. They covered the three basic principles, which formed the foundation of the campaign strategy, some ideas for his announcement speech, and recommendations for personal appearances leading up to the primary.

Just as he finished, Donna walked in. "The staff meeting is ready to go in the conference room. You have a very keyed-up group in there this morning."

"They have every right to be. The two deals we finalized yesterday will provide job security for all of us for years to come."

"Well then, get in there and feed the animals."

Jack headed to the conference room for the staff meeting with a big smile on his face. It was one of those special occasions where the entire staff would be exuberant and one hundred percent in step.

"Hail the conquering hero!" Peter shouted as Jack walked into the conference room.

After the applause died down, Jack replied, "You mean *heroes*. Everyone in this room made a tremendous contribution toward winning this contract. Ladies and gentlemen, there is no better feeling in business than this one. Two major corporations have told us we are the best. They have authenticated our credentials in a most definitive and lucrative way. Now we must go out and fulfill the promise these clients have seen in us. Each and every one of you will touch these projects. Do your best work and we will all benefit for many years to come."

With that said, they got to work assigning the senior staff members who would have overall responsibility for the new client relationships. That group would in turn develop the initial PR campaign outline, present it to the clients for approval, and then select the balance of the account service team based on the resources required to execute the final plan. Peter would oversee this stage of the project, enabling Jack to return, for the moment, to Lindsay Revelle's election campaign.

As soon as the meeting concluded, Jack headed off to Lindsay's house to put the finishing touches on the formal announcement of the Revelle for Congress candidacy.

The ride to Lindsay's house took Jack over the Harbor Bridge and directly past the site where PetroMark wanted to build its depot. He could only hope Robin Revelle's opposition to commercial development of the area would not create a campaign liability for Lindsay or a conflict of interest for Jack. It was naïve of Jack to think it would not become an issue, but he decided to adopt a head-in-the-sand attitude for the time being. He would cross *that* bridge when he came to it. Hopefully later rather than sooner.

When Jack pulled up to the Revelles' house, the parking spaces in front of the house and the driveway were filled with cars. Lindsay had mentioned there would be several members of his election committee present, but from the looks of things this was not going to be an intimate gathering.

When Jack entered the house, his suspicions were confirmed. Lindsay and Robin rushed to meet him and began introducing the congregation. There was Yancey Banks, Jr., the prominent civil rights attorney who would act as the campaign chair; Sylvia Connors, the CPA who would act as treasurer; Jeffrey Shapiro, representing a coalition of liberal groups opposed to the Party; Lindsay's sister, Mary Kay, who would act as Lindsay's assistant; and a collection of local political movers and shakers who would coordinate the efforts in each of the wards in the congressional district. What Jack had hoped would be a strategy session turned into a pep rally.

Yancey Banks opened the proceedings. "We are here today to begin the process of making history. Lindsay Revelle goes to Washington!"

The group applauded and cheered which, in the confines of the Revelles' living room, sounded like the Beatles at Shea Stadium.

Lindsay got up and quieted the group with a wave of his hand. "I am humbled by your support and enthusiasm. This Friday night at La Follette Hall, we will be formally announcing our candidacy. With your help, we will win this nomination on April sixth and go on in November to take our district's congressional seat back from the Liberty Party that has held it for sixteen years."

The group cheered even louder than before. Again, Lindsay quieted them with a wave of his hand. "There is much to do. Each and every one of you will be called upon to play a significant role in this campaign. Yancey will take over the meeting now, discuss your specific assignments, and set up the next meeting where we will lay out our initiatives leading up to the primary."

Again, more applause. This time the decibel level shook the crystal goblets in the Revelles' china cabinet, adding a strange, tinkling sound to the celebration. Jack couldn't help but be amused at the similarities and differences between the two meetings he had attended that morning. Hopefully their outcomes would be equally successful.

Lindsay and Yancey exchanged a handshake and hug as Lindsay headed out of the living room toward the kitchen. He motioned for Jack to follow.

"It appears I have strong support from at least a dozen voters," Lindsay quipped as they stepped into the kitchen.

"Loyal and loud," said Jack. "The best kind. Now we just have to add fifty thousand more and you're home free."

"I hope you've got the plan to get us there."

"I do."

Jack laid out his plan as they sat at the kitchen table. It initially called for a massive show of strength at the announcement. Jack reasoned if they could gather a full house at La Follette Hall, and if that full house was properly seasoned with members of influential activist groups with a few key leaders from the Opposition and a diverse cross-section of the electorate sprinkled in, they just might make the primary a one-horse race. If they could accomplish that, they could then spend all of their energies and resources on winning the general election, thereby dealing the Party a major blow.

"Your speech on Friday night is crucial. If the support is there and the speech is a blockbuster, you will capture the local news for the entire weekend. The leaders of the Opposition will recognize you are far and away their best chance to beat the Party in November and will discourage other Opposition candidates from running in the Primary. Luckily no one has declared yet, which will make their job much easier, assuming your announcement garners overwhelming local support."

"I'm confident it will," Lindsay replied.

"If we can get to unopposed status, another wonderful thing will happen. We will have the Opposition's financial backing from day one. We will have more money to spend, and all of the contributions that would have gone to the Opposition's various other candidates will come to your campaign. It is the only way we can fund a credible campaign in the face of the Party's overwhelming war chest."

"Sounds like I'd better hit a home run on Friday night," Lindsay responded.

"Make it a grand slam, my friend."

"Ideas?"

Jack went over his three-point mantra. He also added a few key concepts, which would catch the attention of the Opposition leaders and a few more that would lend themselves to sound bites for the press to pick up on. Even though Lindsay was accomplished at speaking to groups, a political speech was another thing altogether. A political speech was totally different than a speech about politics. Jack gave him a few basic tips like pausing to let applause die down, speaking into the TV cameras on key points, and acknowledging important people in the crowd. He kept it simple, as he wanted Lindsay's natural appeal to come through. Something overly rehearsed or staged could do more harm than good. Lindsay listened intently and made a full page of notes.

Jack left Lindsay's house feeling on top of the world. The staff meeting left him confident of his firm's future and the "rally" at Lindsay's house left him energized about the campaign. Feeling he was on a roll, he called Mickey for an update on Miles's investigation.

I've got good news and bad news," Mickey said. "The good news is Miles has tracked down the car that hit yours. The bad news is it belongs to a Chicago cop who apparently does a little muscle-type work on the side."

"Are you sure?" Jack was shocked. It was finally confirmed that this was something sinister.

"Of course, I'm sure. Miles knows what he's doing. The cop is a bad apple who's well connected to the Party. It seems his primary off-duty source of income is being one of Franklin Modesky's bodyguards. Modesky is the Party's Illinois chairman. It is not much of a stretch to find him on loan to our local Party's constabulary."

"What do I do?" There was real alarm in Jack's voice.

Mickey tried to sound reassuring. "First of all, get out of your house and move in here. I am sure the attack on your family was unintentional, but they will be safer if you are separated as much as possible. It is unlikely the party will attempt anything so brazen in the future, but we can't be too careful. Just to be on the safe side, Miles will be tailing you for a while to make sure no one is after you."

"I'm not sure I want to see Miles every time I look in my rear-view mirror. That would give me the creeps."

"Don't worry, you won't know he's there. Besides, having him around should give you comfort. He'll be your guardian angel."

"If your theory is correct, I'm going to need more help than one guardian angel can provide," Jack shot back.

"I really think you're safe from bodily harm," Mickey said reassuringly. "Someone in the Party's upper echelon just got carried away. Randall Davies is not stupid. If they want you out of their way, I'm sure they'll likely take a much subtler approach. Some more sophisticated form of coercion."

"Now I'm relieved," Jack responded sarcastically.

"Seriously, they won't be dumb enough to try that again. Not since they botched it so badly the first time. Just move out like you planned and leave the rest to me."

"OK, I'll get some of my stuff together tonight and stay at your place tomorrow night."

"Good. Molly will enjoy having two people in the house to

annoy. See you tomorrow night and don't worry. Miles and I will make sure you stay safe," Mickey said.

Jack was not at all comforted. He knew Davies and his cronies generally got what they wanted, and if they wanted him out of the picture, he was in some form of grave danger. Mickey and Miles were his only compatriots in this battle, and the three of them appeared to be no match for an army of Party operatives.

Maybe the best defense was a good offense, he thought. He would call Randall Davies and confront him with the allegation that he was behind the hit-and-run. Surely once Davies knew they were on to him he would have to back off for fear of detection. Reason prevailed, however. Jack realized Davies would only deny the charge. The accusation would serve only to strengthen the Party's resolve to harm or discredit him. He conceded that he would have to leave the sleuthing to Mickey and Miles for the time being and concentrate on his work and keeping his family safe.

His cell phone rang; causing him to jump. It was Donna. "The Lexus dealer called, and your car is ready. You can pick it up any-time."

Jack headed off to Lee Motors. It would be nice to get behind the wheel of his own car again. When he got to the body shop, his car was sitting out front. The sight of it sent a chill down his spine as he visualized Sandy and Maya being forced off the road careening toward the concrete overpass support. He gathered himself and went inside to return the keys to the loaner and to retrieve his own. After a signature on the repair order receipt, he was on his way.

He headed back to his office with a mixture of emotions churning uneasily in his stomach. Another caustic ingredient was about to be added to the mix. He suddenly realized he was already fifteen minutes late for the next round of collaborative divorce WrestleMania. He called Steven Clark on his cell phone.

"Jack, where are you?" Steven whispered, obviously surrounded and in enemy territory.

"Sorry, my meeting ran late. I'll be there in about five minutes. Can you keep the dogs at bay a little while longer? By the way, did you get my message about the accident?"

"The dogs are no problem. We're all billing $275 an hour. Your soon-to-be ex-wife, however, is another story. Oh, and yes, I got your message."

"Do the best you can until I get there. Offer them dibs on the espresso maker if you have to."

"Will do. Just get here as soon as you can."

When Jack arrived a few minutes later, everyone was seated around the large conference table. Sandy's minions all had their arms folded across their chests in unified disapproval as if to say, "This little transgression is really going to cost you"!

After Jack made all of the appropriate apologies, they began the discussion of finances. Sandy did not work and hadn't since their marriage. Jack's income was the family's sole support, roughly $20,000 per month after taxes.

The experts at Watkins & Relford had determined Jack should pay all of household costs to keep Sandy and Maya in their home, about $4,300 per month; $2,500 a month for Maya's direct support; and $6,000 a month for Sandy's spousal support. That added up to just under $13,000 a month and leaving Jack about $7,000 to pay for a place to live and all of his monthly expenses and walking-around money. In addition, Sandy laid claim to 50 percent of everything else; the equity in their home, their shared possessions, including the motorcycle, Jack's equity in the business, as well as half of the value of their investments, retirement funds, and so forth.

Jack and Steven had a totally different point of view, which included a valuation of Sandy's earning capacity. Their proposal included letting Sandy have the house free and clear. Jack would pay off the mortgage. He would pay Sandy $4,000 per month, but the household expenses et al would be her responsibility. There was no argument over the $2,500 in child support or an equal share of the investments and retirement funds at their value on the day the divorce was final. The issue of the equity in McKay & Associates was another story. He had built the firm long before their marriage. Since the value of the firm was directly tied to his being active in the business, the issue of "lack of marketability" came into play. He couldn't sell the firm and receive its fair value without staying on. That lack of flexibility was not something he was willing to consider and was the source of the offer to buy her the house. Steven proffered that Jack's equity in the firm, discounted for lack of marketability, was roughly equivalent to his equity in the home.

After much heated discussion back and forth, they arrived at an agreement on only one major point. Jack would move out the next day.

Jack spent Thursday night packing a couple of weeks' worth of clothes and some basic necessities for the move to Mickey's. Since this was an interim move, he would leave most of his belongings behind until he had a more permanent landing spot. As he was packing, Maya wandered in.

"Hi, honey. I thought you were sleeping," Jack said as cheerfully as he could.

"Daddy, I don't want you to go." The pout on her face was devastating.

"I know, but Mommy and I need to live apart now. Remember what I told you. You will stay with me several nights a week. You'll have your own room, and while I'm at Mickey's you'll be able to spend a lot of time with Molly. That'll be fun, won't it?"

"I guess so. Take this with you." She handed Jack a photo of the three of them at Disney World. Maya was three at the time, and they were all wearing mouse ears. She had taken the picture from the end table in the living room.

Jack wiped a tear from his eye. "Thank you so much. I'll keep it next to my bed always."

CHAPTER 15

Friday promised to be just as eventful as the day before. Jack had staff meetings lined up on the new PetroMark and Consolidated projects, then there was Lindsay's candidacy announcement, and finally a late dinner at Mickey's to inaugurate his moving in.

Jack donned his charcoal gray chalk-stripe Brioni suit, crisp white Ike Behar dress shirt, and red print Robert Talbot silk tie. The look was stylish but very professional, appropriate for his business meetings and not too fancy for the political rally. It was a little much for the dinner at Mickey's, but he would then, unfortunately, have plenty of other clothes with him to change into when he got there.

He was out of the house before either Sandy or Maya awakened. Another heart-wrenching scene with either would not be a good way to start his day or theirs. He put three suitcases of clothes and two boxes of other paraphernalia into the trunk of his Lexus and headed out knowing full well from now on he would be only a visitor in that house.

On the way to the office, he stopped at Starbucks and had an extra shot of espresso added to his usual grande non-fat latte. He hoped it would jolt him out of the funk caused by a most restless night and the unsettling exile from his home.

When Jack arrived at the office, Peter's car was the only one in the parking lot. He passed Peter's office on the way to his and thought it odd the door was closed. He heard muffled voices, which was odd. He'd ask him about it later.

It took Jack a full hour to get through his email messages. The news of Lindsay's announcement had reached the media and they were all clamoring for the story. Jack formulated a basic response, which he cut and pasted into each return email. Consistency of the outgoing messages was the best way to assure some semblance of order in what was offered to the press from the campaign.

Jack only half-heartedly prepared for the staff meetings. He knew Peter had the game plan wired for each client and that the staff would do a meticulous job on their respective assignments. He was primarily a cheerleader at this point, urging them on to "be the best they can be." Later on, he would jump in as an editor, helping them hone the presentations, and then again when it came time to actually present them to the clients. He was, after all, the lead actor in their repertory company.

After the eight o'clock staff meeting, he approached Peter. "You were in early this morning."

"Yeah, I had a couple of calls to the East Coast I wanted to get out of the way before the staff meetings."

"Anything I should know about?" Jack was trying his best to be nonchalant with his questioning.

"Just routine stuff with Don Buckley," Peter replied.

"Rick Cartwright has put him in charge of managing the relationship from the PetroMark side."

Jack trusted Peter implicitly, but there was something uneasy about this exchange. The early morning closed-door phone call made him a little suspicious. He had a hunch there was something more than "routine" going on, but he decided to leave it alone.

La Follette Hall was built in 1947 to house large public gatherings of all kinds. It was named in honor of Robert "Fighting Bob" La Follette, the famous Wisconsin politician from the early twentieth century. La Follette had served Wisconsin in the House of Representatives, the senate, and as governor. In 1924, he ran for president as an independent against Calvin Coolidge. He earned his nickname as a result of his fiery battles against corruption, staunch support for progressive reforms, and the ability to inspire a crowd with rousing oratory. That legacy made the hall the perfect setting for Lindsay Revelle's coming out party. It echoed the very principles Lindsay would address in his speech and embodied the message of reform that would form the foundation of his campaign.

When Jack pulled up to La Follette Hall, the parking lot was full of trucks from the local TV stations as well as two from Milwaukee. This was a sight that would brighten the day of any good PR guy, satellite dishes atop each truck ready to beam news of Lindsay Revelle's candidacy to several hundred thousand potential voters. His pre-announcement publicity had brought out all of the key media types in the area. Now if only CNN, the Associated Press, and Reuters were here. That would be a clean sweep.

Sure enough, as he entered the cavernous hall, he saw a group of familiar faces congregating at the refreshment table. If you wanted to find the press, find the refreshments. Surprisingly, the group included Jim Clancy of CNN, Beth Jordan of Reuters, and Matthew Gisemar of the *Chicago Tribune* who was, in one thrust, attempting to stuff an entire chocolate éclair into his mouth.

Jack was elated. The presence of the major news organizations provided the type of national exposure that could lead to substantial help from Reform Party Headquarters. And if Matthew Gisemar didn't choke on his éclair, the bonus of the *Tribune's* coverage would carry Lindsay's campaign to Chicago where it could get the attention of key union leaders, as well as activists in its influential African American community. If those two groups took an interest in Lindsay, they could provide enormous strength, stature, and much-needed funding to his fledgling campaign.

"Welcome, everyone. So glad you could make it," Jack said, shaking hands all around.

"Lindsay Revelle could turn out to be quite a story," quipped Rachel Brandel, the AP correspondent who joined the group as Jack was conducting the receiving line. "Jack McKay leading the campaign for an Opposition candidate against the Party and Randall Davies's progeny may be an even bigger story."

"I'm here doing my job, just like you are Rachel," Jack said with a smile. "Lindsay Revelle is your story. Here's a man who really wants to do great things and has the capacity to make those things happen. You know it's my job to hype the candidates who hire me, but you also know I would not have gone with this one, given my past affiliations, if he weren't something special." He was almost scolding now.

Jack had spoken with real conviction and the reporters ate it up. Matthew Gisemar even put down a second éclair to take notes.

On stage, Yancey Banks was approaching the microphone. "Ladies and gentlemen, can I please have your attention?"

The crowd quieted and the reporters turned their attention to the podium.

Banks continued, "I would like to take this opportunity to introduce my friend, Mr. Lindsay Revelle."

The highly partisan crowd broke into thunderous applause. Lindsay walked slowly to the podium, holding Robin's hand in his left and shaking hands with the committee members assembled on stage with his right. When he got to the podium, he kissed Robin, hugged Yancey, and waved to the crowd, just as they had rehearsed it in his kitchen.

Lindsay stepped up to the podium microphone.

"Good evening. I appreciate all of you coming here tonight to hear what I have to say. Robin and I came back to Wisconsin, to our roots, to raise our family but also to make a difference in this community. Since we arrived back here four years ago, it became apparent this district desperately needed new leadership and a new direction, starting with our representation in Washington.

"For too many years, the good ol' boy network has thrived in the Lakeville area. This district has long been controlled by a party that has used cronyism, favoritism, and nepotism to reward a select few of its citizens: those with money and power. In the face of all that money and power, voters have seen any real change as impossible, or at best unlikely.

"That is about to change. I am here tonight to announce my candidacy for Congress in the First District."

There were screams and applause. Shouts of "Lindsay! Lindsay! "Lindsay!" filled the room. Lindsay smiled, gave a brief wave to acknowledge the crowd, and then continued.

"With this campaign, I plan to make each and every one of you a believer in the greatness we can achieve in our district and in our country. Together, we can replace the representation that has created the cynicism and apathy that plagues our district with one that will instill optimism and enthusiasm by initiating positive action and effecting real change.

"For too many years, there was no one who was truly working to ensure the citizens in this district received the attention to the issues that concerned them most, issues that must be addressed to achieve the highest possible standard of living, a standard that each and every person in this district is entitled to.

"I am talking about basic fundamental principles like affordable, high-quality healthcare that will assure the very best that medical science has to offer for each and every citizen regardless of income level.

"Public schools that provide a first-class education for all of our children so they can make the most of the opportunities in their lives.

"Preserving and improving our environment so the air we breathe and the water we drink is safe for us and even safer for those who follow.

"And promoting better jobs for all of our working people so your wages, benefits, and working conditions provide a quality of life you can be proud of.

"Politicians always promise to address these issues when they run for office. You will also hear me addressing those issues during this campaign, but the difference will be that I will address them again and again each and every day after I am elected. During this campaign, I will state my positions on the issues clearly and often, and I will debate this platform with any and all of the other candidates running for this office whenever and wherever possible. When I am elected, I will debate those same issues on the floor of the House of Representatives.

"In closing, I am asking you for your support in the upcoming primary election and then in the general election. With your help, I can go to Washington and give this district an outspoken advocate for all of our citizens, the kind of active representation you want and deserve. With your help we can win this election and begin the task of focusing our government on the issues that concern you the most and enacting meaningful legislation which impacts your life in a positive way.

"Thank you all for coming. I look forward to earning your vote as this campaign unfolds and having the great honor of serving you in the United States Congress.

"Good night, God bless you all, and God bless the United States of America."

While cameras flashed and an ecstatic crowd roared their approval, Jack couldn't help but feel proud of the choice he had made. Robin joined Lindsay at the podium, and they kissed and waved to the throng. Yancey joined them and raised Lindsay's hand as if he were a victorious prizefighter. The three of them walked off the stage while the cheering continued unabated. It was as if the crowd were attending a rock concert and pleading for an encore.

Jack had slipped backstage during the speech and greeted the trio as they left the view of the crowd.

"Very well done. It was a great jumpstart for the campaign. Lindsay, are you up for a little impromptu press conference? The reporters are all stationed outside the stage door waiting for the chance to ask you some questions."

"I suppose we should take advantage of the opportunity, don't you think?" Lindsay said eagerly.

"Yes, definitely. It's nice to see your doctoral studies included exploiting the press."

Jack led Lindsay outside to meet with the press. Lindsay fielded questions for about ten minutes, reciting the three-point mantra at every opportunity. Jack stepped in and ended the press conference when he felt the message had been appropriately delivered. As the crowd of reporters dispersed, he said good night to Lindsay, Robin and Yancey and headed to his car extremely pleased. The campaign had a spectacular kickoff. The momentum felt unstoppable.

When Jack arrived at Mickey's, he pulled his car into the empty stall in the garage. Since the accident, Mickey had no car; instead, he filled the other side of the garage with books, magazines, and other memorabilia from his storied career. Miles had parked near the street.

Jack took the side door from the garage into the yard. He saw Mickey and Miles studying the charcoal grill, its warmth keeping them comfortable in the chilly Wisconsin evening.

"The way you two are staring into that grill, there must be something pretty exciting going on in there," Jack teased.

"You're late," scolded Mickey. "But fortunately, the embers still have sufficient heat to properly cook my famous pork chops."

"Good. I couldn't stand the shame if I somehow ruined your well-timed plan." Jack turned to Miles. "Hello, Miles. It's nice to see you again." As always, Miles looked dapper even when casually dressed in jeans and a polo shirt.

"Nice to see you too, Jack."

"Enough small talk," Mickey interrupted. "One of you guys go inside and bring out the pork chops. We have no time to waste."

Jack had two of his suitcases in tow and offered to fetch the pork chops so he could deposit the suitcases inside. Mickey would surely appreciate the economy of effort. Miles volunteered to go inside to set the table, obviously a cover so he could escape the cold. Jack went inside and returned with a mountain of marinated pork chops.

"We'll never finish these," he said.

Mickey inhaled the sweet smell of the chops. "Leftovers are a bachelor's best friend, Jack. It's the first lesson you learn when you start cooking for one. How did the announcement proceedings go?"

Jack began placing the chops on the grill. "Extremely well, thanks. Lindsay's address was expertly delivered, and the press coverage was extraordinary. We had all the locals, a couple from Milwaukee, three national news services, and the *Tribune*. There were plenty of sound bites to go around."

"I can see Randall Davies now, sitting in front of his TV set screaming profanities at you at the top of his lungs, knowing you have put a major wrench in his plans," Mickey said.

"Yes, but it might only serve to strengthen his resolve to eliminate Jack from the campaign," Miles added as he returned to the warmth of the grill.

"Don't you think now that things are underway, he'll back off?"

said Jack. "He must know we have a strategy in place by now and whether or not I orchestrate it, it will be carried out." Jack was hoping he would get support for his theory. It would certainly help him sleep at night.

"The chops will need to be turned in three minutes," said Mickey, changing the subject. "Seven minutes on side two and they'll be ready to eat. Let's continue this conversation over the dinner table."

Jack turned his attention to the chops and Miles took Mickey inside. Ten minutes later, Jack placed the platter of pork chops on the table alongside the salad and a stack of baked potatoes.

"If my father were only alive to see this," chuckled Miles, "Here I am on Shabbos eating pork chops. He could begrudgingly accept my being gay, but this would have driven him insane."

"You were brought up Orthodox?" Jack asked.

"In my Brooklyn neighborhood, if you were Jewish you were Orthodox. The Conservatives and Reforms all moved to Long Island. Only the Orthodox and the Puerto Ricans stayed behind."

"I assume since you are chewing on a pork chop bone that you no longer subscribe to Orthodox Jewish traditions," Mickey interjected.

"It's like this: I feel very strongly about my Jewish heritage. To me it's a cultural heritage, not a religious one, much in the same way Irish and Italian people look at their backgrounds. Ethnicity far overshadows the religious affiliation. I find the practice of organized religion humorous actually. For a group of people to claim to communicate with a higher power by standing on one foot, rubbing their bellies, and patting their heads is downright comical. Religion started out as a code of conduct and grew into a fanatical display of racism. 'If you don't believe what I believe, you are a heathen. Off with your head.' Definitely not for me."

"Or me for that matter," Jack agreed.

They took time off from their theology discussion to dig in on their pork chops and potatoes. As usual, Mickey had buried his baked potato in sour cream.

"If I can change the subject, please tell me how you tracked down the bad cop from Chicago," Jack said.

"Pretty basic forensics actually," Miles responded. "I took some paint shavings from the damaged fender of your Lexus. I analyzed the black paint and traced its origin. You see, paint manufacturers often formulate based on specifications provided by clients like car companies and large body-shop chains. This formula matched one made exclusively for the AutoMagic chain of body shops. There are three in our area, and eleven in the Chicago area. Also, I got a break when I interviewed the clerk at Leichtman's meat market. He noticed the car parked in the lot had darkened windows and one of those adjustable beams next to the driver's mirror that most police cars have.

"Based on the rest of the description of the car I got from the clerk and your wife, I determined it had to be one of those decommissioned police cars that were sold at auction. Eighty percent of those cars are Ford Crown Victoria's. Since the car was decommissioned, it had to be a least five years old. So I set out to visit the fourteen AutoMagic shops looking for someone who had worked on a decommissioned Crown Victoria police car that had been painted black and was at least five years old."

"Obviously, you found one."

"Very good, my dear Watson," Mickey chimed in, using his English accent.

"Yes, I did. I was also lucky the car owner used the same body-shop chain to repair the damage as the one who had painted it black in the first place. The third AutoMagic place I went to in Chicago had just finished with a car that fit the description. Damage to the front passenger side quarter panel with remnants of pearl paint to boot. I flashed my old badge from the Lakeville Police forensic lab and the body-shop owner came across with the owner's name and address. Once I had that, I made a couple of calls to my Chicago contacts and the rest of the information just flowed."

"Well, now that we've straightened that all out, let's go back to Jack's other question. What do you think Randall Davies's next move will be?"

"I'm the 'after the fact' guy, remember? My expertise is un-covering the evidence and motives once the deed is done. But if I had to venture a guess, I'd say he still plans to go after Jack in some other less obvious way. Not just because he is vindictive, but because Lindsay Revelle is a viable threat to his agenda, and he needs to do everything he can to get his son elected."

"What do I do to stop him?" Jack was getting scared again.

"You do nothing. Go about your business. As the kids say, we've got your back." Mickey was trying his best to be reassuring.

Jack was unconvinced. "What will you do?"

"Don't worry about it. We will be there when you need us. Please trust me on this. We have the advantage of knowing Davies is up to something. Now we just have to anticipate his moves and head him off at the pass."

"Mickey, it's not a matter of trust. You know that. It's just the fact that he could come at me in so many ways that covering all of the possibilities seems like an insurmountable task."

Miles chimed in, "Without sounding too cloak and dagger, we've got some ideas on how to keep him away from you. Just concentrate on your job and we'll do ours."

For some reason, Jack found Miles more convincing. He wasn't sure why, but Jack believed that somehow Miles actually would be able to protect him.

CHAPTER 16

It was the best of times, it was the worst of times . . . Jack couldn't get the opening line of *A Tale of Two Cities* to stop repeating itself over and over in his head. He was parked in front of his old house, picking up his daughter for a Saturday of father-daughter frolicking. Earlier, he'd spent an hour on the phone with Steven Clark trashing his soon-to-be ex-wife for having a drinking problem and showing signs of being unfit for motherhood.

"Hi, Maya," Jack shouted through the open window of his car. "Are you ready for a big day of fun and a sleepover at Mickey and Molly's house?"

"Hi, Daddy," she answered unenthusiastically. Maya looked overburdened both physically and emotionally as she stood next to the driveway with her overnight bag in hand and her backpack full of toys slung over her shoulders.

"Are you okay?" Jack asked as he got out of the car.

She nodded but was unconvincing.

"What's the matter?"

"When I go with you, Mommy's sad. When I go with Mommy, you're sad. I make both of you sad." Tears filled her eyes.

The eloquent Jack McKay was, for once, at a temporary loss for words. He grabbed his daughter and gave her the biggest and longest hug he had ever given her. Then he kissed her salty cheek and whispered, "You are the best thing in Mommy's and my life. You are where our happiness comes from. We just need to learn how to share you better, understand?"

"I guess so."

"Come on, let's go have some fun," he said, attempting to sound cheery.

They loaded Maya's bags into the trunk of the car and headed out. Jack caught a glimpse of Sandy watching them through the sheer curtains in the living room. He looked away for a moment, and when he looked back, she was gone.

Lindsay Revelle slept late on Saturday morning. The festivities of the previous evening had left him unable to fall asleep until well after midnight. The realization that he had taken the leap and was now a candidate had given him an adrenaline rush that would not quit.

He was awakened by a commotion coming from the kitchen. Throwing on his robe, he went in search of the source. There he found a room full of neighbors, mostly African Americans, laden with an assortment of baked goods, roasts, and side dishes. It mirrored a Thanksgiving family get-together except these people were not family. They were well-wishers contributing to the campaign in the best way they knew how. Stock the larder so Lindsay and Robin could hit the campaign trail unencumbered with the responsibility of feeding their family. It was also a way to show their affection and support for one of their own.

Lindsay greeted the group warmly, completely oblivious to the fact he was in his bathrobe, unwashed, and with morning breath. "Great to see you all. What a wonderful thing it is to know we have such terrific friends!"

"We're with you all the way to Washington, Lindsay," Mrs. Phelps cheered. All forms of approval came from the rest of the group.

It was only day two of the campaign and Lindsay was conducting a political rally in his kitchen at nine thirty on a Saturday morning bedecked in a bathrobe. It was the epitome of a grassroots campaign and he loved it. Looking out of the kitchen window, he saw his kids playing in the backyard, seemingly uninterested in the goings-on in the kitchen. He hoped they could stay as unaffected by the rest of the campaign process and, with a little luck, life as the offspring of a congressman.

Jack and Maya pulled up in front of the Revelle's' house. Jack needed to drop off some blank nomination petitions for Lindsay's family and friends to circulate. They needed at least one thousand signatures from valid district voters to get Lindsay's name on the ballot. Based on the enthusiasm of the crowd they discovered in the Revelle's' kitchen, getting the signatures would surely be a slam-dunk.

Lindsay welcomed Jack with a handshake and a huge smile. "Jack, come in and meet some friends of mine."

One by one, Jack greeted the members of the kitchen committee. He also introduced everyone to Maya, who was being very shy and half hiding behind Jack. Robin noticed how uncomfortable Maya was and coaxed her into joining the other kids in the backyard. She was instantly at ease once she escaped the tumult of the kitchen. Robin introduced Maya to Gina, their seven-year-old daughter. The kids were fast friends in a matter of seconds.

Jack deftly worked the room. He talked issues, campaign strategy, fundraising, the Party as the "Evil Empire," and most of all, the need to get out the vote in support of Lindsay's candidacy. Appropriate for a kitchen rally, the supporters ate it all up. They came into the house as curious friends and neighbors and left as proselytized zealots ready to canvass the community to garner support for their favorite son. It was a real-life example of the power of an effective PR effort, one an academician like Lindsay could truly appreciate.

Jack's fortuitous arrival and positive contribution to the ad hoc rally provided Lindsay with absolute confirmation he had chosen his wingman wisely.

After about an hour, the impromptu gathering broke up. None too soon for Lindsay, who had not had the opportunity to wash up since being awakened by the crowd. While he retreated to the bathroom to take care of his hygienic requirements, Robin entertained Jack at the kitchen table.

"Jack, how come you never ran for public office? You know all the ins and outs. You're very bright and articulate. You're handsome and accomplished. Seems to me you'd be a natural."

"Spoken like a true PR professional. How about coming to work at McKay & Associates?"

"Are you planning to open a Washington branch?" Robin said with a smile.

"Touché. I have every confidence this is exactly what you should be doing."

"Me too. Now back to my question. Why haven't you sought public office?"

"Quite simple really. The allure of politics for me is all about the competition. I love it in the same way I loved playing ball. It's the kind of excitement you can only get from hotly contested competition. And if you win, the excitement turns to ecstasy. If I had run and won an office, the ecstasy would turn into drudgery because I'd actually have to perform the duties of a public servant. If I lost, I'd be unemployed. Neither scenario appeals to me at all, and either way I'd only get to run every few years. In my PR role, I get to run elections all the time. And best of all, regardless of the outcome, I still have a job and another election coming up right around the corner."

"Sounds rather cynical to me. You could do so much good for so many people if you were in public service."

"It's not cynical at all. I am deeply involved in public service by being instrumental in electing those who have a calling to serve. If I help Lindsay get elected and he does great things for his constituents, haven't I contributed to those great things?"

"Of course," Lindsay chimed in as he returned from the bathroom. "But maybe you could do even more if you held office."

"Maybe, maybe not," Jack said, wanting to turn to the matters at hand. "For the time being, I need to concentrate on Revelle for Congress. The next few weeks are critical on two fronts. First, if we come out of the box strong, it is likely we'll run unopposed in the primary. If that happens, it will help us with number two, which is funding. Running unopposed will allow us to conserve our resources to a certain extent so we can direct the lion share of them to the general election. We must still invest some to get out the vote. If we invest wisely and demonstrate we can get out the vote even when unopposed, it will pay huge dividends."

"Those dividends will manifest themselves how?" Lindsay asked.

Jack, assuming his most authoritative posture, schooled his pupil.

"Campaign contributions, my friend. If the voters who are opposed to the Party's platform see you have a legitimate shot at winning, the money will flow. It will flow in the ten and twenty-dollar contributions here locally and—here's the big deal of the day—it will flow in the ten and twenty thousand-dollar ones into the coffers at National Reform Party Headquarters and its super PAC. Winning a congressional seat is a big-time score for the Opposition. If they think you have a legitimate shot, they will go all out. Remember, they're only a couple of seats shy of taking back the majority in the House. They will leave no stone unturned if they believe you can win."

"I guess we go balls out for the next few weeks then," Lindsay proclaimed.

"Spoken like a true Rhodes Scholar," Robin scolded, obviously disapproving of the expression, not the sentiment.

"Balls out it is," Jack said with a wink. Robin and Lindsay burst into laughter. Jack really liked these people and they were getting to like him as well. Their friendship and trust would prove to be crucial to Jack's survival as the events of the coming months unfolded.

Over the next few weeks, Jack and Lindsay were virtually inseparable. When Lindsay spoke at a rally, did a meet-and-greet at a high school soccer game, or shook hands at a mall entrance, Jack was there to coach and critique. With each passing day, Lindsay grew more poised as a candidate and the people of the district were taking notice. Contributions were picking up, and, most importantly, filing date had passed without a formal entry of any opposition in the primary. Only a write-in candidate could challenge Lindsay now, and there was no hint of any such possibility. Jack knew it meant Lindsay would in fact be opposing William Davies in the general election. That was when big-time heavy lifting would be needed.

Luckily for him, Peter was minding the store, so Jack was free to run the campaign. McKay & Associates' very capable staff made sure corporate clients like PetroMark and Consolidated were being properly attended to. Nobody was missing a beat. PetroMark had not yet announced their intentions regarding the harbor location for their depot. This saved Jack from having to deal with the fallout, which would certainly come from Robin Revelle's group opposing the project.

During those same weeks, Jack's family life had also found some equilibrium. As far as caring for Maya was concerned, Sandy and Jack had settled into a routine that the three of them were comfortable with—as comfortable as they could be with shuffling Maya back and forth between homes while contending with the ongoing divorce negotiations. Sandy's issues with drinking had taken a back seat for the time being. There had been no further incidents he was aware of, and Jack was content with not stirring things up, although he suspected nothing had really changed in that department. Thoreau's "Simplify, simplify," had become his new motto.

He had also gotten quite comfortable at Mickey's. There was plenty of room, even with Maya, and both Mickey and Molly loved the company. Jack went out of his way to help Mickey around the house while Maya pitched in by becoming Molly's playmate.

It appeared everything was starting to fall into place for Jack.

CHAPTER 17

Randall knew his son, William Davies, had always lived in the shadow of his powerful father. Running for Congress was Randall's idea, but if he won, he thought William would finally be his own man. Randall was, however, a pragmatist and realized William would need all of the influence Randall could bring to bear to win the election. Lindsay Revelle would be a formidable opponent.

Randall and William didn't disagree on the issues. The conservative doctrine ran consistently through both men's veins. Where William differed from his father was methodology. He preferred influence peddling to strong-arm tactics. He preferred innuendo to an outright smear campaign. William would stoop just as low as Randall, but he tried to do so with more subtlety and panache.

"Hello, Father," William said as he entered Randall's office. "Got a minute to talk campaign strategy?"

Randall looked up from the papers piled on his enormous oak desk. "I always have time for the future congressman from the great State of Wisconsin."

William's election to the House of Representatives would be Randall's crowning achievement and absolutely nothing would stand in the way. He always spoke of it as if the outcome were a foregone conclusion.

William took his customary position in the overstuffed leather chair on the far end of the office. His father was far less imposing from that distance.

"How are we going to attack Lindsay Revelle's candidacy?

I mean, are we going to address him now or wait until after the primary?" he asked, looking to his father for direction as he had so many times.

"We will begin immediately, of course. Our public position on the issues will point directly to his political weaknesses, like programs that will raise taxes and the loss of new jobs that will come from his anticipated opposition to the PetroMark depot. Our activities behind the scenes will focus on damaging his reputation, eliminating his principle allies, and arousing the racial hatred embedded in the electorate," Randall said, filling in the blanks.

"Sounds like you've got the bases covered. I assume my job is to pound home the issues-related stuff." William was getting the picture.

"Exactly. However, if we are able to uncover anything about Mr. Revelle or his associates that is improper, you will use your public forum to pound home on that as well."

"You mean I don't get to don the KKK robes?" William kidded.

"No, quite the contrary. You will always take the high road by publicly admonishing any such acts. This way you will play the race card in a way that can only help you. Emphasize his being Black, which is all the White voters will hear. Your indignation at racism will only be perceived as political correctness, not a real position."

"Got it. So what's in the works on the low road?"

After asking the question, Randall knew William likely wouldn't like the answer so he let him off the hook.

"Plenty, but I can't be specific. What you don't know can't hurt you or your campaign. Tell me what is going on with the PetroMark project."

Finally the conversation returned to subject matter William knew well. "They want to go ahead with the project and are prepared to petition my committee for the rights to do their environmental-impact study. We'll fast track the petition, which'll be when the fun starts."

"You mean it's when Revelle's people will begin their protest."

"Yes. It will cost them votes, not earn them any. With the potential of fifteen hundred new permanent jobs and the value of the construction project, they are going to have a tough sell to the voters, particularly in a tight economy. We win big here, not to mention the funds PetroMark will funnel into our PAC."

"How much are we talking about?" Randall asked, hoping to be impressed.

"My contact says they can go at least two hundred grand," William boasted.

Randall was impressed. "Excellent. We have to make doubly sure the money is directed to issue-related initiatives; you can't see a penny of that money directly. Ever since the antics of a certain Senate Majority Leader, the election commissions have really cracked down on the activities of political action committees," he cautioned.

"That's fine. If the money pushes for the approval of the depot and the jobs it will create, we get the rub-off because Revelle opposes it."

"Spoken like a true politician. It warms a father's heart."

As William left, he passed Frank who was waiting to see Randall.

"Hey, Frank. What's new?" he asked innocently.

"Same old, same old," Frank replied without expression.

Randall's secretary motioned to Frank that he was cleared to enter Randall's office.

"Where are we with the McKay situation?" Randall bellowed from behind his massive desk while lighting his cigar.

"I thought you wanted to be kept out of it," Frank retorted, somewhat annoyed.

"I didn't want to know the specifics before," said Randall, "but now I think I need to get involved."

"You take care of your son's campaign. Keep him on track and everything will work out just the way you want it to."

"Actually, I'll make sure it does," Randall said sternly. "I have a feeling something will be breaking real soon that'll do the trick." He had an ominous confidence in his voice.

CHAPTER 18

Jack wasn't sure if he was comfortable with the idea of someone coaching him through the divorce process, but here he was meeting with Mark Bonner to receive his first "treatment." Mark was an accomplished psychologist who specialized in family therapy and came highly recommended by Steven Clark. Steven had taken Jack through how the collaborative process begins healing the wounds of a family breakup during the divorce proceedings. The hope was that everyone would be better equipped to deal with one another during the legal process and to move on with their lives when that process concluded.

When he entered Mark's office, Jack looked around the room for the proverbial couch but only spotted a couple of comfortable chairs to choose from. Overall, the room was somewhat sparse, with only a desk and a couple of lamps to complement the comfortable chairs. Shades softened the sunlight that shone through the windows.

Mark motioned to the chairs. "Please have a seat. Would you like something to drink?"

Jack sat in one and Mark took the other.

"It's more likely I'll need a drink after this session," Jack quipped.

"Funny you should say that. One of the purposes of these meetings is to help you find relief from the stress of a divorce without needing to resort to substance abuse as a release."

"I was only kidding," Jack answered. "My wife's the one who seems to have taken comfort in a bottle."

"I know you were only making light of my offer of a beverage, but the mere fact it occurred to you means it's out there. If you have concerns about your wife's drinking, we can address them as it relates to how you can deal with her and with your daughter. But first we need to deal with how you're coping with the changes in your life."

"I think I'm coping quite well, actually. I've moved in with a friend and have settled into a nice routine juggling my work and my time with my daughter Maya."

"How are you sleeping?"

"About the same. Some nights I get six or seven hours, others less."

"So, no change in your pattern."

"No, not really."

"Good. How are things going with you and Maya?"

"She was very sad at first, but now she seems to be doing quite well. I see her a lot, and she particularly enjoys her sleepovers. We do pretty much what we did before, just that it's never as a family. My friend Mickey, who's putting me up, has a big house with a dog Maya adores, so it has been as comfortable as it could be under the circumstances."

"Do you feel any resentment from her?"

"Just the opposite. She seems to be, well, almost overly affectionate and trying very hard to be helpful. It is as if she doesn't want me to be sad or to blame Sandy for the divorce or to have to do the things for myself Sandy once did. She's only six, but she seems more like twenty-six in some ways."

"I would guess she feels she needs to take care of you since you don't have a wife anymore."

"Exactly," Jack said.

Mark nodded. "Jack, it is extremely important that each of you try to maintain your roles within the context of the family. Maya needs to know you're the parent and she's the child and that you will provide for her. I'm not saying she can't try to help you out with chores and such, but she needs to be the six-year-old and not forced by circumstances to be the twenty-six-year-old."

"You're right. I get it."

They went on for another half hour discussing ways to help Maya cope with the divorce and how to establish a new family unit between them. After covering the ground he had planned for the first session, Mark asked, "Are there any specific issues about the divorce that you'd like to discuss?"

Jack gathered his thoughts for a moment before answering. "I mentioned earlier that I am concerned about my wife's drinking, both as it affects Maya and just how bad it is in general."

"You're right to be concerned. First off, neither you nor I will be able to get Sandy to stop drinking or to seek help. She needs to do it with the help of her own support structure. You certainly need to make Steven aware of your concerns so he can discuss them with Sandy's attorney. Hopefully, Sandy's people can convince her to seek help from her coach or another professional. For the time being, you and I will concentrate on how you deal with Sandy and Maya both in light of your concerns about her drinking and in the context of the overall state of your marriage. We can begin our next session on that topic." Are you available next Wednesday in the afternoon?"

"That should work. I'm booked solid until after the primary election next Tuesday. Shall we say two?"

"Perfect. If you don't mind my asking, how are you involved with the election?"

"I am advising Lindsay Revelle's campaign." Jack said proudly.

"Good for you. He seems like a very special guy."

Jack could sense Mark had more to say but, ever the professional, was keeping his opinions to himself.

"Any thoughts about the election you'd like to share?" Jack was hoping for a story which would provide something useful in the upcoming battle with the Davies' and their Party.

"Let's just say I'm hoping it all works out well for the community and leave it at that," Mark said diplomatically.

It was encouraging to hear someone from the upper middle-class strata express their displeasure over the way the Party had wielded power in Lakeville. He left Mark's office with renewed vigor, more resolved than ever to find a way to get Lindsay elected and equally resolved to work through his family issues with Mark whom he'd taken a genuine liking to right off the bat.

When Jack got to his office the next day, his laptop was on his desk, which was unusual since he generally put it in the desk's locked drawer if he wasn't taking it with him when he left. That way he could leave his office unlocked if Donna or Peter needed something on his desk. On days when he left it behind, it was his way of unplugging, if only for a few hours. Maybe it was also his way of protesting the intrusion that technology had made into his life: computers, cell phones, voicemail, email, navigation systems, MP3 players, TiVo, digital everything. Or maybe simply an attempt to relax. As a small concession to the twenty-first century, he often checked his smart phone to keep abreast of any important emails, only answering the important ones immediately.

He sat down to transcribe his handwritten notes from the campaign announcement event. The notes were very brief. They covered his critiques of Lindsay's recitation of the three basic principles, some ideas for his upcoming speeches and recommendations for additional personal appearances leading up to the primary.

Once converted to a Word document, the notes scribbled on paper were expendable. He rolled them into a ball and was about to attempt his customary eight-foot seated set shot into the wastebasket, when he noticed the wastebasket was not in its traditional spot next to his credenza underneath the team picture from his senior season at Madison. Right on cue, Donna appeared in his doorway, basket in hand.

"Looking for this?" she said.

"Don't move," Jack said as he launched the paper projectile. The ball of paper landed softly in the basket. Jack held up both arms in exaltation.

"You can take the boy out of the gymnasium, but you can never take the gymnasium out of the boy," she quipped.

"I guess not. How come you had my waste basket in the first place?"

"Every time they have a new person on the cleaning crew, they mix up the baskets. I assume they had someone new again last night."

There was so much going on at such a continuous pace. Jack's thoughts turned back to the campaign. The primary was only a couple of weeks away and there was much to do.

CHAPTER 19

The final days leading up to an election were always frenetic. They were exhausting and invigorating, even when your candidate was running without opposition. Jack often knew the outcome of elections before the polls opened because his charges frequently ran unopposed. This time it was very different. He still had butterflies. It was because he really believed in this candidate and was truly excited about the ultimate outcome still some months away. This was a mission, not a job.

Jack and Lindsay knew they would have a difficult task getting people mobilized over an election that had already been decided. They also knew if Lindsay could get out the vote and garner a broad base of support, particularly in predominantly conservative, white neighborhoods where the Party usually dominated, he would have tremendous momentum for the general election. That momentum would be further fueled by financial support a good showing would generate. Money was, after all, the lifeblood of any campaign, especially if you were the underdog.

Jack and Lindsay met at Kathryn's for an early breakfast. This had become their routine in the days leading up to the election. The corner booth across from the kitchen became their campaign headquarters annex each morning between seven and eight thirty. They talked strategy. They rehashed the previous day's highs and lows. They reviewed finances. And they fantasized about the future.

They were also the center of attention even though they were tucked away in their corner booth. The staff fawned over them, keeping their coffee cups filled with hot chicory-blended java and their table loaded with grits, waffles, fresh fruit, and frittatas. Jack had become family at Kathryn's, and he loved it. It gave him a genuine sense of belonging, which he sorely needed in light of the collapse of his marriage. He often brought Maya on Saturday mornings now. She, too, loved the food and the attention from the staff.

The patrons also made a big deal out of the two well-dressed men in the corner booth. They would come to the table offering well wishes or a high-five laced with a "go get 'em." This was the same reaction Lindsay was getting all over the district. Jack was exhilarated by the groundswell of support for Lindsay. He had gone from cautiously optimistic about Lindsay's chances to quietly confident. He now felt sure if things continued on this track the seat in Congress was attainable.

Jack got down to the business at hand. "We've got a little logistical problem next Friday. Channel 7 wants to do an interview with you during their five o'clock news broadcast and you need to be across town shaking hands at the Elks Club fish fry no later than five thirty."

"Can't they do a remote from the Elk's?"

Jack chuckled. "Spoken like a truly media-savvy political veteran. That would be nice, but their truck will be covering William Davies's speech at the Chamber of Commerce dinner at that time. They wanted to have something from each of you for the broadcast, and I convinced them to have you on after Davies. It gives you a chance to counter any points he makes in his speech but no time to get across town."

"Isn't the Chamber dinner at Harbor Place?" Lindsay asked as if he had something up his sleeve.

"Yes. Why?"

"Well, Harbor Place is two blocks from the Elk's. They could cover William Davies's speech and cut to me outside Harbor Place for my reaction. I love the 'he's on the inside and I'm on the outside' analogy it would convey. I can finish the interview as late as 5:27 and still make the fish fry on time."

"You obviously don't need me anymore. I'm going back to store openings and charity ball announcements," Jack said teasingly.

"Now, now, we'll find something important for you to do." Lindsay was laying it on thick because Jack had shown that he could take it.

Jack laughed. "Fuck you. Without me you'd still be teaching high school poly-sci, and the only elections you'd be involved with would be advising one of your students who was running for class president."

Their talk was a surprisingly great way of relieving the tension they both felt.

"Faye, Special Agent David Harris is on line three for you," Jill announced without the aid of the intercom.

Visibly annoyed at Jill's lack of decorum, Faye took a moment to collect herself and then picked up the phone. "Hi, David. What's new?"

"Looks like we have sufficient evidence to issue warrants on several cases. We've got two child enticements and three for possession of child pornography, with two of those including intent to distribute."

"When will we get the files?"

"The AG wants me to deliver them in person. Are you available tomorrow around noon? I'll buy lunch."

"Sure. Why don't you stop by around eleven thirty and we can go over the cases before lunch? Should I invite Detective Malory?"

"Good idea. We can finalize our entire action plan in one meeting. I'll see you tomorrow morning."

"Thanks, David. See you then."

The game is on, Faye thought. This would be her chance to bring some real lowlifes to justice and boost her career in the process. She couldn't wait to call the DA and let him know.

CHAPTER 20

Randall could not have been more proud than watching an extremely confident William Davies stand in front of the gathering at the Chamber of Commerce dinner. The audience was seeded with prominent business and civic leaders who owed much of their success and stature in the community to the Party. Most had curried favor directly from Randall Davies and thus owed his son their total allegiance.

"Good evening, ladies and gentlemen, fellow citizens of Lakeville. This city has become great because of you, its leaders in both business and government. Strong leadership has guided this city as it has grown and prospered. I intend to do my part in continuing that progress. When I am elected to Congress, I will be representing the interests of this community by insuring the federal government does its part in ensuring the wellbeing of Lakeville's citizens. The Party I represent has always been successful in getting support for Lakeville's most important projects like the Harbor Bridge and Niles Point nuclear power plant. I will do everything possible to ensure the process continues."

The audience erupted into applause. They realized their enthusiastic support was ultimately in their best financial interest, not to mention their apprehension of ruffling Randall Davies's feathers.

William continued for another ten minutes extolling his virtues and those of the Party. He was careful not to say anything controversial nor to mention his opponent. Jack's replacement, Kevin Lauterbaugh, had written this speech personally. He was a campaign specialist brought in from Party headquarters in Washington to get William's campaign off and running. Randall had called in a few markers to gain the services of the Party's number one strategist for this congressional race. Lauterbaugh would map out the campaign strategy and oversee its progress from Washington. Randall was confident the Party's local clout along with guidance from Washington was more than Lindsay Revelle could overcome. Add to that the behind-the-scenes activities orchestrated by Frank Ryder, and Davies had become a virtually unbeatable candidate.

William wrapped up his speech. "I appreciate having had this opportunity to share my ideas with you about the continued growth of Lakeville and look forward to serving you in the United States House of Representatives. Thank you all for coming."

The perfunctory standing ovation followed. Wanting to appear dignified, William waved politely at the crowd, and as he made his way off stage, he smiled broadly into the Channel 7 TV camera. What he really had wanted to do was one of those end zone celebrations he'd seen at pro football games. In his mind, the election was his, but he knew that in order to ensure victory he had to keep his composure in public, tell the right people what they wanted to hear, and not make any false moves. He forgot to include the behavior of others in that equation.

As soon as William finished his speech, Channel 7 cut to the remote of Lindsay outside Harbor Place. From the studio, the newscaster asked Lindsay for his reaction to William Davies's speech.

"As usual, my opponent told the crowd only what they wanted to hear. Specifically that he was all about business as usual. This campaign needs to address the pressing issues on the minds of the majority of Lakeville's citizens: affordable healthcare, funding for our schools, and protecting our environment for future generations."

"Mr. Davies was addressing the Chamber of Commerce," the

newscaster returned. "Don't you agree that a business theme is appropriate in that forum?"

"Absolutely, but only in the context of how business in this community can be best served by a well-educated, well cared for citizenry and how a cleaner environment makes this city a magnet for new business development and continued growth."

"Thank you, Dr. Revelle. And now here's Don with the weather."

Jack was impressed with Lindsay's poise under fire. "Short, sweet, and on message," he told him. "Very well done. Now on to the fish fry."

CHAPTER 21

Faye spent most of the night lying in bed watching the minutes on the clock tick by, one by one. Her vigil ended when the alarm went off at six. Even though she had not slept much, she jumped out of bed and got dressed, energized by the exciting prospects of the day ahead.

Heading off to work, Faye couldn't help projecting out how her professional life would change when David Harris delivered the child porn cases. High-profile cases made or broke careers in the DA's office. If she successfully prosecuted these cases, she would, at the very least, move up to the very top of the department. Because the initiative emanated as a priority from the governor's office, the ramifications of these cases could carry her on to a position in the attorney general's office, an appointment to the US Attorney's office, or even a partnership offer from a high-profile private law firm.

Being a single mother who had struggled mightily to get where she was, this was the big payoff and she would not let it slip by without taking full advantage of the opportunity. Best of all, she could proceed with strength of conviction because she knew those who would be indicted were the scum of the earth and deserved to be prosecuted and put behind bars.

She pulled into the parking lot. Ted Erickson walked into the building with her.

"Good morning, Faye. This should be a most interesting day for you."

"If we get the kind of strong cases we're hoping for, it will be extremely interesting. Do you want to sit in on the meeting with

Harris and Malory?" she asked.

"No thanks. This is your baby, Faye. You handle the meeting and brief me after you've had a chance to look over the cases."

Just as she had watched the alarm clock, Faye watched the wall clock in her office as it ticked off the minutes to her meeting with Harris and Mallory. She occupied her time filing the loose papers on her desk and returning a few unimportant phone calls she had neglected. It was imperative for her to clear the decks because she knew these new cases would fill her dance card for the next several weeks, or maybe even months.

There was a knock on her door. It was Jake Mallory, who apparently was equally anxious to see what Harris had come up with.

"You're early, Jake. Nothing important going on at headquarters?"

"Nothing as interesting as a series of sex crime arrests."

"Hopefully it will be arrests and convictions."

Faye was glowing with pride and wondered if the people she passed in the hallways could see what she was feeling from the glow on her face. She promised herself that the confidence Ted showed in her would be rewarded by an unwavering effort to win the cases they would prosecute.

"Good morning, David," Faye said, greeting Harris, who had stopped by her office and joined the discussion.

"Faye, Jake, good to see you both. Are we meeting in here?" he replied. Apparently Faye's office was insufficient in size and stature for such an important meeting.

"We're moving to larger quarters," she said, seemingly unfazed by Harris's implication. "I've reserved Conference Room A down the hall."

As they walked down the hall, Faye felt all the eyes in the department on her. She knew everyone anticipated something big was happening, and they were jealous they were not in the know.

The rather stark, government-issue conference room was in

the center of the department. It was equipped with a large heavy wooden boardroom table and chairs that would seat twenty, an old-fashioned schoolroom chalkboard, and a credenza equipped with a stack of legal pads, a water pitcher, and glassware. It also had one glass wall that provided a window into the proceedings for Faye's nosy associates. This was one time she didn't mind an audience, as this was to be the beginning of her finest hour.

"Well, David, whatcha got?" Faye opened, trying to seem nonchalant.

"We have five cases which we believe are very strong. The evidence we have is solid. In a few instances, the caught-in-the-act portion of the evidence will rest with Jake's department. In the others, some additional evidence will be needed to make them airtight, but we believe all of the cases are chargeable and convictable based on what we already have."

Harris proceeded to lay out the way they developed the cases. He explained how the DOJ's investigators had used the internet to identify suspects involved in illegal sexual activities with minors. Two types of criminal activity were the focus. The first was adults attempting to entice children into involvement in sexual activity of one kind or another. The second was possession and distribution of material containing child pornography.

Faye interrupted, "How current are these alleged incidence?"

"They're fresh. All culminating within the last few weeks. In our first three cases, we have had members of our task force posing as children in online chat rooms. In these cases, they have been corresponding with adults who are attempting to set up meetings to have sex with minors. We have been able to trace the suspects via their email accounts. If they show up at the appointed time and place, we've got them. The only part of the process that remains is the actual sting. Jake, we need to set up 'meetings' between the suspects and your personnel. Then you'll arrest them at the scene.

The evidence to back it all up is in these files."

Harris tossed the three files onto the conference table and looked at Jake as if to say, "It's all up to you now. Don't screw it up!"

Jake stood and went for a glass of water. "I assume all of the suspects are males and in the city of Lakeville," he said, returning to the table.

Harris continued, "Everyone is squarely within your jurisdiction, Jake. Your assumption that they are all males is way off base, however. We have three different scenarios. One is a man who sought out a young girl who wants to give up her virginity. One is a man seeking sex with a young boy who is afraid to let anyone know he's gay. The third is a woman seeking to lure a young boy by offering to show him 'how it's done.' All in all, quite an assortment."

"Sounds like you've got a pretty diverse group of sickos," Jake responded.

"That's the whole point," Faye chimed in. "We need to demonstrate that predators come in all shapes and sizes and with many different types of desires. The cases are perfect. They graphically demonstrate the depth of the problem, and this initiative shows the community that we will not allow our children to be exploited by sexual deviants."

"Sounds to me like you're already formulating your closing arguments," Harris quipped.

"If the cases are as solid as you say they are, the closing arguments will write themselves," Faye responded.

Harris nodded, "True. Now about the other two cases. These are the possession of and possible distribution of pornographic material depicting children. We set up a website tracking system to identify individuals who were downloading child pornography. We have been able to track actual downloads to confirm possession and then further investigated to determine if there was any actual distribution of those materials."

"And?" Jake said from the edge of his seat.

"One with and one without," Harris said, sounding like a short-order cook.

"What's next?" Faye said, asking the obvious.

"We need to go to the judge to obtain search warrants," said Harris. "And then, depending on the findings, we'll go to the grand jury to get indictments. I'll get moving on the warrants shortly. We need to have all of our ducks in a row before putting the hammer down."

They all nodded in agreement. Faye knew it was her signal to get going.

CHAPTER 22

Jack needed a distraction. The long campaign and working on the Consolidated and PetroMark project at the same time, was taking a toll on him both physically and mentally. The remedy, he thought, could be found in the garage. He headed to his now former home to fix the broken seat in the minivan since his trip to the dealer had been sidetracked by Sandy and Maya being run off the road. Hopefully, he'd get to spend some time with Maya as well. Halfway there he realized he'd better call Sandy to see if it was okay. Another confrontation would defeat the purpose of the visit and further antagonize Sandy. Things were tough enough in that department already.

"I have some time and would be happy to come over to fix the broken seat in your minivan," he told her. "I could use some mindless wrench twisting about now." Hoping she'd say yes, he added, "And Maya can help me so you can have some alone time, if you'd like."

"Ever the negotiator," Sandy said, only half disapproving. "OK, but don't turn this little repair job into an all-day stay."

"Works for me. I'll be there in twenty minutes or so." He hung up before any objections could be raised.

When he arrived, he felt the strangeness of pulling into his own driveway but feeling like a visitor. It was a feeling that he was going to have to live with from now on. Thankfully, the garage door opener still worked. He was certain Sandy would have changed the code and the locks on the doors once she realized they gave him access.

His mood changed immediately when he saw Maya running out to greet him.

"Hi, Daddy!" she shouted gleefully. "I'm ready to help you fix the minivan."

"Great. Go ask Mommy for the keys to the minivan so we can get started."

While Maya fetched the keys, he grabbed a few tools from his workbench. Once Maya arrived with the keys, he opened the side door to access the broken seat hinge. The bolt at the center point of the hinge had popped out, which caused the collapse. With any luck at all, it would be somewhere on the floor of the van. It was likely a size he'd have trouble replacing if it could not be found.

His search bore fruit. In fact, more fruit than he had intended. There was the bolt and next to it was a torn wrapper. A torn condom wrapper. Making sure Maya didn't see it, he slipped it into his pocket. Its presence explained both the broken seat and Sandy's appearance that night when she returned home with her clothes in disarray.

He went about fixing the seat, with Maya's help, all the while not letting on that he was upset about the result of his hunt for the bolt.

Sandy peeked out the door to the garage from the house. "Well, was the surgery successful?" she said in an almost-friendly tone.

"We fixed it, Mommy," Maya shouted triumphantly.

"Great. Thanks, Jack. Maya and I have some shopping to do so we're going to take off."

"You're welcome. I had a great helper," Jack said.

There was much more he wanted to say but that would have to wait for another time. He had to consider how to approach the obvious. Was she just craving some temporary attention? Or was it something more? Either way, he had to decide how best to handle this. He expected to be angrier, but something inside him recognized that even though the divorce was not even close to being legally complete, the marriage was over. It was inevitable that they each needed to move on.

He drove off feeling a tremendous sense of loss.

By the time he got back to Mickey's, he was back in campaign-management mode. Jack had a real talent for compartmentalizing, so he boxed up thoughts of Sandy's indiscretion and stashed it away for another time.

"Where ya been?" Mickey inquired casually.

"Stopped by the house to fix the seat in Sandy's minivan."

"And to spend some time with Maya, I suspect."

"Of course, she's my daughter. It's what dads do." As soon as it came out of his mouth, he knew he misspoke.

"Unfortunately, not all of us have that opportunity," Mickey lamented.

"I'm sorry, Mickey. I didn't mean to reopen an old wound."

"I know you didn't. Hopefully you and Maya will be as thick as thieves forever."

"Bobbie loves you, you know. She just hasn't figured out how to deal with things quite yet," Jack reasoned.

"It's been seven years, which should be long enough. She'd better figure it out soon, otherwise I might be gone." Mickey sighed.

"Maybe I could talk to her," Jack suggested.

"No, she has to come to it on her own. Like I did with my drinking."

"What's for dinner?" Jack asked to change the subject.

"Pot roast," Mickey said as he disappeared into the kitchen.

Jack couldn't get the circumstances of Mickey and Bobbie's estrangement out of his mind. Bobbie Martin was a top-notch lawyer just like her father. When her mother was killed and her father sent to prison, she left her position at the public defender's office in Lakeville and moved to Madison. She originally hooked on with a firm specializing in representing employees with workplace discrimination cases. Her experience as a litigator and her left-leaning politics were a perfect fit. She ultimately decided she wanted to go it alone to focus on criminal defense. Even though Mickey had asked him not to, Jack decided to give her a call. He believed they both desperately needed the reconciliation, and he was determined to try to facilitate one.

"Hi, Bobbie. It's Jack McKay."

There was a pause. Jack thought he heard Bobbie gasp.

"Long time, Jack." she said, after a moment.

She was right. The last time Jack had seen Bobbie was before her parents' fatal accident.

"As they say, only fools rush in where angels fear to tread."

"So this isn't merely a social call. I assume you want to talk about Mickey and me. It's not a topic I'm interested in discussing." Her tone was anything but friendly.

Jack realized he would have to deliver his most persuasive pitch. He'd been so successful doing that in his business world, but this was something altogether different.

"You've made your position on the subject perfectly clear, Bobbie. That said, I want you to know how devastated he still is over losing you *and* your mother. Isn't it time for the two of you to start healing together?" he implored.

"I can never forgive him for what he did," she said emphatically.

"So you don't believe in contrition or forgiveness?" Jack pleaded.

"Contrition is fine, forgiveness not so much." Bobbie wasn't giving in.

"Bobbie, your father misses you more than you can possibly imagine. He's been sober for seven years. He's your father, and the two of you need each other."

"Says you," she responded pejoratively.

"It's time, Bobbie. Please reconsider before there isn't any time."

"He ran out of time years ago. Don't you understand?"

"I don't doubt you carry a lot of pain. I can hear it in your voice." Jack was trying his best to be conciliatory. "Please give it some thought."

"Thanks for the call, Jack," she said hanging up.

CHAPTER 23

There was nothing more exciting than Election Day. Even when Jack's candidate was running unopposed in a primary. Today would be the official kick-off of Lindsay Revelle's run for Congress. It would also be the official start of William Davies's campaign, so the race was on and the lines were drawn. The contrasts couldn't be more clear. The voters would have two very different candidates and platforms to choose from. Jack relished this campaign more than any in recent memory. His candidate wasn't merely a client; Lindsay Revelle was someone he truly believed in.

Shortly after arriving at the hotel ballroom that night for the victory celebration, Lindsay approached the podium to a rousing ovation. Once the crowd calmed down some, he thanked them for their support and then shifted into reaffirming his platform and asking for their help in getting out the vote.

As Lindsay left the stage, he gave Jack a hug and a smile. No monetary payment could have provided as much remuneration.

Jack imagined that the mood wasn't as festive at the Liberty Party headquarters. Sure, there was the perfunctory victory lap at William's victory celebration, but he was far from guaranteed the congressional seat. Under Jack's direction, Lindsay Revelle would mount a strong campaign and prove to be a formidable adversary.

After the rally, Jack was spent. He pulled into Mickey's driveway not remembering any details from the ride home. Thankfully, he made it there without incident. When they sat down to eat, Jack regaled Mickey with excerpts from Lindsay's speech and the plans for moving the campaign into combat mode.

"You know full well the resources Randall Davies has at his command," Mickey said in a foreboding tone.

Jack nodded. "You needn't remind me."

"So what's your strategy to battle the evil empire?"

"This may sound trite, but our greatest asset is our candidate. His charisma, his ideas, his grassroots support and so on. We can use his strengths to energize the voters and hopefully use the underdog label to garner media attention."

Mickey responded with the million-dollar question. "What about money?"

"Well, that's the rub," Jack conceded. "We'll do well with the small contributions from supporters, but we need to get some help from larger donors and PACs. The Reform Party's national fundraising arm will assist as well. One of my biggest challenges will be to get support from local movers and shakers who, up until now, have benefited from the Party's pro-business policies and legislation."

"Sounds like a monumental challenge. How in the world do you fight that?"

"I only know one way: convince those people Lindsay's going to win, and if they don't back him, they'll be left out in the cold."

"Like I said, a monumental task," Mickey repeated, this time with more emphasis.

"That's why they're paying me the small bucks. I will have to earn my kingmaker nickname this time for sure," Jack said, trying to sound confident.

"How can I help, Jack?"

"For starters, keep me well fed," Jack mumbled through a mouthful of corned beef and cabbage.

"I can handle that. Remember, I've been in the game a long time and still have some good contacts who could help."

"I appreciate that, old friend. Rest assured, I won't hesitate to solicit your help. What's for dessert?"

"Nothing after calling me old," Mickey chuckled.

They enjoyed the rest of their meal. Jack had told Mickey everything about the night, but he also felt a heaviness and guilt about calling Bobbie behind Mickey's back. When the time was right, he would tell him.

CHAPTER 24

Jack needed to check in with Lindsay to make plans for the afternoon interview at the Lakeville Examiner, the lone surviving printed newspaper in the area.

"Hi, Jack." Lindsay's distracted tone told Jack he had interrupted the family's morning routine.

Jack could make out Robin Revelle's voice in the background ushering their kids off to school. "Is this a bad time?" he asked politely.

"Nope, just the normal morning routine at the Revelles'. Actually your call probably gets me out of dishes duty."

"I trust you aren't calling to ask for a raise just 'cause we won." Lindsay teased.

"Based on the size of the campaign bank account, you sure couldn't finance it anyway," Jack said.

"Now that we have the preliminary pleasantries out of the way, what can I do for you, Jack?"

"I just wanted to confirm the pick-up time for the interview. We need to be there no later than one thirty. I could pick you up around noon if you want to have lunch—"

Lindsay cut him off. "Jack, I can certainly handle this on my own. You don't have to babysit me."

"Well, actually I do," Jack shot back. "It's my job to be in your corner, like Angelo Dundee was for Ali. Besides, you never want to do an interview for print without a witness. It's so easy to be misquoted. If need be, it's much easier to keep the record straight this way."

"I doubt the public would take the word of my campaign manager over a reporter, but OK," Lindsay conceded. "Then pick me up and we'll do lunch. Since you pointed out the sad state of the campaign's bank account, you're buying."

"Works for me," Jack said, ending the call.

Jack headed out to meet up with Lindsay for lunch and then the interview. On the drive over, he considered how strange it was that Peter's office door had been closed the night before when he stopped in. Jack had reviewed the Consolidated Foods action plan, moving some things around until he was fully pleased. But Peter had been having a hushed conversation over the phone when he knocked on the door. It seemed unusual.

As his car rounded the corner onto Rogers Street, he saw Lindsay holding court in front of his house. A group of neighbors had gathered to congratulate him and offer support. When Jack parked and got out of his car, Lindsay shouted, "There's the guy who made it all happen!"

The neighbors applauded even though they had no idea who Jack was or why he deserved credit for making it all happen.

"It's all about the candidate," Jack said, attempting to sound humble.

"Let's just say we're a good team and leave it at that," Lindsay conceded.

"Where would you like to go for lunch?"

"Somewhere other than Kathryn's. Too much noise and too much food."

"How about one of those new poke places that have popped up all over town?" Jack offered.

"Perfect. There's one downtown on Fifth near the Examiner's office."

With that, they headed downtown. Once they arrived at the restaurant and were seated, they got down to business. Jack asked the questions he thought the reporter would ask and then helped Lindsay polish his answers a bit. The polishing wasn't particularly necessary, as Lindsay had his positions well thought out and his delivery was, as always, impeccable.

"Jack, I have a few questions for you," Lindsay said, changing gears. "How did you come to fall-in with the Party?"

"Fall-in is actually what happened. When I was just starting out, I ran into an old college teammate, Nick. I told him I had just one client, Mickey Martin, and I was looking to hook up with a PR firm to grow my portfolio. Nick suggested I talk to his uncle, who was on the Party's election committee and was looking to beef up their support staff."

"Let me guess, the uncle was Randall Davies."

"Bingo," Jack replied in a joyless tone. "I parlayed a short stint with the Party into a one-man consultancy. Gun for hire, you could say. From there, I added staff as my client list grew. Within a couple of years, McKay & Associates was off and running."

"I assume the Party was one of those clients and you stuck with them out of loyalty for them helping you get started." Lindsay offered.

"I stuck with them out of greed, truth be told. It was easy. They had the money to pay me. The work was steady and their well-oiled machine practically guaranteed success," Jack conceded.

"Remember, Jack, they stayed with you because you delivered!"

"Agreed, but it became an uncomfortable dependency. Thanks to you, I believe I'm now in recovery." His analogy amused them both. "Now, let's get back to preparing for this interview."

The *Lakeville Examiner*, the long-standing local newspaper, had occupied the same red brick building since the 1920s. Inside, however, it was a typical modern-day operation. Cubicles filled with reporters on their computers, phones ringing and the hum of a vibrant operation.

The receptionist escorted Lindsay and Jack into a wood-paneled conference room with an expansive view of the harbor. "Mr. Reynolds will be with you shortly," she said.

Hank Reynolds, the editor-in-chief, was a hometown product who had learned his trade over three decades of newspaper and wire service work with various news organizations both in the US and abroad. He had returned home thirteen years ago when offered the job of leading the *Examiner*. As he put it, "his final resting place."

"Great to see you, Jack. It's been awhile," Hank said.

"Hank, this is Lindsay Revelle, the next congressman for this district."

Lindsay extended his hand. "Nice to meet you, Mr. Reynolds. You'll have to excuse Jack, he has a tendency to get a little ahead of himself."

"No problem. It's Jack's job to add the hype," Hank said, joyfully needling Jack. "Lindsay, may I call you Lindsay? I'm going to conduct this interview myself. It's not often we have a candidate whose campaign has raised the profile of a local election to a real competition."

"You can certainly call me Lindsay. I appreciate your perspective on the viability of our campaign."

"Let's all sit down and get started."

Hank took three bottles of water from the mini-refrigerator in the corner, gave one to each of them, and began the interview.

"Lindsay, what has been the driving force behind your decision to run?"

"There were a number of factors. First, I'm from this town. I love it here and I want to see it have a representative who looks out for all of its people. Second, there are a number of issues that I believe speak directly to the needs of this community. If elected I intend to push forward initiatives that address those issues."

"What are those issues?"

"We need to promote jobs for working-class people. Those jobs need to provide a living wage and benefits, like healthcare coverage, which will provide working people with the opportunity to prosper. Investing in infrastructure will be a major factor in providing those jobs and improving the living conditions for all our citizens.

"I have been extremely fortunate to have had a great education. Because I could play basketball, I received a college scholarship, which I used as a springboard to earn my degrees. The opportunities I have had should be afforded to all qualified students, not just those who can sink a three-pointer."

"Any others?" Hank continued.

"Many others. Tax laws that provide relief for working-class people while ensuring the wealthiest among us pay their fair share. Women's initiatives granting them equality of pay, protection from workplace harassment, and their right to choose. I also believe we need more responsible gun laws. Our children need to feel safe both at school and where they live. We need to prioritize the environment and invest in clean energy and other methods of combating climate change while providing clean water to drink and clean air to breathe."

"Quite a list. Changing subjects for a moment, do you have any thoughts about your opponent, William Davies?"

"Yes, of course. Mr. Davies, like his father, stands on the opposite side of the fence from me on most, if not all, of the issues I just mentioned. He is for providing tax breaks for the rich, spending public money to support corporate projects—"

Hank interrupted, "So you're not in favor of using government funds to help companies provide the jobs and taxes which support the initiatives you've outlined?"

Jack wanted to chime in but knew Lindsay had to be able to defend his views without prompting from him.

"Of course, I favor public investment in corporate projects but only where the payback to the community is commensurate with the resources invested. My opponent, who sits on the public service commission, has openly supported the use of prime land in the harbor area for an oil depot."

"So you think it's a bad idea?"

"It's a bad idea if it's approved without an intense environmental study and a series of public hearings to let the residents of the community have their questions and concerns addressed. As it stands now, the commission can proceed with impunity."

"Isn't that simply a local issue? You're running for national office."

"I will represent the people of this community's interests wherever it may be necessary. Besides, Lake Michigan is of vital interest to the four states it borders, and the health of the Great Lakes affects the entire country in one way or another."

The interview went on for another thirty minutes or so. At its conclusion, Hank stood up offered his hand to Lindsay and then to Jack.

"Thanks for the time, gentlemen. We look forward to covering the campaign."

As they left, Hank gave Jack an approving nod. Lindsay had definitely impressed this seasoned journalist.

CHAPTER 25

"Now that we've taken care of Jack McKay, we need to press on with the campaign like it's still a contested election," Randall told William as he reveled in his plan.

"Well, we haven't 'taken care' of him yet. No charges or public condemnation have surfaced at this point," he reminded his father.

"Correct, which is why we must carry on with business as usual. Once the shit hits the fan, we must be able to show righteous indignation while implicating Revelle with guilt by association. The voters will not tolerate any candidate who is tainted by such an inexcusable crime so close to the election." Randall was relishing the double whammy his son's election would be putting on Jack and the Opposition.

"It should also negate Robin Revelle's efforts to thwart the PetroMark depot, which will allow them a clear path for their support of the campaign, correct?" William noted.

"Sure, but you need to get the Planning Commission ready to approve once everything is lined up."

"How soon do you expect the news to break?" William asked.

"Within a few days, I expect. It's likely they'll go to the grand jury with the evidence for all the cases and seek indictments. Once the indictments are in hand, they go about making arrests. Then the real fun begins." Randall could not contain his excitement.

"Well then, I'd better get the PetroMark harbor depot approval process ready for a vote."

"Yes, get to it!" Randall demanded in closing.

Jack always felt bad drinking around Mickey. He kept a bottle of Scotch in his room, but Mickey could certainly have uncovered it. An hour ago, Steven had called him and told him the final papers were ready and he just needed to swing by and sign. And that was just what he did. It was a lifeless process, putting his John Hancock on paper after paper. Now, he needed a stiff drink. Regardless, he felt a twinge of guilt as he retrieved the bottle.

Mickey's place was perfect for unwinding. Because Mickey couldn't see, the place was dimly lit. No need for bright lights when it was just Mickey and Molly hanging out. Jack had become accustomed to the low-light conditions. In fact, he found it quite soothing. Pouring three fingers of Scotch into a rocks glass, Jack settled into his designated place on the couch and, after a few sips of his drink, began to recount the highs and lows of the day's events to Mickey.

"The interview with Hank Reynolds went extremely well. From my perspective, Lindsay came off as sincere, knowledgeable, articulate, and very well-suited for the job. He answered the questions in a very straight-forward manner, with only a touch of candidate-speak."

"Could you tell if Hank was tracking with him?"

"I could. I even detected a slight nod of approval when we left," Jack said confidently.

"A possible endorsement?" Mickey's tone struck a hopeful pitch.

"Maybe. Hank's an old pro who's unlikely to tip his hand. That said, he was definitely impressed, and I can't see him feeling the same way about William Davies."

"Or his father," Mickey added contemptuously.

"True. Then my day turned south. I went to Steven Clark's office and signed the divorce papers." Jack took a big sip of his drink.

"That must have been very hard for you. Now your focus will

shift to reestablishing your lives and ensuring Maya is loved and nurtured even more than if you and Sandy were still a couple."

"Exactly. You missed your calling, Mick. Maybe being a psychologist would have been a better fit than a judge."

"Different skill set. It's easy for me to see your path forward. Guiding you there is altogether different."

"For sure. Enough about politics and divorce. Where should we go for dinner?" Jack got up and poured himself a little more Scotch.

"You assume I didn't make anything?" Mickey deadpanned.

"I don't smell anything cooking, so I assumed . . ." Jack said, not finishing his sentence.

"You assumed right. Where are you taking me?" Mickey demanded.

"Johnson's?" Jack offered as he downed the rest of his drink.

"Perfect. A steak will do nicely."

Faye stepped out for a bite to eat around 6:00 pm and then returned to the office. Working late was going to be the norm for a while. When she returned, she found a sealed file marked "Confidential" on her desk. Jill had told her Agent Roger Obregon would deliver a package signed for by Ted. A note was attached asking Faye to stop by the next morning to discuss the file and Roger's comments.

The plan was to seek search warrants for the computers and any other evidence of wrongdoing, with the intent of following up with arrest warrants for the offenders. Faye was to go to the grand jury and seek the warrants. Then, if substantiating evidence was discovered, criminal indictments.

Faye called home. "Mom, can you stay with Abby a little while longer tonight? I have some work I need to finish before heading home."

"Sure, no problem."

"As long as you're being so agreeable, can you handle things with Abby tomorrow?"

"Specifically?"

"Just everything. Make her lunch, take her to school, pick her up, and stay with her until I get home." Faye knew what the answer would be but asked in the most appreciative manner she could.

"I'd be happy to," her mother said without hesitation.

"Thanks, Mom." Faye was glad to have that covered. Tomorrow would be a very busy day.

She returned her attention to the file and opened it. She was startled to see who the target of this facet of the child pornography investigation was going to be. It was Jack McKay.

The evidence against Jack included a laptop computer belonging to him on which he had apparently downloaded several videos and numerous still shots of children engaging in sexual activity. The downloads came from the site the DOJ had been tracking in order to uncover offenders. These downloads were precisely the criminal activities the task force had set out to find. This evidence would, hopefully, lead to arrests and then convictions once they had the offenders and the evidence they needed rounded up. It would also help the DOJ shut down and prosecute the operators of the site. That all made sense, that is, except the inclusion of Jack McKay as a suspect.

CHAPTER 26

Jack had a very busy day ahead. A conference call with the lawyers on the Consolidated and PetroMark contracts and then a staff meeting with the election team to discuss the next steps in the Lindsay Revelle for Congress campaign. And that was just the morning schedule.

On his way to work, Jack picked up Maya early enough for a trip to Brown's Bagels for a quick breakfast before dropping her off at school.

"Hi, Daddy," she said half-heartedly as she got into the back seat.

"You sound sad."

"It's just that I miss having you home all the time," she confessed.

"I know, but you know I can't live with you and Mommy anymore. You have two homes now, and one has a dog!" Jack was trying his best to make her feel better. It wasn't working.

"I know" was her sad response.

Changing the subject, Jack asked, "What would you like to do on Saturday?"

"The zoo?" she responded.

"It's a date!" Jack was glad to end the conversation on a high note.

When they arrived at Brown's, Maya had a sesame bagel with peanut butter. Jack had a pumpernickel bagel with salmon cream cheese spread. The chewiness of the bagels kept the additional conversation to a minimum, which was fine with Jack.

After breakfast, Jack dropped Maya at school with a hug, a kiss, and a "See you Saturday!" He left wondering what he needed to do going forward to be a successful part-time dad.

Upon arrival at the office, Jack was ambushed by a host of staff members with questions ranging from campaign next steps to a press release about PetroMark's depot plans. He artfully directed each to meet with him individually, at specific times, throughout the morning. Setting off toward his office, he ran into Carol Meyers.

"Got a minute?" she asked.

"Sure, what's up?"

"I just heard you've scheduled strategy meetings with the teams for PetroMark and the Revelle campaign. As Head of Strategy, I feel I should attend both, particularly since there's a good chance these projects will intersect at some point." She didn't come off as angry, but Jack interpreted it that way.

"I was planning to call and ask you to attend once I got back to my office. Haven't even had a chance to hang up my coat," Jack shot back.

"C'mon, Jack. I'm not angry. Just doing my job."

"I know, Carol. I'm just feeling a little harassed this morning. By the way, I want you to know I think you do your job extremely well, and I wouldn't move ahead on any of these things without your participation."

"Thanks, Jack."

Jack closed his door and sat down at his desk. He needed to prepare for the onslaught of morning meetings, so he began organizing his thoughts in longhand on a legal pad, as was his typical modus operandi.

As he laid out the projects, each with their own set of objectives and challenges, he kept going back to Carol's comment about the likelihood of these two projects intersecting. Now that Lindsay had survived the primary, a collision, not merely an intersection, was almost inevitable.

Faye set her briefcase down on the credenza behind her desk. She had just returned from the grand jury case. They had issued indictments for the three original cases but weren't totally enamored with the evidence in the McKay case.

Just then, a knock on the door, and Ted poked his head in. "How'd it go?" he asked.

"They felt there was insufficient evidence in the McKay case to indict." She was disappointed in the decision.

"Let's get the judge to sign off on a search warrant so our men can uncover more corroborating evidence."

"I'm going to call Roger Obregon's office to see if they want investigators from the task force to work on this, either with our folks or on their own."

"Good idea," Ted said as he started back to his office.

Faye wanted to hang onto these cases and move them ahead under the control of the Lakeville DA's office. Bringing the DOJ back into this seemed unnecessary, but she knew it was proper procedure to ask how the DOJ wanted the case pursued. She called Roger and told him what had happened in court.

"Are you fucking kidding me?" Roger said.

"I still think there's a strong case against McKay," she said. "We just need a search warrant so we can seize the computer in question and pursue additional evidence. If he's guilty, we'll get the goods on him. We'd be happy to handle all the leg work on this end, if that works for you." She hoped her confidence would convince him to let them handle the case through to its conclusion.

"So you're suggesting we skip the 'contact' stage?" Roger replied. The usual procedure was to have a contact meeting with a suspect, without specifically discussing the crime they were investigating, to see if they would offer any incriminating evidence or even confess.

"Yes, we feel skipping the contact makes sense. We're dealing with a very smart suspect. If he feels we're on to him, he might destroy some evidence or cover up his crime in another way." Faye was confident she was recommending the right methodology.

"That's fine, but I want you to keep us informed of your progress every step of the way. We'll jump in if and when necessary."

"Thanks. You'll be hearing from us shortly," she said, relieved. This case was important to her on so many levels. On a selfish level, charging and convicting these criminals would certainly be a feather in her cap. Keeping it local would enhance the prestige of the department and instill confidence that law enforcement in Lakeville was doing a proper job protecting its citizens.

Faye called Jill into her office and the two of them proceeded to prepare the request for a search warrant.

Jack sat in the eighth row, a little off center. The stage was decorated with cutouts of coral and fish, all neon painted. The auditorium was packed with eager and proud parents for the first-grade production of *The Little Mermaid.* He spotted Sandy a few rows up.

As they waited for the curtain call, Jack mulled over what Peter had said earlier. He wanted to meet Jack tomorrow, off campus, to talk about the looming issues between them representing Consolidated and PetroMark while still managing Lindsay Revelle's campaign. Now that Lindsay was officially in the race, they needed to figure some things out.

The music played, and the children performed their hearts out. The audience oohed and aahed as the children fumbled over their lines and missed their dance cues.

Maya's performance as a fish was, by Jack's standards, nothing short of Tony Award worthy. He stood and cheered at the curtain call. Sandy was also standing and cheering wildly.

The kids all took their bows and then quickly disappeared backstage to remove their costumes so they could rejoin their adoring fans. Jack joined Sandy to wait for their daughter. When Maya appeared, she was smiling ear to ear.

"Great job!" Sandy exclaimed.

"Really great job!" Jack echoed.

"Can we all go to dinner together?" Maya implored.

"Of course, honey," Sandy said. She nodded to Jack.

"Maya, your amazing performance means you get to choose," Jack offered.

Maya selected Scarfido's. Besides being Jack and Mickey's go-to place, it was her favorite. She had artfully maneuvered her parents into a family dinner. He realized his daughter was quite the six-year-old politician.

CHAPTER 27

As Jack was leaving what was now Sandy's house his phone buzzed. "Please hurry home" the text message read. Jack was confused. This could only mean trouble. Mickey would never send such a text otherwise. It was nice to see, however, that he was using the dictation app's capability on his phone. A godsend for the visually impaired. He just wished this use of it wasn't because of a problem.

When he arrived at Mickey's, he found Miles and Mickey with long faces and trouble in their voices.

"We also have some serious stuff to discuss." Miles's tone was foreboding.

"Sounds ominous," Jack responded.

"It is. Let's sit down and discuss it over dinner." Miles was already headed to the kitchen table.

"I've already eaten," Jack said impatiently.

"Then just sit with us as we eat." Mickey served himself and Miles each a healthy portion of his very special homemade chili. He added a loaf of French bread, a bottle of light beer for Miles, and diet root beer for himself.

"So, what's the serious matter you want to discuss?" Jack was growing more impatient by the minute."

"I have a friend at the DOJ." Miles spoke in his serious detective voice, which could only mean trouble. "My friend wouldn't have called unless this was big. He's not one to divulge anything about the goings-on at the DOJ. He did tell me it was bad enough that he felt it warranted his breaking protocol. I also suspect he thought it was of dubious nature. He's no friend of the Party and probably had a feeling or saw some indication they were behind it."

What's your friend's name?" Mickey was probing for the friend's identity. It hadn't worked before and wasn't about to now.

"Sorry, Mickey. He remains anonymous. By the way, how did you know it was a 'he'?"

"Because I assumed it was, shall we say, a bed partner of yours," he teased.

"Former bedpartner, yes, but still a friend. That's all the identification you'll get on him. Now on to the important stuff. My friend says you're in trouble, Jack. A heap of trouble. He wouldn't elaborate, but said we need to be prepared for some ugly stuff that's about to come down."

"Prepare how?" Mickey temporarily put aside his shock.

"I'm not really sure yet. But I intend to start by investigating all the ties the Party has to Jack's clients. Until whatever is going to happen actually happens, it's about all I can do."

"So you suspect the Party is behind this trouble for Jack, whatever it is?" Mickey asked.

"I certainly do. The Party has declared war on you Jack, whether you know it or not. How could they not? You betrayed the Party, told them to go fuck themselves, and now you're running a candidate against Randall Davies's son, the Party's candidate. Revelle's wife wants to scuttle the PetroMark project, which the Party has a vested interest in. This all has to be at the core of whatever is about to happen. Jack, listen . . . if you're sure you've done nothing wrong—"

"I haven't!" Jack interrupted.

"If you're sure you've done nothing wrong, then we'll get to the truth of who and what's behind this," Miles finished.

"I'm sure," Jack stated emphatically.

"Good. Now Mickey and I will get to work. If Davies is behind this, we'll see to it you're cleared and hopefully take them down in the process."

Mickey nodded. Miles's logic was obviously sound. But the real question was what trouble was about to befall Jack?

"Miles, please get on this right away. I'll cover any of your time and any expenses you incur." Jack could not have been more emphatic.

"Jack, this one's on me. I hate that you are about to suffer some undeserved *tsuris*."

"*Tsuris*?" Jack's Yiddish was obviously lacking.

"*Tsuris* means 'trouble.' Sorry, sometimes I assume everyone knows basic Yiddish expressions. Anyway, I'm on it."

Miles was not only engaged now, he was pissed.

Jack headed to his room and lay on the bed, staring at the ceiling. *What crime could they possibly try to pin on him,* he wondered. He had heard of many shady things the Party had done behind closed doors. He thought about his career, analyzing the work he did for each corporate and campaign client, trying to find anything criminal in nature in the work he did. There were many questionable tactics employed but nothing he thought remotely illegal. The same thing in his personal life. A few bar altercations when he was young or nights out at the clubs with his guy friends before he was married. Not any of it qualified as criminal activity.

He got very little sleep as his mind kept spinning as he wondered what in the world could he have done, or what the Party could have conjured up.

Faye and Jake arrived at the door to the judge's chambers. Judge Joan Thompson had been on the Circuit Court bench for seven years. She was known as a tough and extremely competent jurist and had been reelected twice without opposition. Early in her law career she had been underestimated even though she had graduated from the University of Chicago Law School with honors. Thompson was often dismissed as just another pretty woman, but she had worked hard and succeeded in overcoming that unfair stereotype while earning the respect of her peers and the voters.

Ironically, she became a judge when she was appointed to fill the remainder of Mickey Martin's term when he was forced to resign.

"What can I do for you, Ms. Villareal?" Judge Thompson asked without looking up from the papers on her desk.

"I'm here to ask for a search warrant in a child pornography case I'm working on," Faye responded. "Here are documents outlining the evidence for probable cause."

The judge looked up. "So the DOJ is planning to prosecute these cases in their local jurisdictions. I think that's smart on a couple of levels. It separates the cases so their whole task force operation doesn't come under fire if a particular case falls apart and it brings more resources to bear."

Judge Thompson began reviewing the preamble to the specific case Faye was working on. Then her face turned pale as a ghost.

"Jack McKay is being accused of possession of child pornography?" she exclaimed, not really asking a question.

"Yes, Your Honor."

"Wow. Well, based on this information, I'll grant your request for a search warrant. A word of caution. This better be an ironclad case if you're going to publicly prosecute a well-respected member of the community. Particularly one with so many political connections," the judge warned as she signed off on the warrant.

"I totally understand, Your Honor. We have no interest in ruining any innocent person's life and will take the utmost care in not going to trial without a provable case."

"See you do just that," the judge cautioned. "I will not look kindly on your office if this turns into a media circus and the case is found to have no merit. The stakes are high for you, the DA, and DOJ. Be doubly sure you present the jury with a proper case for conviction in this matter."

"I will, Your Honor." She left the judge's chambers both excited about the high-profile case to follow and with the judge's cautions ringing in her ears.

CHAPTER 28

Jack got out of bed foggy from a night without rest. He proceeded with his morning rituals preparing for a typical day at the office while knowing it was unlikely to be typical at all. Something terrible was going to come down, and he had no clue what it was going to be.

It was his day to drive Maya to school. He texted Sandy and asked her to give Maya breakfast because he was running late. Truth be told, he didn't feel up to the typical morning "daddy talk" today. He picked her up and drove straight to the school, a five-minute drive. She gave him a hug and said, "Have a nice day, Daddy."

"I will, honey," he said, knowing full well it would not be the case.

Jack walked into McKay & Associates amidst a bevy of stares and half-hearted good mornings. Looking down the hall, he could see several men standing in the doorway to his office. Two were uniformed police officers and two others were dressed in black business suits. As he entered, one of the men in a suit approached.

"Jack McKay?" he asked.

"Yes, who are you?"

"I'm Detective Jake Mallory of the Lakeville Police Department. I'm here to serve you with a warrant authorizing us to search your office."

"What are you searching for?" he demanded.

"It's all here in the warrant, Mr. McKay," he said as he and the other officers proceeded to rifle through Jack's office.

While the cops went about searching, Jack looked at the warrant more closely and was astonished to see they were looking for evidence of child pornography. At first he was relieved because he didn't have anything of the kind at the office or elsewhere. But his heart sank when he realized the Party had likely planted something incriminating somewhere and his office was the perfect spot. It would provide a big, embarrassing scene, doing maximum damage to his business and reputation. Once you went against the Party, there was no turning back.

Within a few minutes the police entourage emerged from Jack's office with his laptop and a file folder.

"We're done here, Mr. McKay." Detective Mallory handed Jack his copy of the warrant and a receipt for the evidence seized.

The group then made their exit, leaving the office personnel aghast.

Peter rushed over. "What was that all about?"

Jack pulled him aside and spoke in as calm a voice as he could. "It appears the Party has found a way to punish me for choosing to work with Lindsay Revelle instead of William Davies. They're accusing me of possessing child pornography, which I assume was the evidence they planted, and the police just seized."

"That's ridiculous," Peter exclaimed indignantly.

"Ridiculous or not, it's what just happened. I need to get a lawyer."

"Jack, whatever you need, I'm here."

"Thanks, Peter."

Jack closed the door to his office. He sat down at his desk, took a deep breath, and called Mickey. He filled him in on what had just transpired.

"I'm going to need a real good lawyer. It's likely the Party has provided the DA with a strong case. We will need to not only prove my innocence but also prove the evidence was planted. If the Party is trying to take me down, I need to take them down as part of the process of defending myself."

"I know just the man, I mean person, for the job," Mickey offered.

"Who?" Jack asked, already knowing the answer.

"Bobbie, of course," Mickey said. "She is the best criminal defense lawyer I know, and I know a lot of them." Mickey was pleading his case, and Jack knew he was right.

"All right, I'll call her. I suspect you're hoping that this will help you reestablish contact with her."

"Of course I am. But getting you out of this mess is the first priority!"

Jack hung up and debated whether or not to call Lindsay to alert him to the impending media blitz, which would follow the leak of the case to the press. He was sure the Party had that at the top of their to-do list. Realizing what the implications were for the campaign, he called Lindsay.

"Hi, Jack. What's up?" Lindsay said in an unsuspecting tone.

"I have some very disturbing news," Jack said, getting right to the point. "It appears the Party has unleashed an attack designed to destroy me and your campaign in the process."

"I don't understand, Jack. What attack?"

Jack proceeded to recount the pertinent events of the morning emphasizing his innocence and how this was Randall Davies's handiwork.

Lindsay exploded. "Those bastards! What do we do now?"

"First thing you do is fire me once the story comes out."

"Isn't that just playing directly into Davies's hand?"

"Yes, but realistically we have no choice. In order to save your campaign, you must distance yourself as best you can from all of this." Jack was being pragmatic but knew deep down that unless he was acquitted well before the election, Lindsay would be unfairly victimized.

"Okay, Jack. We're going to beat this."

"Of course we will, Lindsay." Jack tried to sound confidant. "We'll talk again as soon as this all unfolds a little more."

The moment he hung up, his heart sank. He quickly gathered his things and raced out of the building to pick up his daughter.

CHAPTER 29

Jack watched the sun come up after a restless, mostly sleepless night. Unfortunately, the morning brought no relief. He did, however, decide what to do next.

"Roberta Martin," Bobbie said, answering her private line.

"Hi, Bobbie. It's Jack McKay."

"Is this another plea on Mickey's behalf?"

"No, this time it's on my behalf." Jack then proceeded to tell her all that had transpired along with the theories as to why the Party was behind it, and the fallout for all concerned: his daughter, his business, Lindsay's campaign, and so on.

"Jack, I'm so sorry about this. Should I assume you're calling means you want my help?"

"Bobbie, I need a top-notch defense lawyer who I trust will go all out in my defense. And one who will implicate all those who are behind it."

"Any good defense lawyer will do just that," she said.

"I don't need just any good defense lawyer, I need a great one. I need you." Jack was practically begging. This was a deal he really needed to close.

"All right, Jack. I'm in on one condition. No forced get-togethers with Mickey."

Even though he wasn't sure how he would navigate the request, he agreed.

Bobbi made a quick to-do list in her head and rattled it off to Jack.

"It is likely you will be arrested any minute, so I will get a friend of mine, Carl Rafferty, who practices in Lakeville, to deal with the niceties of getting you through the charging and bail process. Call Miles now so he can assist you in lining up a surety bond so you can make bail. That way it'll be ready to go when you need it. No sense spending a minute longer in custody than necessary. After you're out, let's meet right away to discuss the charges and how we'll go about proving your innocence."

Her reassurance notwithstanding, Jack knew it would be a rough road to acquittal.

"Any thoughts on how to handle this with my family?" he asked. "Not sure I told you, but I've just signed my divorce papers. This, I assume, will impact my parental rights, at least temporarily, not to mention how Sandy will react. Most of all, how do I shield Maya from the trauma of my being arrested and the stigma which will be attached to it considering the nature of the charges? This could all be devastating for her." Jack was on the verge of tears.

Sensing Jack's sadness, Bobbie's voice took on a less business-like and more comforting tone.

"First of all, call your divorce lawyer. Who is it, by the way?" she asked.

"Steven Clark."

"Explain to Steven what's going on with the authorities. Tell him, in no uncertain terms, that you are innocent and need his help to protect your family and your parental rights. Then—and this will be really hard—stay away from your family unless Steven sets up some sort of supervised visit. *Capisce?*"

"Got it." Jack's voice had become barely audible.

"Jack, you're strong. You'll get through this. It may be tough sledding for a while, but you will prevail." Her attempt at comforting him was not particularly effective, but he appreciated it nonetheless.

"Thanks, Bobbie. I can't tell you how grateful I am to have you in my corner."

"With you all the way, Jack."

After they hung up, Jack was anything but reassured. In fact, he was filled with anxiety about Maya, the firm, and the campaign, not to mention the personal price he was about to pay regardless of the outcome of the legal proceedings.

His next call was to Peter.

"Hi, Jack. How are you holding up?"

"Not very well, I'm afraid. This is an awful situation, and not just for me. I feel terrible in so many ways. I know I can count on you to handle everything there while I sort things out." Jack knew Peter would be more than happy to take charge.

"Of course. Will you be taking care of things with Lindsay Revelle, or do you need me on call to take care of that too?"

"No, I've spoken to Lindsay and told him to fire us. Hopefully that should provide some cover for him and the firm."

"Anything else?" Peter could hardly contain his feeling of relief.

"Not at the moment. Peter, I really appreciate you stepping up. There will be a lot to do to keep things afloat. I'm grateful for being able to lean on you."

Jack was genuinely comforted to have Peter to rely on. After he finished his call with Peter, he poured himself a cup of much-needed coffee and joined Mickey at the kitchen table. He had decided to hold off calling Steven until he had a chance to collect his thoughts.

"Any progress?" Mickey asked.

"Your daughter has agreed to represent me, and Peter is ready to take on all of my responsibilities at the firm." He knew Mickey would be elated about Bobbie taking Jack's case.

"That's progress," said Mickey, sounding predictably cheerful.

"Of sorts, I guess. It's so weird just sitting here—"

Suddenly, there was a loud knock at the front door.

"Police! Open the door!" someone shouted in a booming voice.

Molly went bounding to the front door squealing and barking with delight as she went. Little did she know that the visitors were not friendly.

Jack opened the door. His body was shaking.

"Jack McKay?" the officer asked.

"Yes," Jack replied.

"Mr. McKay, you are under arrest." The officer read Jack his *Miranda* rights, placed him in handcuffs, and proceeded to escort him to the police cruiser parked in front of the house. Molly growled throughout, somehow knowing Jack was in trouble.

The short ride to the police station was painful both physically and emotionally. The officers who took him into custody obviously knew what the charges against him would be and must have viewed him as among the lowest form of criminal imaginable. It was the most humiliation Jack had ever faced, uncomfortably handcuffed and dragged out of the house in broad daylight.

Once at the station, he was booked, fingerprinted, and put into a dingy temporary holding cell. Soon he was moved to an interrogation room where he was "greeted" by two detectives. One was Jake Mallory, who had executed the warrant at Jack's office. Jack pegged Detective Mallory to be about fifty and possessing the intimating gaze of a seasoned cop. The other, barely thirty, looked as if he was fresh out of the academy.

"Mr. McKay, do you know why you've been arrested?" Detective Mallory asked.

"No, I don't," Jack said defiantly.

"You've been booked on suspicion of possession of child pornography. We would like to ask you a few questions if you don't mind." Mallory emphasized the words "child pornography" in a most disapproving tone.

"I do mind. I must insist on contacting my attorney before saying anything. I believe it is my right," Jack declared.

"Okay, then. One of our officers will provide you with a phone so you can call your attorney. Until he arrives, we'll just put you back into the holding cell."

Shortly thereafter, Jack was led down a long corridor by the younger detective to a small room with a phone. He had memorized the mobile number for Carl Rafferty that Bobbie had given him. Carl was expecting his call and told Jack he would head right over. Jack was then escorted back to the holding cell to wait for Carl.

When Carl arrived, Jack was led back to the interrogation room to meet him. Also in the room were the two detectives and a woman dressed in a sharp gray suit. He and Carl sat down at the table across from the trio.

"I'm Deputy Faye Villareal, and we're here to secure a statement from you, Mr. McKay, regarding the charge that you were in possession of child pornography, which is a felony."

Before Jack could say a word, Carl took over. "My client will plead not guilty and will have no further comment at this time. We request an immediate bail hearing."

"Why do you feel he's entitled to an expedited bail hearing, particularly given the severity of the charges?" Faye asked, obviously annoyed.

"My client is a longstanding member of the community with no criminal record. He deserves the opportunity to be released quickly so he can mount a defense against these baseless charges." Carl had obviously done this before.

Bobbie picked a good associate, Jack thought.

"I'll see what I can do," said Faye. "In the meantime, he'll have to go back to the holding cell."

As they were whisking Jack away, Carl assured him he'd get him out as soon as possible and that he'd get in touch with Miles about posting bail.

Two hours later Jack, Carl and Miles were in court securing his release on a $100,000 surety bond. A preliminary hearing date was set for Friday.

Miles drove Jack back to Mickey's. Neither said a word on the way. Jack dreaded the next call he would have to make. Once back at Mickey's, Jack placed the call.

"Steven, it's Jack McKay . . ." He laid out the horror story of what had befallen him and asked for Steven's help in minimizing the damage to the divorce decree and, most importantly, the impact on his daughter.

"Jack, I'm sure you've been falsely accused. That said, the court will almost certainly forbid you to have any contact with children, especially Maya. I think it's best to have me contact Sandy's attorneys to get them engaged before they hear about it from the media. As soon as I connect with them, I'll be back to you."

"Steven, I can't thank you enough."

"You're welcome, Jack. Keep your head up, my friend."

Exhausted, Jack plopped down on the couch, hoping to drift off for a much-needed nap. That plan was briefly interrupted by Miles.

"Jack, I'm off to do what I do best: snoop. We know you were set up. Now we just have to find proof as to who it was and how they did it."

"Well, we know who ordered it." Jack lamented.

"We still need the 'who' actually did it and the 'how' they actually did it."

"Go get 'em, Miles," Jack said with all the enthusiasm he could muster. He dropped his head back onto the couch pillow. This was going to be a long, hard fight, but he would never stop working to prove his innocence.

CHAPTER 30

Waking up to a sixty-degree spring day in Wisconsin was like finding a $100 bill. You just couldn't wait to go and spend it. Jack decided to spend this one riding his Harley to his meeting with Bobbie in Madison. He dressed in a suit and tie, but he also wore rain pants over his Armani slacks. He folded the suit jacket nicely and put it in the storage compartment he and Maya had installed on the back of the bike. Donning his leather jacket and helmet, he headed out.

Once he got underway, Jack remembered what an exhilarating feeling he got riding his bike instead of being insulated in his fancy car. Every sense was heightened on the bike. He saw vast vistas instead of viewing the scenery through a narrow windshield. He heard the rumble of the engine not the sound of the radio. He felt the vibration of the bike over the road instead of floating surreally in a moving easy chair. Rather than filtered air, he smelled a complex mixture of outdoor aromas so strong they'd created a unique flavor he could actually taste.

As Jack rode through the Wisconsin countryside toward Madison, he realized what a contrast it was to the daily life in Lakeville. Life, like the passing topography, had so many different appearances.

I guess this is why some people love the quiet, straight-forward life of the country and others love the tumult and unpredictability of the city, he thought. *It's all a matter of what you consider the perfect setting.*

His life, to an outsider, might seem like a perfect setting: lovely wife, adoring daughter, exciting job, nice house, stature in the community, all the things which make up the idyllic American Dream. Now that had all changed.

As he approached Bobbie's office on the Square in Madison, he shook off the self-pity and gathered himself. Jack parked the bike in a lot across from the building. He removed his rain pants and packed them with his helmet and leather jacket in the storage compartment, put on his suit coat, straightened his appearance in the bike's rearview mirror, and walked across the street.

Bobbie's office was in a very non-descript mid-century steel-and-glass building on the Lake Monona side of the Square. As he exited the elevator, he could smell the antiseptic odor of the internist's office across from Bobbie's. He couldn't help but think how similar the two businesses were. Diagnose, treat, and hope for the best.

The office was small: a reception area, conference room, and her private office. As a sole practitioner, Bobbie had developed a solid criminal defense practice and saw no real advantage in having a larger firm. Bobbie's assistant greeted him.

"Mr. McKay, I presume," she said. It struck Jack as funny as he flashed to the famous "Dr. Livingston, I presume" line. Jenna was somewhat perplexed as she noticed him trying to hold back a smile and couldn't figure why.

"I'll tell Ms. Martin you're here."

Bobbie poked her head out of her office door and invited him in with a wave of her hand. The office was tidy and well-appointed with an eclectic blend of office antiques and modern conveniences. But it was the view that made it special. There was Lake Monona with dozens of small crisscrossing sailboats adorning its sparkling blue water. The other window offered a panorama of downtown Madison dominated by the State Capitol building, considered by many to be the most beautiful one in the country. In the distance was the university. Jack was transported back to his college days there when the most complicated part of his life was which party to attend on a particular night. Bobbie had chosen well for her self-imposed exile.

"I never figured you for the pedophile type," she greeted him sarcastically.

"So you think I'm guilty. Some defense attorney you are," he snipped as he moved about sizing up the place.

"I'm sorry, just trying to lighten things up a little," she said, her sincerity returning. "The attorney general's investigation and resulting indictments will soon make headlines in every state paper. Your arrest will be very prominently mentioned. We need to get this to trial quickly to minimize any long-term damage it may cause, even after your acquittal."

She gestured for him to sit.

"Bobbie, you're the best defense lawyer around as far as I'm concerned. It's also better you're someone not tied into the political scene in Lakeville. By the way, thanks for recommending Carl. He did a masterful job getting me out without undue fanfare."

She smiled as she changed the subject. "I know Mickey's behind selecting me."

"He's the one who suggested I hire you, but you are the right choice to defend me," Jack proffered. "Besides, you know he's a great legal mind and we'll need his help. Kind of a Mr. Inside and a Ms. Outside combination."

"You know Mickey and I are not speaking," she said somewhat angrily.

"Isn't that something you'd like to change?" Jack replied, hoping for a crack in the ice.

"Don't think so. Besides, we covered that on the phone awhile back, remember?" A sharp-and-to-the-point answer.

"Yes, we did. Back to why I'm here. I really need your help. Please join my defense team," Jack implored.

"Who else besides Mickey, Carl, and Miles is on your team?"

"Just you, which I'd say makes quite a formidable team."

She was staring out the window, running the argument through her mind. He sensed a slight thaw in the ice. As Jack watched her, he couldn't help thinking how she had transformed from the cute, pony-tailed law student at Marquette he first met into a very attractive, accomplished professional with a coiffed 'do and a chip on her shoulder. But most of all he was struck by how her eyes were as deep blue as the Monona waters they reflected.

"It's going to be very hard to work so closely with Mickey on this, given my feelings," she said softly.

"If you clear the air first, it might just be the elixir each of you needs. You know, something to fill the holes in your hearts."

"Let's save the discussion about Mickey and me for another time. I'll take your case without promising any form of reconciliation with him. Okay?"

"Deal!" Jack was genuinely pleased to have her onboard. He was optimistic that somewhere along the way, she and Mickey would patch things up.

Peter knew he had to advise Drew Tucker of Consolidated about Jack's predicament before it hit the papers, so he placed a call.

"Hey, Peter. What can I do for you?" Drew asked.

Peter gulped and started in. "Drew, there's been a development here at the firm that I need to discuss with you. It's about Jack and unfortunately it's not good news."

"Go on."

"There's no gentle way to say this, so here goes. Jack has been arrested on suspicion of possession of child pornography."

"What?" Drew screamed.

Peter filled him in on the few details he had. Then he tried to soften the blow. "We're confident the charges are a big mistake and that Jack will be cleared soon."

Drew wasn't the kind to mince words. "This is awful for all concerned. I'm not sure what else to say except I don't see any way you can continue representing us."

"What if Jack takes a leave of absence?" Peter was hoping that would suffice.

"Not sure it would adequately insulate us from his problems."

"What if he were to resign and relinquish his ownership stake?" Peter offered.

"That would be better, but if he's innocent, he would lose the firm unnecessarily. Besides, he's one of the main reasons we selected you."

"I've thought of that. If he resigns and agrees to sell his shares, we could agree to let him buy back in once he's acquitted or at least consult for us."

Drew paused, then said, "Sounds like you've gotten a plan together rather quickly."

"I had to. There's too much at stake for too many people not to have a contingency plan in place." Peter's plan to save the firm obviously positioned him to take over the operation completely. If it worked, Jack's predicament would be Peter's goldmine. "If we can extricate Jack from the firm, can we count on keeping your business?"

"Peter, you know I can't unilaterally agree to it. As VP all I can do is take it up with Bill and the executive committee once Jack has stepped aside. It is crucial he do so before all this stuff hits the papers." Drew was more than emphatic in his demand.

"I totally understand. I'll be back to you as soon as we have the plan in place."

"Don't forget to bring Don Buckley at PetroMark up to speed. We all need to march in lock step on this regardless of the outcome."

"Don's next on my call list. Thanks, Drew." Peter hung up. Things would certainly fall into place for him and the firm if all went well.

Jack's ride back from Madison wasn't as enjoyable as his ride up had been. While he was even more sure Bobbie was the right choice to defend him, he knew that dealing with Sandy and Maya as well as the future of the firm loomed large on the horizon. As he approached Lakeville, an overwhelming feeling of anxiety gripped him. It was a feeling unlike anything he had experienced before. And this was just the beginning.

As he put the bike away in Mickey's garage, he felt his cell phone humming. It was Steven Clark. He told him precisely what he had anticipated was coming.

"Sandy's attorneys have informed us that under no circumstances are you to have any contact with Maya until you are acquitted," Steven said. "Further, she has decided to take Maya out of school and move temporarily to her parents' house."

Jack knew it was the right decision. They would be safe there. All the uproar surrounding his trial would be too stressful for them to remain in Lakeville. Maya loved Sandy's parents, Sam and Diane Freeman. They lived in the quiet residential Milwaukee suburb of Shorewood with their calico cat Sadie. Thankfully the school year would be over in a couple of weeks anyway, so the loss of a little time out of school wouldn't be an issue.

"I guess it's best for all concerned," Jack conceded.

"It is, Jack. As soon as things are favorably resolved with your case, you'll have your placement schedule reinstated immediately."

Steven went on to explain that Sandy had told Maya that Jack had to go on a long business trip and so they were taking the opportunity to visit the Freemans. Steven also said he had appealed to Sandy's attorneys to let Jack call Maya. He was awaiting their response.

"Okay, thanks," Jack replied dejectedly as he hung up.

"I guess I know why you're so cheery this afternoon, Frank," Randall said without looking up from his afternoon newspaper. The headline and first paragraph read: "DOJ Cracks Down on Child Pornographers: Prominent Lakeview PR Executive Implicated."

The article stated:

The State Department of Justice Sex Crimes Task Force has arrested four local men in connection with a wide-ranging investigation into sex crimes, primarily focused on child pornography. One of the suspects is Jack McKay of Lakeville. McKay is the prominent CEO of McKay & Associates and a well-known adviser to political campaigns, most recently that of Lindsay Revelle, who is running for Congress in the First Congressional District, which includes Lakeville.

"Nice article in the *Examiner*, I'd say." Frank could not contain his pride over their handiwork.

Randall beamed. "Yes, it's exactly what the doctor ordered. The best part is that even if Jack is acquitted, he's ruined and Revelle has no chance to win the election."

"So I guess we just sit back and let the whole thing play out."

"No, Frank. We need to be sure none of this comes back on us. Rest assured, McKay's attorneys, and anyone they employ, will be looking at every angle and possible source for the evidence against him. If we detect even the slightest notion of this set-up falling back into our lap, you'll need to act to protect us from any implication.

The Party must be lily white as this case unfolds."

"Don't worry, I have this under control. We've been very careful not to leave a trail that leads back here."

"You'd better be right, Frank, or we'll all be heading to prison."

Frank nodded and headed out the door. A professional always covered his tracks.

CHAPTER 31

The smell of burnt toast and scrambled eggs filled the room. Jack lay on the bed staring out the window. His eyes were burning. He didn't sleep much. He forced himself out of bed and headed into the kitchen. Molly greeted him with the usual squeal and rapidly wagging tail. He wondered how dogs could be so eternally cheerful. The answer was simple: because they didn't have people problems.

"Sleep well?" Mickey inquired.

"Not really. I keep running over in my mind the question of how the evidence they found got onto my computer and into my desk." Miles walked into the kitchen. He had joined them at the breakfast table for what turned into an impromptu strategy session and the beginning of his investigation.

"They got into your office somehow and went about their dirty work," Miles said. "I assume your building has security set up to control access and hopefully video surveillance. Once inside, the placing of the printed stuff is a piece of cake. Breaking into your computer requires a certain level of expertise. Did they simply hack into your computer or did someone supply them with your password?"

Miles was not really expecting an answer. It was more like he was thinking out loud. He scribbled a few things in his notebook.

"Yes, we have security to enter the office suite," said Jack. "Typical keypad system. The office staff and cleaning service each have their own access code. There are no security cameras, however. A couple of people have my computer password, just in case."

"Who?"

"Let's see, Peter, of course. Donna, my assistant. Our IT guy and the office manager. Maybe a couple of others. I'm not sure," Jack recalled.

"So at least five people including you?"

"Yes, I think that's correct. By the way, when I got to the office that day, I found I had left my laptop on my desk overnight."

"Well then we have some possible suspects to look into. Please get me the full names of the employees in question as well as the people you deal with at the security company and the cleaning service." Miles continued his note-taking.

"As soon as we've finished breakfast, I'll email you the list with their contact information. Anything else?" Jack asked.

"Send me the password to your computer, the access code for the building's security system, and the name of your security system provider," Miles said.

"No problem, but why do you need the password for my computer since it's already in the hands of the authorities?"

"Just covering all the bases," Miles replied, not fully disclosing his reasoning. "By the way, I assume you'll use a different password on the new laptop."

"Yes, of course!"

With that they returned to their burnt toast and eggs. Once they finished eating, Jack did the dishes and went off to his room to reset the password on his new computer.

Later that morning, he was reading the *New York Times* online when his phone rang.

"Good morning, Lindsay," Jack said, trying to sound cheerful.

"How you holding up, Jack?" Lindsay's voice showed genuine concern.

"It's hard, but knowing I'm innocent really helps."

"I want you to know I am one hundred percent behind you in that belief. I'm having a press conference this afternoon, and I know

I'll be asked about your status with the campaign. Just so you know, I will answer that, while I believe in your innocence, you are no longer employed by the campaign."

"That is exactly what you need to do." Jack appreciated Lindsay believing in him but knew this had to happen. "Who will you name to replace me?"

"Robin. She's qualified, identified with our positions on many of the issues, and has the skills."

"Great choice. Just don't forget to give your marriage a little campaign downtime. Sorry, I'm not the one who should be giving marital advice."

"No apology required. It's good advice. One more thing. Robin and I want you to advise her on an informal basis. If that works for you, we can work some compensation once the campaign is over."

"What a generous offer. I'd love to stay involved. As for compensation, nothing monetary is required. Just having something important to focus on other than defending myself against trumped-up charges is a godsend. I really appreciate it."

"It's settled then. Robin will be in touch with you soon. Hang in there, Jack. I trust we will both prevail."

Jack was in a happier mood. Having the opportunity to continue helping Lindsay get elected and to bring down Randall Davies and his son in the process was just the lift he needed.

If the number of news station trucks parked outside the hall was any indication, Lindsay's press conference was going to be much better attended than expected.

Robin had helped Lindsay with his opening statement and his responses to the obvious questions that would follow. They spent extra time on the ones concerning Jack.

"Good afternoon, everyone. I'm here to state my case as a

candidate for Congress in Wisconsin's First District and then to answer your questions. For too long, the congressional seat I seek has been held by one party. That party has catered to the wealthiest members of our district. They have stood against proper funding for public education and a cleaner environment. They have stood in opposition of legislation that would provide affordable healthcare for everyone. They have fought against common sense gun laws, paid family leave, and so many other programs that help the vast majority of our citizens. We can change all that. I need your vote on November 2 so I can go to Congress and help enact the programs that will have a profound and positive impact on your life and the lives of our fellow citizens. With that I'll take questions."

The first question was from Lesley Townsend of TV station WBGR from Janesville. "Mr. Revelle, your campaign manager, Jack McKay, was recently charged with possession of child pornography. What changes, if any, have you made in your staff as a result?"

"Thank you, Lesley. Your question is an important one. While I firmly believe Jack is innocent and will be cleared of all charges, we have relieved him of his duties as campaign manager. My wife, Robin, has assumed those duties going forward. Robin has successfully spearheaded a number of political movements and is uniquely qualified to take over and run our campaign."

Thankfully, the questions moved on from Jack to the issues. Lindsay's knowledge of the issues and his ability to articulate his stance on each question was on full display. The voters would certainly have a clear choice between him and William Davies. His populist message had broad appeal and would play well with the predominantly working-class urban voters, a segment he needed to carry in overwhelming numbers.

After the press conference concluded, Lindsay walked off the stage, and Robin greeted him with a hug. "You did great!" she added.

"Let's hope the voters felt that way too. If the Jack thing doesn't raise its ugly head again, we have a fighting chance to win this election."

Lindsay was unsure just how the voters would ultimately view his association with Jack once they got to the voting booth. They packed up and headed toward the car.

"I'm sure the Party will try to use it," said Robin, "but we'll steer clear of engaging them on that topic, at least until they bring it up at the debate in October."

"Agreed." Lindsay acknowledged as he closed her car door. Just then his cell phone rang. It was Jack.

"Very nicely done, Lindsay," Jack said.

"Thanks, Jack. Listen, Robin and I are concerned that any semblance of interaction with you might be traceable and fall back on the campaign. I meant what I said earlier about wanting Robin to be able to rely on you. She will contact you as needed, but we need to keep those contacts to a minimum until your legal battle is over."

"A smart strategy. I'm here when you need me."

"Robin will be in touch."

Even though Jack knew this was the proper course, it stung. The gravity of his predicament kept delivering gut punches to his attitude. He desperately needed something to go his way. As if on cue, his cell phone rang. It was Miles.

"I've found something interesting. It appears someone from your office called the janitorial service on two occasions asking them not to send their crew. One of those instances seems to coincide with the time you mentioned finding that you'd left your laptop on your desk at the office. Do you remember anything which might connect those events?"

"Actually, yes. That morning Donna commented that the

wastebaskets were not where they were supposed to be. She thought it was another substitute janitor."

"I suspect the substitute janitor may well have been more skilled than your typical cleaning service staff member."

Miles continued to lay out his theory. Someone posing as a McKay employee could have called the service and then sent in their own hacker who downloaded the porn and put the printed stuff in Jack's desk.

"But how did they gain access to the offices without the security code?"

"A couple of ways. The easiest was someone on the inside or at the janitorial service gave it to them. The other is that the hacker was adept enough to hack the alarm system as well as your computer."

Jack had real trouble imagining one of his people being in on this scheme, so his preferred theory was the hacker did all of it. Miles, however, was leaving all possible options on the table.

"I think we now have a real solid possibility as to the 'how', the 'who,' and the 'why' are next. Stay tuned."

CHAPTER 32

After moving the rest of his things from his old house to Mickey's, there wasn't much else to do. Jack's work life and time with Maya were gone, if only temporarily, so he spent some time fiddling with his motorcycle. But mostly he focused on his case.

Jack was really looking forward to his meeting today with Bobbie. They were going to meet for lunch at Busby's in Lake Geneva. It was a cozy roadside diner just north of town on Highway 12 about halfway between Lakeville and Madison. A relatively quiet place just far enough away from the tourist haunts in town to afford them some privacy.

Jack decided to go by car this time and arrived first. He staked out a table in the corner and ordered coffee. Bobbie arrived a few minutes later with a briefcase and cell phone in tow.

"I'll have coffee as well," Bobbie told the server when she sat down.

"Thanks for agreeing to meet me here. I needed to get away from the office routine and taking the drive from Madison allowed me time to gather my thoughts," she said, taking a deep breath and adding a smile.

"I was happy to get out of town as well. Everywhere I go, I can feel the disapproving stares of everyone even though I'm sure most of them don't have a clue about who I am or what I've been accused of," Jack lamented.

The server returned with Bobbie's coffee and took their order. Bobbie opted for a garden salad with grilled chicken. Jack, ever the carnivore, ordered a cheeseburger.

Bobbie returned to the business at hand. "I had a chance to speak to Miles and he filled me in on his latest findings. He's come up with some good circumstantial evidence, but we need to turn that information into provable evidence which links the specific acts to specific people with the motive and the intent to wrongly incriminate you."

"No small task," Jack pointed out.

"True, but absolutely essential in proving your innocence." Moving on, Bobbie quizzed Jack on a number of subjects. Most were basic, and some were unpleasant to say the least. Some questions like "who had access to his computer password" were just to confirm what Miles had told her. Some of the unpleasant questions covered topics such as any possible history he might have had with pornography. Did he have any interactions with his daughter which could be viewed as inappropriate? On and on like that for about an hour.

As she spoke, Jack realized he was becoming totally taken with her. Not just by her obvious good looks, but by how smart and capable she was. He wrote off some of his feelings to his being sad and lonely, but there was definitely something more there. He wondered if she also felt any attraction. That investigation would have to wait for another place and time.

Bobbie continued filling Jack in on their defense strategy. "Remember, the burden of proof is always on the prosecution, so it is not our responsibility to prove you're not guilty. In this case, however, for the sake of your family and your reputation, we must prove you're innocent by proving who set you up and why. I will first focus on discrediting the evidence the prosecution provides in discovery. Then we must introduce our own evidence implicating the real criminals. Jack, I have an assignment for you. Please work on a list of who within your organization might have helped Davies's people get into your office and your computer. You should coordinate the list with Miles so he can follow up your ideas as possible leads."

They finished their lunch and went their separate ways. Jack was angry at himself for not working Mickey into the conversation. He was on a mission to reunite father and daughter and had missed an opportunity to further that effort.

As he headed back to Lakeville, Jack's thoughts were consumed about who within McKay & Associates may have betrayed him. His mind was spinning.

"Who in my organization would want to harm me, and what could they possibly gain by doing so?" he said to the empty car. He came up with two hypotheses. The first theory was probable. Maybe some lower-level staff member was promised a big job with the Party when the firm was brought down. He hated his second theory: Peter was hiding something. Peter was the only one who could really capitalize on Jack's downfall. He'd inherit the firm and its clients and then likely be set up as the Party's PR firm du jour. He hoped Miles would uncover the insider, if there was one, before he shared his suspicions with his defense team.

The ride home was smooth other than the nagging feeling that Peter might be an accomplice in the plot to destroy Jack. He got off the freeway and took a quieter route home. He wanted some time with his thoughts. A few moments later, his concentration was interrupted by his ringing cell phone. It was his father-in-law, Sam Freeman.

"Jack, sorry to bother you but I need to share something with you." Sam was obviously troubled about something.

"No problem. I'm just headed home from a meeting. What's up? Is Maya OK?"

"Maya's fine. And let me start with this. Diane and I want you to know that we don't believe a word of what you're being accused of doing. Regardless of your issues with Sandy, we are behind you."

"Thanks, Sam. That means a lot. What is it you want to share?" Jack wasn't sure he wanted an answer.

"Well . . . since Sandy and Maya have been here, Sandy has been spending many nights out late at the places on Oakland."

Shorewood's Oakland Avenue was loaded with upscale bars and restaurants, often called gastropubs, places that in the early evening were frequented by young adults with their children and then a more traditional bar crowd later in the evening.

"She sometimes goes to one of those places with Maya, and sometimes we would join them. On those occasions, we would take Maya home and Sandy would stay. Either way, when she comes home, she's intoxicated." Sam's voice broke as he spoke.

"Sam, I understand your concern, but I'm not sure what I can do to help."

"First of all, we wanted you to hear about it from us, not your divorce attorney. Secondly, we want you to know that we are making sure Maya is always safe. After many unpleasant discussions, we've finally convinced Sandy to seek help. She will be voluntarily entering a rehab facility later today."

Jack was not surprised that Sandy's drinking had gotten out of hand. He'd certainly seen plenty of evidence of it. Given the circumstances, he was grateful Sandy saw fit to get help with her drinking problem. Both he and Sandy were also very fortunate to have Sam and Diane's support, particularly where Maya's welfare was concerned. Longer term, both he and Sandy needed to get their respective lives in order for Maya's sake as well as their own.

"Sam, I know all of this must be putting a terrible strain on the two of you. Obviously, I can't help directly, but if you need some help with Maya's care, I'll gladly provide financial support. The same goes for Sandy. Whatever she needs—"

"Don't worry about any of it, Jack. We've got all of it under control. We need to work together and ask the attorneys to see if they can get the court to at least let you talk to Maya by phone. Will you work on it with your attorney?"

"Of course. You can't imagine how much I miss her and would love to hear her voice. I can only imagine how sad she must be. I have asked my attorney to try to set up a call, but I'll ask him again and emphasize just how much more important it is now. Oh, and Sam, we are all so lucky to have you and Diane looking out for us." Jack's voice cracked. Tears were running down his face as he said goodbye to Sam.

He pulled into Mickey's driveway, turned off the ignition, and sat alone in his car for several minutes feeling sorry for himself. Finally, his moment of self-pity over, he got out of the car and marched into the house intent on turning things around.

But when he stepped inside, he found Mickey on the floor barely breathing with Molly at his side whimpering as only a loving dog could.

"Mickey!" he shouted as he knelt next to him. He quickly called 9-1-1 and gave the operator the needed information. While they waited, he comforted Mickey and Molly until help arrived. He held his friend's hand and told him that everything was going to be all right.

The paramedics were there within a couple of minutes and tended to Mickey. He was conscious but struggling to breathe. Jack held his hand. "You're going to be all right, Mickey," he said. Mickey looked up and winked but was too weak to speak. The paramedics put an oxygen mask over Mickey's nose then loaded him into the ambulance and took off for Memorial Hospital.

"I'm following right behind," Jack yelled. "I'll see you at the hospital!"

Jack quickly took care of Molly then texted Miles before heading to the hospital. On the way, he called Bobbie.

"Forget something, Jack?" she said.

"Your father has had some kind of an attack, from his COPD I think, and the paramedics have transported him to Memorial. I'm on my way there now." Jack tried not to sound panicked, although he most certainly was.

"Is he going to be all right?"

"I don't know, but if I were you, I'd get over there immediately to see him." The tone of Jack's voice convinced her of the gravity of the situation.

"I'll leave as soon as we hang up. Please call me on my cell if anything changes, good or bad."

"Will do." Jack had finally convinced Bobbie to see her father. Hopefully, it wasn't too late.

His whole world was crumbling, and Jack felt powerless to stop it.

CHAPTER 33

Jack and Miles were chatting in the waiting room of the ER when Bobbie arrived.

"Hi, Bobbie." Jack tried his best to sound calm.

"Any news?" she said.

"Nothing yet. Since we're not family, they're not forthcoming with information or letting us see him. You will need to get through the nurse at the desk. She's the gatekeeper."

With that, Bobbie sprang into action. She approached the nurse behind the desk and politely, but firmly, announced her presence. Bobbie's growing impatience was apparent, but she held it together. Handing the nurse her driver's license, she asked, "Now may I see my father?"

"I'll check with attending staff to see if he's in treatment or can have a visitor." The nurse got up and disappeared behind a doorway.

Jack saw Bobbie motion for him to join her at the desk. To his surprise, she wrapped her arms tightly around him in an embrace. He could feel she was trembling.

"Jack, he can't die. Not now. There is so much we need to say to each other."

"I know, and you will," Jack said, continuing the embrace.

The nurse reappeared and asked Bobbie to follow her into the examination area. She exchanged a hopeful smile with Jack, and then disappeared through the door.

Jack returned to his seat next to Miles, embarrassed at how

much he had enjoyed holding Bobbie. Miles smiled as if he knew what Jack was feeling.

Mickey was still being treated in the triage area of the ER. The attending physician came out to speak to Bobbie before allowing her to see her father.

"Your father has an advanced case of COPD. Do you know what that is?" she asked.

"I do."

"He's had a major flare up of the disease, similar to an acute asthma attack. He's going to be OK once we get it all settled down, but this disease only gets worse. You can see him now."

As they entered, the doctor said, "Mr. Martin, your daughter's here."

Mickey was barely able to lift his head, but broke out into a broad smile, tears flowing freely down his face.

"Hi, Dad" was all Bobbie could muster. Unable to speak with the oxygen mask on, Mickey simply held out his hand. She took it in hers, signaling she was warming to the idea of starting anew.

She sat with him in silence for a short while before the attendants came in to move him from the ER to the intensive care unit. They gave her the room number and told her she could rejoin him there but to allow about an hour for the staff to get him situated.

Jack and Miles were reading magazines in the ER lobby when Bobbie returned.

"How's he doing?" Miles asked.

"He has a bad case of COPD, but I'm sure you knew that. This was a big-time attack. He's stable and they're moving him to intensive care. Once they get him settled, I'll go up there to be with him. Once I get the lay of the land, I'll let you know about visiting him. I assume it'll be awhile."

"In that case, Miles and I will go back to Mickey's to attend to the dog. On the way back, we could stop and pick you up something to eat if you'd like."

"Thanks, but I'm not hungry. You should get something for yourselves though."

"I like that idea, I'm starved," Miles interjected.

"OK, we're off then. Don't worry, Mickey's tough as nails," Jack said in parting.

Bobbie smiled half-heartedly and headed off to see her father.

As they got into the car, Miles chuckled. "Do you two have something happening?"

Jack blushed. "Maybe something at some point, but not now." Given Mickey's illness and his pending trial, Jack thought he should put any romantic thoughts about Bobbie aside for the time being, but he couldn't help himself. He was smitten.

Miles and Jack stopped by Sammy's Deli to pick up some provisions on the way back to Mickey's. When they got back, Miles took Molly for a walk. Jack took the opportunity to check his phone for emails and missed calls. The emails were mostly ones trying to loan him money or sell him things he didn't need. The only missed call and voicemail was from Steven. He played the message.

"Jack, good news! It looks like the judge will allow you to have a supervised phone call with Maya. I'll work out the details with the authorities as soon as possible and be back to you."

Maybe, just maybe, things will actually start turning around in a positive way, he thought.

Jack poked his head into Mickey's room and saw Bobbie had fallen asleep in the chair next to Mickey's bed. She was awakened by a nurse who was helping him sit up. The oxygen mask that had covered his face had been replaced with a smaller one, which was just a tube with two small hose nozzles that fit under his nose. Jack stayed long enough to overhear their brief conversation.

"Hi," he said in labored speech.

"Hi, Dad. How are you feeling?"

"Better, now that you're here. I'm sorry . . ." He broke down.

Bobbie gently touched his hand. "We both have apologies to make. We'll get to them later. I'm here now. Let's focus on your recovery. Once you're feeling better and home, we can go into all that." With every word she spoke, Mickey's eyes brightened.

"Deal," he declared, and soon after, he fell asleep.

It was apparent to Jack that Bobbie had realized the time had come for her to begin her long overdue reconciliation with her father. A step she was finally willing to undertake. Given his condition, they would have plenty of one-on-one time together to figure out their path forward, he thought.

CHAPTER 34

Ted Erickson had a habit of poking his head in Faye's office when she was at her busiest. She only had three weeks before the trial.

"How are the cases coming together?" Ted asked.

Faye shuffled a few files on her desk and barely looked at him. "Lots to do! All but the McKay case are ironclad. Lots of evidence, multiple infractions, corroboration, the whole nine yards—"

"Take a breath," Ted said as he stepped into her office. She paused for a moment. She could only imagine how frantic she must look.

In a slower pace, she said, "In the McKay case, all we have is stuff downloaded onto his personal computer and some pictures in a folder in his desk drawer. We're likely going to need something more substantial to get a conviction."

Ted sighed. "You better find something or we're in a pickle. If we don't have enough for a conviction, he walks, but a prominent citizen has had his reputation and career ruined and we're to blame. We cannot lose this one now that we've charged it. Get on the phone with the folks at DOJ. They brought the case to us, so they need to help us wrap it up."

"I'll do that right now," Faye promised as Ted headed out the door.

She sat back in a huff. Her desk was piled with files, and she was shaking from her third cup of coffee. Focus, she chided herself. With a shaky hand, she called the DOJ. A half hour later, she was on a conference call with Obregon and Harris. She shared her concern about not having more corroborative evidence, and if that was the case, Jack McKay may be acquitted. They got the message and promised to see what else, if anything, their investigators could come up with.

The call to Maya was made from Steven's conference room with a court-approved social worker sitting in. Jack sat there feeling irritated that this was how he had to talk to his daughter but also grateful that he would hear her voice.

Sam answered the phone.

Trying to sound cheery, Jack opened with, "Hi, Sam. How are you?"

"Fine, Jack. How are things going for you?"

"As well as can be expected. Particularly, since the court has approved my calling Maya. Any word on Sandy's progress?"

"Nothing yet. I'll get Maya." Sam was obviously not up to discussing Sandy's situation with Maya within earshot.

"Hello," Maya said in a hesitant voice.

"Hi, Maya. It's Daddy. How are you?"

"Daddy, when are you coming home?" Maya asked in her whiniest voice.

"Soon, honey. I still have work to do." It was true, considering how much work it would take to get acquitted.

"Mommy's gone too. Grandma says Mommy is sick and had to go to a hospital where I can't see her."

"I know, and I'm sure she'll be home soon. Are you having fun with Grandma and Grandpa?" Jack tried his best to change the subject.

"Yes, I guess so," Maya whined.

She and Jack chatted for a few more minutes. When they ran out of small talk, Jack finished with, "I love you, sweetheart."

"I love you too, Daddy."

The call ended. Jack felt sadder than he did before the phone call. He thanked Steven and left.

The ride back to Mickey's was a blur. He had to feed Molly and then go to the hospital to visit Mickey. After the call with Maya, Jack reflected on all that had happened to his family. He thought about his honeymoon with Sandy. How they walked hand in hand down the Malecón in Puerto Vallarta, eating tacos from street-side carts, how they made love on the balcony of their seaside hotel room. He recalled the excitement when he found out Sandy was pregnant, the joy when Maya was born, and what a wonderful child she had turned out to be. Now all that was shattered.

It took a while, but Jack collected himself and headed off to the hospital. When he got to the room, Mickey was holding court. In attendance along with Bobbie and Miles was Carl Rafferty.

"Quite an entourage, Mickey. Lucky for you the hospital doesn't charge by the number of visitors you have."

"Lucky for you that you have such an esteemed group working to save your ass." Mickey, who was obviously feeling much better, loved sarcastic repartee.

"So where are we?" Jack asked.

Bobbie took over the proceedings. "For starters, I've asked Carl to join our team until your case is resolved. He'll be invaluable. Particularly in the courtroom. Miles has more information on the call made to the janitorial service and the download log from the McKay & Associates network server."

Miles took over. "According to the phone system log, the call to the janitorial service's number was made from the office conference room at 5:23 p.m. on March thirteenth. It matches the information we had previously. Also, on that same night, the network internet server log shows there was a substantial download made to your workstation from a site on the dark web. Turns out—drumroll please—it's a porn site. This all ties together perfectly. Unfortunately, nothing in this establishes who canceled the janitorial service or who initiated the download."

"I won't even ask how you came by all that information," Carl interjected.

"Good idea," Miles said with a chuckle.

"I suppose the same person, or an accomplice, could have placed the pictures they found in my desk drawer." Jack surmised.

"Of course," Mickey added. "Bobbie will find out if there were any fingerprints on those pictures at discovery."

"I'll also have to share the information Miles has uncovered during discovery, assuming they don't already have it," Bobbie conceded.

"So what's next? Do we simply wait to see what evidence the prosecution has?" Jack was impatient to find some evidence that would establish his innocence.

They discussed, at length, the names and possible motives of others at the firm who might have been accessories to the crime, how the Party—assuming they were behind all of this—became aware of the DOJ Task Force investigation, and then devised their plot to bring Jack down and Lindsay's campaign with him.

There were obviously a lot of moving parts and people involved, so a trail of clues inevitably was out there. They just had to find that trail in the short time left before the trial.

"Peter Evans," Peter said picking up his office phone.

"Peter, it's Drew Tucker. The executive committee has agreed to continue with McKay & Associates, provided Jack remains on leave from the firm. However, if he's convicted, we're done with your firm. At least as it's presently configured."

"So if Jack were to be convicted, we'd have to reestablish ourselves as a different entity to maintain your business."

"Yes. But I'm sure you'd have to do that anyway, wouldn't you? Besides, it would let you back into Randall Davies's good graces as well." Drew was showing Peter his path to future prosperity, and he was very grateful.

"Makes total sense. Thanks for the encouragement and guidance, Drew."

"You're welcome. Keep moving on our collaboration with PetroMark. It's a top priority around here."

"We will and thanks again."

Excited, Peter called Carol Meyers into his office.

"I just hung up with Drew Tucker. He gave us a vote of confidence and a path to maintain their business if Jack should be convicted."

"That's amazing. Things couldn't have fallen better for us under the circumstances."

"Agreed. Now let's redouble our efforts on finalizing the Consolidated-PetroMark marketing plan. The sooner we get it moving, the sooner we get the revenue stream flowing."

Mickey had been released from the hospital and was resting back at the house. Jack sat at his bedside. After some "can I get you anything?" small talk, the subject turned to the future.

"Listen, Jack. We both know my time is short."

"Stop it!"

"No. We have to talk about this stuff. I'm leaving the house to Bobbie, of course, but I want you to make sure Molly is properly taken care of. Maybe Maya will want her."

"With Sandy's situation in flux, we'll have to see. Regardless, I promise Molly will have a good home. Speaking of homes, Bobbie lives in Madison, so I guess you're leaving it to her to sell."

"Probably true, but it's the only thing of real value I have to leave her. My pension and Social Security payments leave with me.

Hopefully she'll invest the proceeds from the house wisely and have some security down the road. Besides, this is her childhood home. She should have the right to do with it as she pleases."

"Of course," said Jack, changing the subject. "Enough future planning. What would you like for lunch?"

"Haute cuisine. A peanut butter and jelly sandwich accompanied by potato chips. Your specialty."

"Yum!" Jack replied as he headed to the kitchen. Walking away, he considered how empty his life would be without Mickey. He also wondered just how much his relationship with Maya would be altered. Both scenarios frightened and saddened him.

CHAPTER 35

Bobbie and Carl met at the courthouse steps for the discovery phase of the pre-trial. The evidence exchanged was enlightening for both sides.

In addition to several members of local law enforcement, including Bill Timmons, the forensic expert from the crime lab, and representatives of the DOJ Task Force, the prosecution's witness list included Gil Lattimore, a forensic technology expert, and, surprisingly, Victor Forsch, owner of an adult video store on Grant Street.

Jack's witness list included among others, Miles, Peter Evans, McKay's Executive VP, several other members of the McKay & Associates staff, Phil Thomas, owner of KnowIT, a renowned information technology company, and Eric Irons, owner of the janitorial service McKay & Associates used.

The prosecution's evidence list was short. It consisted of forensics results from Jack's laptop and the folder of illicit pictures found in Jack's desk, logs from the internet and phone servers, and some DOJ internal memoranda. Jack's list, in most cases, duplicated the prosecution's, but with one more notable exception. The specific list of the individuals from Jack's firm who had the password to his computer.

After a routine exchange of some documents and a short discussion, the session concluded. Each side had some new and interesting unanswered questions they'd need to address before the trial.

Bobbie and Carl headed back to Carl's office, where Bobbie had set up shop. On the way, they called Miles to have him meet them. Once they were all together, their first order of business was to bring Miles up to speed on the prosecution's case and get him started in his investigation.

"I'm going to focus on their IT guy and adult video store owner. See if there are any Party connections or other stuff we can use to call their credibility into question," Miles offered.

"Don't forget the McKay people," said Carl. "We need to see what, if anything, they have that we can use. By the way, what about your DOJ contact? Was there more to his tipping you off than just a heads-up about Jack?"

"I think so, but he didn't share anything specific with me."

Bobbie chimed in. "See what you can find out from him. If this plot against Jack was set up with help from someone at the DOJ, this thing will explode."

"Got it." Having received his assignment, Miles was out the door.

Carl chimed in to provide his perspective. "Bobbie, the more I see about this case, two things jump out at me. Number one, the case against Jack is really flimsy, unless one of the witnesses has some very incriminating testimony to offer. Number two, our suspicion that the Party is behind this as revenge against Jack and for William Davies to win the election seems to be more likely by the minute. If Miles can get his DOJ contact to talk, we may have the key to connecting those dots."

Bobbie nodded. "I agree, but right now we have to focus on discrediting the witnesses and evidence we have. First things first."

After a long morning at home, getting her daughter ready for school, and doing the dishes from last night's dinner, Faye put on her lawyer outfit and waited for her mother to arrive. A moment later she burst through the door.

"Sorry I'm late," she said catching her breath. "I missed my usual bus and had to take the next one. I ran from the bus stop because I knew you needed to leave."

"No problema, mamá." Faye often interjected a little Spanish when chatting with her mother, knowing it made them feel more connected to each other and their heritage. They both made sure Spanish was passed along to Faye's daughter, Abby.

Faye kissed them both and headed off.

When she finally arrived at her office, Ted was waiting for her, full of questions.

"Any surprises at discovery?"

"Well, they have included the owner of the janitorial service on the witness list. We didn't have him on ours. They are also subpoenaing more members of the McKay & Associates staff."

"What do you suppose they want to establish with them?"

"My guess is they're going to try to prove that additional people had access to McKay's office and could have planted evidence. Also, could be as character witnesses. Not sure what the owner of the janitorial service can offer. We'll see if we can find whatever they've uncovered, if anything, before we go to trial."

"Good plan. Faye, I know I sound like a broken record, but we must nail this case down before we go to trial. The other cases are open and shut but we cannot afford to lose this one or we, and our friends at DOJ, will pay a big price." Ted was more than emphatic. Their careers could hang in the balance.

"I know. I know. We will have our case ready with a likely conviction in-hand."

"Make sure it's more than likely. What are your thoughts about jury selection?"

"I'm inclined to seat as many female jurors as possible. I believe they're much more likely to convict than male jurors will be. Also, people with kids are preferable to single ones. Other than that, we'll just have to see what information we can pull from the pool during *voir dire*."

Faye's plan for jury selection was sound. She was confident that, given the right pool of prospective jurors, she could find the necessary votes to convict.

Having done what she could at work for the day, Faye headed home to see Abby and relieve her mom.

"Mommy, can I watch *Frozen* again tonight?" Abby had seen that movie dozens of times but was still asking for a rerun. Faye usually gave in even though she knew it was, at least in part, a stall.

"Okay, honey. But then it's off to bed."

Abby had a huge smile and a hug to give. "Thanks, Mommy."

Dinner was next. A tuna sandwich for Abby and a veggie salad for Faye. They sat down in front of the TV and got lost in the icy kingdom of Arendelle.

CHAPTER 36

After a long day for each of them, Mickey, Bobbie, and Jack gathered around the dining room table to discuss trial strategy while they waited for Miles to arrive with the Chinese takeout from Wei Lu's.

They had barely finished setting the table when Miles appeared carrying three large brown paper bags filled with Asian delights. They couldn't wait to dig in.

Bobbie laughed. "I guess the six sets of chopsticks indicates Wei Lu's assumed this was a meal for six."

Miles defended himself. "It is a meal for six. So if two more people show up, we're covered. Always good to be prepared."

"Be prepared? Were you a Boy Scout?" Mickey asked Miles.

"No, but when you're brought up in a Jewish home, you always have food for two more."

"Even kung pao shrimp?" said Mickey.

"We weren't *that* Jewish," said Miles.

Once the joking subsided, they passed the containers and filled their plates. As they ate, they discussed jury selection, questions for the witnesses, how to discredit the prosecution's evidence, and any additional information Miles should be tracking down. The dinner meeting was adjourned before any of them slipped into a Wei Lu's-induced food coma.

His illness having sapped his strength, Mickey returned to his room. Miles said good night and headed off to do more sleuthing. Bobbie and Jack headed out to the front porch with Molly.

"Jack, with all that's going on with your court case, I haven't wanted to pry." Bobbie had a soothing tone and a real concern in her voice. "But I do want you to know I feel badly for you that your marriage is dissolving. It's remarkable to me how you're holding up so well with all that's happening."

Jack felt softened. "I've read that most men are good at compartmentalizing aspects of their lives. At least better than most women. It's the case for me, I guess. The toughest part of all this is the effect it's having on my relationship with Maya, especially with Sandy's issues compounding things for our little girl. It's killing me. I know I'm innocent of the charges against me, and with your help that will be resolved soon. Favorably, I'm sure."

"What about McKay & Associates? Assuming all goes well at trial, will you go back to business as usual?"

"I really don't know. Before all this happened, I was having my doubts about what I wanted to do with the rest of my life. Typical mid-life crisis thoughts. Add to that my impending single life, and you have a whole fresh basket full of unknowns."

"Well, I'm sure you won't be single, or at least alone for long."

Jack thought her words sounded almost flirtatious. He hoped he was reading it right, and despite the circumstance, he decided to push his luck.

"Do I start accepting applications?"

"Depends." She wasn't totally shying away from his obvious interest.

"On what?"

"Whether or not you're prepared to prove yourself worthy." She was teaching him some of the rules of being single.

"I hope to. I would welcome the opportunity to prove myself worthy," he confessed.

"Get through this trial first. . . . Staying out of jail will help your dating life immensely."

"OK," he conceded, wondering if, at some point, she might be interested in an application.

On the way to his room, Robin Revelle called Jack's cell.

"How are you, Jack?" she asked.

"Holding up pretty well. Thanks for asking. I see where Lindsay's poll numbers are strong."

"We're close but still trailing. We took a hit over the unfortunate situation you've found yourself in, but we're coming back." Thankfully, there was no blame in her inflection.

"If my case is resolved prior to the election, it should help."

"Yes, particularly if the people responsible are who we think they are."

"Agreed." Knowing she likely called for advice, Jack went on. "I assume you called for a reason other than a status report on my well-being."

"True. I have a question related to the use of donor information in promoting the campaign. Should we name names, amounts raised, etc., in our advertising?"

"Good question. Naming names is a double-edged sword. For every person who is positively influenced by a name on the list, another is turned off. I recommend against it. I feel taking a macro approach is the way to go. Saying you raised a certain amount from over thousands of contributors has a greater impact, especially if the math shows a lot of people contributed small amounts and the total is impressive. It supports the 'candidate of the people' narrative and shows the campaign's viability."

"That's what I thought but wanted confirmation. Thanks, Jack. Hope you get through this legal business quickly. We'd love to have you back working with us."

"Robin, that means a lot. Feel free to call me again with any other campaign questions you may have."

"I will. Good night."

Jack wasn't sure if the call was a genuine outreach for advice or just Robin and Lindsay checking up on him. Either way, he appreciated the call. Adding that positive feeling to the one he was savoring from his conversation with Bobbie gave him a modicum of peace. Something he had not had in quite a while.

CHAPTER 37

Frank was summoned to Randall's office to provide an update.

"What's our guy in Madison saying about the McKay case?" barking his question as Randall most often did.

Frank pulled his notebook out and checked his notes before answering.

"From what I've been told, based on what they provided at discovery, their case must totally center around discrediting the evidence we planted. It's going to be really hard for them to come up with conclusive proof to discredit anything the prosecution has to offer. My guy at DOJ says they have solid, hard evidence and the corroborating testimony we've provided should help."

"You'd better be right or we're all in deep shit. You in particular." Randall's eyes were wide and a vein on his forehead was bulging, leaving no doubt about what he meant. "I want a conviction! What else can we do?" Randall could not have been more emphatic.

Frank seemed a little puzzled. "I thought we win with or without a conviction."

"Yes, we do. We've already effectively ruined Revelle's campaign, which will get William elected. But tarnishing McKay's reputation isn't enough. I want to bury the bastard! What else can we do to ensure a conviction?"

"Well, Miles Darien has been snooping around trying to discredit the evidence we've 'provided.' I will see what I can do to throw him off the scent."

"Don't just throw him off the scent. Do whatever is necessary to make sure he doesn't mess this up. Do you get my drift?"

"Yes, sir." Frank got the message and was out the door.

Jack awoke well past nine after a decent night's sleep. After a cup of coffee, he decided to check in at the office, so he called Donna. She was always so cheery, but today her voice had a sadness to it.

"You sound down, Donna. Is everything OK?"

"Just that everyone here seems to be fine with 'business as usual,' and I can't act as if nothing has happened. I can't stand what's happening to you. It's so unfair."

It was a strange role reversal, Jack consoling her about his situation. "I'm going to get through this just fine. I've done nothing wrong and we'll prove it."

"I know," she said. Jack could almost see her pouting through the phone.

"What have you been up to? Peter keeping you busy?"

"Of course. I'm spending a lot of time working on the Consolidated–PetroMark paperwork. Contracts and the like. Speaking of which, I heard Peter say in one of our meetings that you would need to provide a formal resignation letter, which would be on file in the event you're convicted."

"Makes sense." Jack made sure he didn't sound surprised or upset by the revelation. He made a mental note to let Bobbie know what Donna had told him.

After some small talk about Donna's dog's visit to the vet and the Packers, Jack thanked Donna for the update and promised to check back in with her again soon.

Sure enough later that afternoon, Jack received an email from Peter:

Hello Jack,

First and foremost, let me share with you that everyone here, myself in particular, supports you as you fight against the trumped-up charges you are facing. While you're preoccupied with your defense, I will continue to do my best to run the company and maintain the standards you have set. I have checked and it appears your weekly salary checks have been electronically transmitted. Should you need an advance to cover any expenses, please let me know and I'll make whatever arrangements are necessary.

One order of business I do need your help with is a request from Consolidated that we have a resignation letter from you on file in the event the negative publicity from the trial somehow mentions them. That way they will be covered for continuing to retain us while this litigation gets resolved. I'm sure you see the wisdom of their request.

Again, I trust this nightmarish incident will be behind you soon and you will be able to rejoin the firm ready to continue leadership of McKay & Associates.

Warmest regards,
Peter

Jack was so incensed by the email that he had to get up and walk around for ten minutes to calm himself down. He finally sat back down at the computer and wrote a response.

Peter,

Thank you and everyone else at the firm for your good wishes. I will, undoubtedly, be exonerated of these false charges and will then return to the firm ready to resume my leadership responsibilities.

Since I am innocent and will be acquitted, there is no need for a letter of resignation. Please communicate to our client, that if under the circumstances they feel at risk, they should terminate our agreement. I expect you to back me up on this and to communicate to Drew your full support.

Thanks,

Jack

There had been questions in Jack's mind about Peter's loyalty and possible involvement in his troubles. This email exchange did nothing to dissuade him from those feelings. He sent a copy of the email exchange to his team along with his suspicions.

Jack wanted to escape from all this for a while and decided to relieve his tensions with a motorcycle ride along Lake Michigan. Riding along the tree-lined road with gaps exposing the lake's multiple shades of blue and pristine sand beaches was the perfect elixir. An hour on the bike, with nothing but the rumble of his Harley ringing in his ears, was just the tonic he needed.

His relaxation didn't last long. As soon as he placed his helmet on the shelf in the garage and checked his cell phone, he saw he had a voicemail from Peter.

"Jack, I just got your response to my email about the resignation letter. You need to understand it is a requisite of our continuing with Consolidated and PetroMark. I hope you'll reconsider for the good of the firm."

Unlike Jack's usual method of meeting opposition head-on, he decided not to respond. He had stated his position and was going to let his email stand as his last word on the subject.

Jack was very concerned how his and Sandy's absences were affecting Maya. He decided to place a call to Sandy's parents to check on

Maya's well-being and Sandy's rehab. Diane Freeman answered the phone.

"Hi, Diane. It's Jack. How is everyone doing?"

"We're all fine here. Maya's been making new friends every day and seems on the surface, at least, to have adjusted pretty well to all of this."

"What do you hear about Sandy's progress?" Jack was genuinely concerned about her.

"From what she's told us, she's making real progress on several fronts. Her physical withdrawal symptoms seem to have all but gone away, aided in no small measure, I think, by her newfound enthusiasm for exercise. Her mental state appears to have improved dramatically as well. At least from what I can pick up over the phone."

Jack was certainly relieved by Diane's accounts of how both Sandy and Maya were doing. He had enough other things to worry about, so it really helped to know they were both holding up well under the circumstances.

"Thanks, Diane. I really appreciate all you and Sam are doing for them. I know they do too."

"Jack, we're here for them. You need to focus on you right now."

"True enough. I'll check in again soon. 'Bye, Diane."

Late that afternoon, Peter was busy putting the finishing touches on his edits of the press release formally announcing the Consolidated–PetroMark joint venture. Carol poked her head in his office door.

"Hey, there. Have you finished with the press release? I'd like to get it sent out before the end of the day."

"Just finished. I'll send it over to you for a final once-over."

"Thanks. If I can change topics for a moment, were you able to get Jack to write a resignation letter?"

"Unfortunately not. He said since he has done nothing wrong, it's pointless. I don't agree. The point is to preserve the Consolidated relationship and ultimately the firm." Concern was written all over Peter's face.

A similar expression appeared on Carol's face. "That's not good for us at all . . . I mean for the firm."

"We'll just have to move on and do our best not to bring it up in any of our discussions with either the Consolidated or the PetroMark folks."

"Peter, I want you to know I am with you one hundred percent regardless of what happens with Jack. You and I are a great team, and I know we can make the firm viable no matter what happens." By the tone of her voice, this "great team" seemed to refer to both their professional and personal relationship.

Peter tried to ignore the complication. "I agree," he said.

He continued his work as she left to send out the press release.

CHAPTER 38

The team was covering every angle in anticipation. With only a week to go before the trial, Jack was getting a real insight into what the prosecution was likely planning to present. He might have actually enjoyed the education had his life not hung in the balance.

"So what will the adult video store owner likely testify about?" Carl asked Bobbie, kicking off the day's strategy session.

"I suspect he will make a claim Jack did or tried to purchase child porn from him."

"He'd better have something more than just an alleged conversation. He'd need something to corroborate his claim in order to be credible, wouldn't he?" Miles interjected.

"You'd think so," said Mickey, "but the more damning testimony they can pile on top of their case, even sketchy evidence, the more impact it will have on the jury. They're simply looking for the straw that breaks the camel's back."

He had a point, thought Jack. It would become more and more difficult for the defense to discredit the prosecution's case with every new piece of evidence and damaging testimony they brought forth.

"Well then, I'd better get crackin' to find the holes in each piece of their so-called evidence." Miles had real fight in his words.

"Yes, Miles. Keep at it and report anything, even the smallest sliver of information, which might assist us in discrediting their case." Bobbie then provided Miles with a complete list of the items and witnesses the prosecution had provided. She had made some notes on each to give Miles some direction for his investigation.

Miles took the notes and was off. Carl, Mickey, and Bobbie then began peppering Jack with questions the DA was likely to ask him on the stand. Jack's experience in contentious business meetings and political campaigns would be helpful when on the stand. They had concluded that he needed to take the stand in his own defense to answer the allegations the way only an innocent man could. The toughest questions would center around his alleged crime since he had a six-year-old daughter.

He did fine with the mock trial questions they posed. Whether or not he could weather the storm that would most assuredly take place when he was on the stand remained to be seen.

After the strategy session broke up, Jack decided to call his in-laws to see how Maya was doing at her new school. He felt safe calling, as she would still be in class and he would not be violating his restraining order.

To his surprise, Sandy answered.

"Hi, there. So glad to see you're back home," he said.

"Thanks, Jack. I can't tell you how glad I am to be here. How are you holding up?"

"OK, I guess. Obviously, all that's going on is incredibly stressful, but hopefully it will all be resolved soon." Changing subjects, he said, "Are you finished with your treatment or just home for a visit?"

"A little of both as it turns out. I'm home but still in outpatient treatment, three times a week."

"Maya must be thrilled."

"I suspect she will be. I just got home an hour ago. You must have called for a reason."

"Just wanted to see how our little girl was doing. The fact that you're there now tells me everything I needed to know."

"Thanks, Jack. That's very kind of you."

This was the most civil conversation they'd had in months. Jack smiled. Her therapy was already paying dividends.

Continuing the civility, she added, "By the way, I've asked my attorney to hold off on any divorce proceedings until after you're done with that ridiculous trial."

"Thanks. I appreciate you taking one thing off my plate, at least temporarily."

"Anything else?"

"Nothing really except to say I'm happy you and Maya are back together. Please give her a hug for me when she gets home from school and tell her I called."

"I will. Bye, Jack."

He hung up the phone feeling about as good as he could, given his current troubles. Sandy was doing better, which meant Maya would be doing better. It also helped that the animosity he had been feeling from Sandy before she entered rehab had dissipated somewhat. A healthy change for both of them.

He rejoined Mickey and Bobbie in the living room where they were watching a story on CNN about gun violence.

"Wouldn't you two prefer some lighter subject matter?" he scolded.

"Compared to your life, this is lighter subject matter!" Mickey returned fire.

"Touché," Jack conceded.

Frank was convinced that whatever information McKay's team had to discredit the prosecution's case most certainly had been acquired by Miles Darien. He had worked closely with Miles a few times on Party business over the years and was confident Miles had been dogged in his pursuit of facts that could exonerate Jack. Frank decided to pay an unannounced visit to Miles's apartment to find out what he had.

It took a while, but after two hours sitting in his car, Frank saw Miles leave his apartment. He waited a few minutes more to be sure Miles didn't return. Convinced the coast was clear, he walked across the street and entered the building. The directory said, "M. Darien #204." Wanting to reduce the chance of being seen, he chose the stairs to the second floor, avoiding the elevator.

Picking the lock was surprisingly easy, given that Miles was an experienced detective and should've taken additional precautions. He donned a ski mask and a pair of latex gloves before fully opening the door and then double-checked the entrance for electronic alarms and cameras. Finding none, he entered.

Miles was what you'd call an organized slob. All of his junk was kept in a series of neat piles. A bachelor's filing system to be sure. Frank found the pile with file folders and began carefully reviewing each of them. He only found one that had any relevance to the case, but it only contained lists of the prosecution's witnesses and evidence and a few innocuous notes. It was likely that all of the material Miles had accumulated was in the computer sitting on the dining table.

Since he probably wouldn't be able to get into the computer's hard drive quickly, he decided to take the unit with him and make it appear as if the apartment had been robbed. To cover his tracks, he ransacked the apartment, upending the neatly kept piles of junk. In addition to the laptop, he grabbed Miles's thirty-six-inch flat-screen TV and the Amazon Alexa smart speaker. Items a common thief would have immediately grabbed. He stuffed the items into the satchel he had brought and slung the TV under his arm.

Before he left, he closed the door and then broke the lock to make it seem as if an ordinary thief, in a hurry, had broken in.

Any cop would certainly view the evidence as a simple robbery. To avoid detection as he left, Frank took the back stairs out of the building. After removing the ski mask and gloves, he walked down the alley a few hundred feet and dumped the TV and the Alexa into a dumpster behind Freddy's Red Hots. He then crossed the street, got into his car, and headed off to his place to see what he could find on Miles's computer.

Bobbie had given Jack a grocery list. Provisions had run low at Mickey's, and Jack was happy to go and do a "normal life" chore. What he didn't bargain for was the woman at the meat counter screaming at the top of her lungs at him, "Child molester, pornographer!" He had several choices. Confront the woman, leave his basket and walk out of the store, or go about finishing his shopping. He chose to finish. While others in the store stared, no one else said anything. Jack paid for the groceries, loaded them into the Lexus, and headed back to Mickey's. It was extremely difficult to drive as both his legs were shaking uncontrollably.

Jack just had his first taste of what it felt like to be found guilty in the court of public opinion and it had a most profound effect on him. It would be difficult to get him to venture out again until his legal problems had been resolved.

"What happened?" Bobbie asked when he came into the kitchen carrying groceries.

"Just some woman screaming at me at the store. Calling me names."

"Oh, I have a pretty good idea of what she said. So sorry. Are you okay?"

"I will be," he said unconvincingly.

Bobbie's phone blared and she answered. Her eyes grew wide. "Hold on a minute," she said as she put her phone on speaker.

"You're not going to believe this," Miles said over the phone. "My apartment was robbed."

Jack gasped. "What happened?"

"Someone broke into my home, and they took my Alexa device, which is connected to my smartphone. If the device is unplugged for any reason, I get an alert on my smartphone. Assuming the worst when my phone pinged, I disconnected my computer from the cloud storage on my Google Drive. As a precaution for just such an event, I keep all of my important files on the cloud, not on my computer's hard drive. I quickly downloaded the files pertaining to Jack's case onto my phone and set off home to survey the scene. When I got there, sure enough my place was ransacked."

"Holy shit," Jack said.

"The Party is behind this," Bobbie said.

"I don't believe it for a minute that this is a typical break-in," Miles said.

"It's gotta be one of Davies's goons looking for any evidence to come up with to gain your acquittal," Bobbie said.

A shiver crawled down Jack's spine. They would stop at nothing to ruin his life. "It wouldn't surprise me if this was the handiwork of Frank Ryder, Davies's number one goon," Jack offered.

"At this point, it doesn't matter, right Miles?" Bobbie said. "Please assure us that no information was taken and whatever was on your computer is now in safekeeping."

"I can guarantee that," Miles said.

Mickey, who had been listening quietly from the living room, chimed in, "Now that we have established the security of the evidence, what's for dinner?"

Bobbie and Jack broke into much-needed laughter, easing the tension.

"I have ribeye steaks for you and me. Salmon fillet for Bobbie. Asparagus for all. I'll cook all that stuff on the grill if someone will cook up some rice." Making dinner was a welcome distraction for Jack.

"By someone, you mean me, right?" Bobbie replied sarcastically.

"You're very perceptive, Counselor."

With the appointment of the chefs having been made, they went about preparing the meal.

After dinner, Bobbie and Jack retreated to the den to check email and do some work on their computers. On his way to bed, Mickey stopped by.

"I know I'm a fossil, but it scares me that so many people today, particularly young people, feel access to information, vis a vis the internet, is a viable substitute for knowledge. Real knowledge requires comprehension, analysis, and context, which can then be translated into rational thought. It's where new ideas are born and, goodness knows, the world desperately needs more good ideas on so many fronts."

"Well, Dad, you are a fossil, but you're not wrong. Most people couldn't locate Chicago on a map without Google showing them."

Mickey smiled. It was clear to Jack that Mickey loved hearing his daughter call him dad.

Jack chimed in, "Yes, but knowing the outcome of the Battle of Hastings isn't a life lesson."

"We could argue the point further but I'm tired and going to bed." Having said his piece, Mickey set off very slowly up the stairs.

After he left, Bobbie turned to Jack with a tear in her eye. "He doesn't have much longer, does he?"

"No one really knows. I choose to take it one day at a time. None of us is guaranteed tomorrow."

Bobbie sighed. She shut down her laptop and followed Mickey up the stairs.

Jack worked a few minutes longer and then also went to bed. On his way to his room, he could hear Mickey laboring to breathe.

He knew Bobbie's prediction was probably correct but decided to revert to his "one day at a time" philosophy if for no other reason than to avoid sadly waiting around for nature to take its course.

Even though his days were less physically active, he was exhausted. For Jack, the mental strain of his predicament took a greater toll on his stamina than any day of manual labor ever had.

Just as he was about to turn off the light on the nightstand, his door opened slightly. Dressed in a nightshirt, Bobbie walked by. Knowing this was not the time or the place, he resisted the temptation to speak and closed his eyes.

CHAPTER 39

When Bobbie arrived at the breakfast table, she found Mickey scooping grounds into the coffee maker and Jack at the kitchen table reading emails.

"Morning, Dad."

"Hi. Please put two cups of the dog food into Molly's bowl. If her water dish is low, please fill that too."

"How about, 'Good morning, my lovely daughter' for a greeting?"

"You're right. Good morning, my lovely daughter, please feed and water the dog.'"

"That's better. What's for breakfast?"

"I'm making coffee. You're on your own for anything additional."

She gave Jack a smile before she took three sesame bagels out of the freezer, defrosted them in the microwave, and began the process of toasting them.

"What would you like on your bagel?" she asked Mickey.

Before he could answer, Jack said, "I like cream cheese and strawberry jam on my bagel."

"Both of those are in the fridge. Help yourself," she shot back.

"I'll have the same," Mickey added.

"Thought so." Jack had shared bagels with Mickey many times and knew the drill.

After finishing their bagels and coffee, the threesome began another trial strategy session. Today's discussion centered around whether someone at McKay & Associates was in on setting up Jack. While there were several possible candidates, they kept coming back to one person: Peter Evans. He had motive, opportunity, and the wherewithal. As much as Jack hated the idea, he, too, had felt Peter was likely involved. Proving it would be difficult.

Miles finally arrived. They brought him up to speed and then listened to his latest findings.

"I was able to coerce my contact at DOJ into revealing some additional information. Turns out that the case against Jack was added very late in the Task Force's investigation. From what I can piece together, it would appear the addition of the case was right around the time Jack opted to take on Revelle's campaign instead of William Davies's. It would seem to support our contention that the evidence was planted in retribution."

"Good work, Miles, but it's only circumstantial in nature," Bobbie pointed out. "No hard evidence there. Any chance we can identify the task force member who was responsible for including Jack's case file? If we could tie that individual to the Party, or to Davies, we'd have a very strong conspiracy argument."

"We need to tie the task force's actions to some skullduggery by Davies or we really have no way to effectively use Miles's information."

"What about running my car off the road, almost killing Sandy and Maya?" Jack interjected.

"It's a stretch to connect it to the case. Obviously, once we prove your innocence and the Party is implicated, we'll provide the information to the DA's office, assuming they decide to indict."

That wasn't what Jack wanted to hear. He wanted to be acquitted, sure. But he wanted those responsible for attacking his family to pay dearly.

Bobbie concluded the meeting with assignments for the team. Miles was to determine if his DOJ contact could provide any clues that could link the Party, Davies, and the task force. Jack was tasked to see what he could do to find out if Peter had actually betrayed him. Carl needed to finalize the individual files they had created for each article of evidence and each witness. Bobbie was pleasantly surprised by the collection of new items they had all come up with. Exhausted, Mickey went back to bed.

The trials on the other three cases of child pornography were already in various stages of completion. It was apparent that convictions were virtual certainties in each.

Faye was singularly focused on Jack McKay's trial and seemed a little uneasy when Ted stopped by to check in.

"Everything OK?" he asked. "You look perplexed."

"I am a little perplexed. All of the evidence we have lines up well with the charges, but something is missing. All of the other individuals we've charged show a pattern of behavior where the illegal actions of those individuals seem in character. Nothing in Jack McKay's life would lead you to believe he was into this sort of thing."

"Isn't that often the case?"

"Sure, but this one is different. Our evidence basically centers around his activities on this one day."

"What about the video store owner's testimony?" Ted pointed out.

"Well, it's a 'he said, he said' testimony from a rather sketchy witness about a brief encounter similar to ones he'd likely had with scores of other customers. Not sure it's particularly compelling."

"Seems to me that unless the defense has come up with evidence to refute all or at least most of what you have, you'll get the conviction."

"You're right, but I'm still uneasy."

"Back to work, then. Button up your case with additional evidence or stronger support for what you already have."

Faye knew her investigators and the ones from the task force had been diligent in their gathering and corroborating what she had. She decided to spend the remaining forty-eight hours before jury selection re-examining all the evidence and witness testimony as well as what she expected from the defense. None of it stopped her from feeling uneasy.

Frank knew he'd better do what he could to find out what Miles had, or Randall would have him drawn and quartered. He decided on a full-frontal attack. He found Miles at his usual lunch place, Sammy's Deli.

"So your buddy's trial is coming up in a couple of days. Never picked him to be into kiddy porn."

Miles didn't take the bait. "Nice to see you too, Frank."

"C'mon, Miles. We both know he's going to do some hard time."

"What we both know is that you and your 'associates' are trying your best to see that he does."

"Don't know what you're talking about, Miles. We have nothing to do with what's happening to him."

"If you say so." Miles wasn't giving an inch.

"What makes you think we're behind any of this?"

"Just call it instinct."

Miles wasn't about to show his cards, so Frank left empty handed.

He decided he would contact his informant inside the DOJ. With a little pushing, he could get an edge on the case. His hand would not remain empty for long.

CHAPTER 40

At the *Lakeville Examiner* morning staff meeting, the editors and reporters were pitching stories to Hank Reynolds for the next edition. The usual local stories included school funding problems, a rash of car thefts, public transit debates, and high school football. The stories they all really wanted in on were the upcoming elections and the child pornography crackdown.

Hank looked up from his note and began handing out the story assignments.

"The politics desk will continue to cover all the elections. Richard will handle the specific assignments. I'm going to handle the McKay trial with help from Wendy, who has already begun looking into the case. Maureen and Andrew will cover the other trials."

Associate Editor Paul Schmitz asked, "Why the focus on the McKay case and so little coverage of the other cases?"

"Simple," Hank replied. "The McKay case is a much more complex story given the election implications and Jack McKay's standing in the community. The other cases are, from what we've learned so far, basically open and shut. Still important to the well-being of the community, but with motives and verdicts hardly in doubt."

Once the other perfunctory assignments were handed out, the meeting adjourned.

As the others filed out of the conference room, Hank pulled Wendy aside. "There is going to be a lot going on with this case. I suspect the defense will claim that McKay was framed, possibly implicating the Party in the process. The prosecution will try to show McKay as a wolf in sheep's clothing. It will be a real courtroom drama that will pique the interest of a large portion of our readers. We not only need to cover what goes on in the courtroom, but we need to run down any leads which could potentially impact the verdict and what happens afterwards."

"Okay. Since the McKay trial starts this afternoon with jury selection, I'll be at the courthouse anyway so I'll see if I can get anything from the DA or the defense team," Wendy said, taking the initiative. "I do have something else I've come across to run by you," She added. "I was able to obtain copies of the evidence and witness lists, and—"

Hank immediately put up his hand as a stop sign and interrupted. "You have what? How did you come across those lists?"

"Well, I was interviewing Miles Darien, the PI working on the defense team, seeing if he would provide any insights for our coverage. He offered me a deal. He'd share their lists with me if I would, in return, share any important information we uncover about the case." Even though Wendy spoke matter of factly, Hank sensed her apprehension about how he would react.

"You're on some potentially shaky ground here. Not with receiving information about the case but with promising to share what you uncover with the defense. Anything you plan to offer in return needs to be cleared by me. Understand?" Hank said, emphasizing the last word.

"Yes, sir."

"Good work, by the way."

"Actually turns out I have uncovered something else you'll need to clear. I've also checked into each of the defense witnesses and found out Eric Irons, the owner of a janitorial service who was subpoenaed to testify for the defense, left town unexpectedly. His office said he was suddenly summoned to Flagstaff, Arizona to tend to his mother. They had no idea when he would return. Obviously, he's under subpoena for a reason. If I share this information with the PI, maybe we can find out what the guy was going to testify about."

Wendy had already been successful running down significant leads. Hank was impressed.

"That's an angle worth pursuing. When you talk to Miles Darien, approach it like this. 'Thanks again for the witness lists. When I looked into your list, I found out Mr. Irons had left town and no one at his office knew when he would return. Did you know he was unlikely to appear as planned?' Then follow up with, 'Can you share anything with me about what Mr. Irons was going to testify to?' That way you can provide information in the form of a question and ask for information in another question. Which is the way good journalists, like you, should do it."

"Thanks. Will do." Wendy was beaming as she left Hank's office.

CHAPTER 41

The time for the trial had finally arrived. Jury selection was the first order of business. A pool of prospective jurors was brought into the courtroom for the jury selection process. Bobbie, as head of Jack's defense team took charge of the back-and-forth questioning process, *voir dire*, in which each side struck various prospective jurors. Each side used their six "strikes" to eliminate people they thought would favor the other side. The DA struck several single men. The defense struck several moms with young children. Judge Thompson struck one woman for cause because she had worked on a campaign Jack had run and admitted knowing him.

Finally, a jury panel of twelve, with two alternates, was selected. The group was split evenly male and female. All of the women were married with two having grown children. Two of the men were single. One of the married men had a teenage boy.

Bobbie and Carl left the courtroom after the jury selection was completed and found Miles waiting for them in the hallway. He greeted them with some unsettling news. "Eric Irons has skipped town."

"What?" Bobbie was not happy.

"My guess is Frank Ryder is behind it. Likely made him an offer he couldn't refuse."

"That's a real blow to our case, isn't it, Bobbie?" Carl chimed in.

"Not totally. Since the beginning we've suspected who was behind all of these shenanigans, so we took extra measures to insure our evidence. When Miles and I interviewed Mr. Irons, we were able to get a sworn affidavit from him recounting the events that would have been his testimony on the stand. If we can get the judge to allow us to introduce it as evidence, we can still make our argument."

"I suspect Frank Ryder never thought to ask Mr. Irons if he'd provided a sworn statement. Gangster types seldom ask questions. Instead they rely totally on their intimidation tactics." Miles had been down this road many times with guys like Frank Ryder and knew thinking a move or two ahead, like chess, wasn't their forte'.

"What now?" Carl asked.

"We need to double back on all of our witnesses to make sure no one else breaks ranks." Miles and Carl parsed out the list of witnesses, each taking a few. Armed with their lists, they headed out to secure their witnesses.

Just before five, Wendy was back at her desk transcribing her notes when Hank came over for an update.

"Did you run into Miles Darien at the courthouse?" Hank asked.

"Yes."

"How did he react to your information?"

"He was appreciative and didn't seem to be very surprised."

"He's a real pro and would certainly keep his game face on, regardless of the magnitude of the revelation. Did you question him further providing an opening for him to share more?"

"I did. He said he'd be back to me as things progress with the trial. I actually think he might."

"Likely he will, particularly if he needs someone to help with some legwork."

"Is that a bad thing?" she asked.

"No, quite the contrary. Miles asking you to help with some specific task is the best kind of lead we could hope for from him. Just keep at it."

"Okay. See you in the courtroom tomorrow."

"Bring your notebook." Hank said with a wink.

Frank stopped by to see Randall, feeling almost boastful that he had put a roadblock into Jack McKay's defense strategy.

"So what have you accomplished?" Randal inquired anxiously.

"They had the owner of their janitorial service prepared to testify that on March thirteenth he received a call from McKay headquarters telling him to cancel service for the evening."

"Enlighten me on the significance of that."

"His testimony would prove that on the night of the download of the porno material onto McKay's laptop, they were called off and by someone at McKay's office. It would certainly provide some evidence of a set up."

"Okay, but what have you done to remediate the situation?"

"I assume you mean fix it." Frank wanted to be sure he understood what "remediate" meant.

"Yes. How did you *fix* it?"

"First I got, Mr. Irons, the owner, to tell me what he knew. Then I convinced him to leave town until the trial was over."

"Dare I ask how you did that?"

"I simply suggested it would be in the best interest of his children's health that he do so."

"He could have called the cops on you."

"He wouldn't. We've had dealings in the past and he knows I back up what I say."

"OK, good. Did you ask him if he provided any other evidence to anybody?"

"No."

After a busy morning in court and an even busier afternoon looking for more evidence, Jack's team reconvened at Mickey's for a late dinner. Jack stopped at Wei Lu's. Miles returned with two Scarfido's pizzas. Not exactly a healthy meal but filling and an easy clean up.

The dinner talk was minimal. They all craved a little peace and quiet except for Mickey, who wanted a full accounting of the day's events.

Bobbie explained the choices they made in jury selection. Miles recounted the news about the disappearing janitorial service owner, and Carl covered the limited additional information they acquired about the prosecution's witness list.

When they had all finished, Mickey asked the obvious question. "Are we going to get Jack acquitted?"

"Yes," was the response delivered in unison. Some yeses were more enthusiastically positive than others.

The trial would begin in earnest at nine a.m. sharp the next morning. Carl and Miles headed home early. Mickey was the first to bed less than an hour after the meal ended. Jack and Bobbie were each in bed, alone, by ten thirty.

CHAPTER 42

As they downed their cups of coffee and pieces of toast, Jack and Bobbie went through a mental checklist to be sure they had everything packed up for their day in court. When they headed off, Mickey was still in bed.

They met Miles and Carl on the front steps of the courthouse and went inside. Once in the courtroom the two lawyers and Jack set up camp at the table on the left facing the judge's bench. Miles took a seat in the gallery behind them. Joining him in the gallery were several members of the press, including Hank and Wendy of the *Examiner*. He also noticed Tim Mathews, an alderman and one of Randall Davies's associates, who was there undoubtably to keep Randall apprised of any significant developments in the proceedings. The gallery's seating was soon totally occupied.

The prosecution's team arrived a short time later. On the way to their table, they stopped to shake hands with Bobbie and Carl. The jury was then ushered in and everyone waited for the judge to enter.

The muted murmur in the courtroom was silenced by the bailiff. "All rise. The Circuit Court Branch Six of Lakeville County is now in session, Judge Joan Thompson presiding."

The judge took her seat and asked everyone to be seated as well. The clerk then read the case information into the record after which Judge Thompson asked the prosecution to begin with their opening statement.

DA Faye Villareal took the floor and addressed the jury.

"Thank you, Your Honor. The Department of Justice of the State of Wisconsin created a task force with the sole intent of tracking down and prosecuting individuals who were in possession of pornographic material which contain graphic images of children who were nude, and in some cases, engaging in sexual activity. Possession of this type of material violates State Statute 948.12 and constitutes a Class I felony, punishable with up to three-and-a-half years of imprisonment and a fine of up to $10,000. This particular case is being brought against one such individual, the defendant Jack McKay, who resides in Lakeville. We intend to prove, at the time of his arrest, he had acquired and was in possession of such illicit material, in both printed and digital form.

"The witnesses and forensic evidence we will present will authenticate the defendant's acquisition of the pornographic material found on his computer and in his office. Further we will produce a witness who will testify to the defendant's attempt to acquire additional child pornography. We believe that this evidence will prove, beyond a reasonable doubt, that Mr. McKay is guilty as charged and that you will vote to convict him of this horrible crime."

Judge Thompson then turned toward the defense table and inquired, "Is the defense ready with an opening statement?"

Bobbie rose from her chair and moved around the table. She stood behind Jack, facing the jury, and answered the judge.

"Yes, Your Honor. Ladies and gentlemen of the jury, while we fully support the work of the DOJ's special task force, we will show that, in this case, they have been misled into charging Jack McKay in this matter. As the judge will instruct you, Mr. McKay is entitled to the presumption of innocence. The burden is on the prosecution which must prove their case beyond a reasonable doubt. Even though we are not obligated to do so, we will provide exculpatory evidence that will show the case they have brought against our client is based totally on falsehoods.

"Further, we intend to show that my client is, in fact, the victim in this case. An evil conspiracy has brought us all here today. We will show that the conspiracy seeking to destroy Jack was politically motivated as revenge for Mr. McKay's choice of which candidate he chose to help get elected. Further, you will see how those same sinister forces were behind planting the evidence, which will be introduced by the prosecution. We also intend to show how some witnesses who will testify have been tainted by those same sinister forces. In the end, you will clearly see that the charges brought by the state against Jack McKay are baseless and misdirected. We trust you will, therefore, find him not guilty."

Jack's palms were sweating. He looked over at Wendy from the Examiner, who was furiously writing notes. Then he looked at the jury. From what he could see in the body language of many of the jurors, they were skeptical of Bobbie's claim. The evidence the defense planned to supply in rebuttal to the charges had better be very convincing if they were going to get Jack acquitted.

After Bobbie finished her statement, the judge turned to the DA. "Ms. Villareal, are you ready to call your first witness?"

"Yes, Your Honor. The prosecution calls Agent David Harris to the stand."

Harris took the stand, stated his name, and was sworn in. Faye began her questioning.

"Mr. Harris, please tell the court where you work and what you do there."

Ever the confident professional, Harris explained in great detail about his job at the DOJ, his role on the task force, and the initiative the task force was undertaking statewide.

"Mr. Harris, are you familiar with this case before the court?"

"Yes, I was involved in the review of evidence against the accused. And then, based on that evidence, the grand jury issued an indictment which was referred to the Lakeville County DA's offices for prosecution."

"Would you share with the court what the evidence was and why you referred it for charging?"

"Sure. One of the key components of this type of investigation is tracking the downloading of illegal material via the internet, both the traditional internet and the dark web. We have the ability to use highly sophisticated technical methodologies to detect when these downloads occur and where the content ends up."

Villareal stood and approached the witness with feigned ignorance. "You mentioned the dark web. Can you explain the dark web for those of us who are not acquainted with it?"

Agent Harris said, "The dark web is internet content that exists on darknets, which are overlay networks that use the internet but require specific software, configurations, or authorization to gain access to the otherwise hidden information. In layman's terms, you have to have specialized software and knowledge to access information from the dark web. It's not accessible to the general internet user. Much of what is contained there is illegal."

"Thank you. Specifically, what information did you detect which was downloaded by Mr. McKay?"

Bobbie stood. "Objection, assuming facts not in evidence. No evidence has been provided that shows Mr. McKay personally downloaded anything."

"Sustained," said Judge Thompson. "Please rephrase your question, Ms. Villareal."

Faye continued her questioning. "Mr. Harris, how did any of the illegally downloaded information lead you to suspect Mr. McKay was involved in such activity?"

Straightening up in his chair, he looked directly at Faye and continued, "The information download we tracked was downloaded via McKay & Associates' company server to the IP address of Mr. McKay's personal computer. In other words, the downloaded material ended up on his personal computer. Our experts then worked with the Lakeville PD to authenticate that what they found on the computer was actually the illegally downloaded material we tracked."

Jack felt sick to his stomach.

Faye handed him a file folder of documents. "Is this a copy of your report detailing the findings you just testified to?"

Harris nodded. "Yes. It includes the findings of our forensic experts, as well as copies of the illegal material we found on the computer and the pictures found in a file folder in Mr. McKay's office."

"You mentioned a file folder with pictures. Can you elaborate on the contents of that file folder?"

"Yes. It contained a stack of pictures inside in a sealed plastic wrapper. Upon opening the plastic wrapper, Lakeville PD uncovered nude pictures of minors and, in some cases, those minors were engaged in what appeared to be sexual acts."

"Your Honor, we would like to have this report admitted into the record as State's Exhibit A," Faye requested.

Bobbie energetically rose from her seat. "Objection, Your Honor. We submit there is no evidence the defendant ever saw the downloaded images on the laptop, and since the pictures were in a sealed plastic wrap, he could never have seen those photographs. Having the jury see those images and photographs would be unfairly prejudicial to the defendant's case."

Bobbie's point obviously hit home with the judge.

"Members of the jury, I will rule on the admissibility of the exhibit and whether or not you will see the material in question after the lunch break. Ms. Villareal, you may continue."

"Thank you, Your Honor. I have no further questions for Mr. Harris."

"Ms. Martin, would you care to cross-examine the witness?"

"Yes. Thank you, Your Honor," Bobbie said. She stood and

approached the witness. "Mr. Harris, were you able to establish that Mr. McKay, himself, did the downloading?"

Mr. Harris shook his head. "Unfortunately, we can only confirm his computer was used for the download and that it was his password which was used to sign onto the computer."

"Is it then totally possible anyone with access to that computer, who knew the password, could have downloaded the material in question?"

"Yes."

"Thank you. No more questions at this time."

Faye resumed calling her witnesses. First calling the police detective, Jake Mallory, who supervised the raid on Jack's office and confiscated the laptop and the file folder containing pornographic pictures. He went over the details of the raid and what was discovered. Bobbie declined cross-examination but reserved the right to recall the witness.

Faye then called Bill Timmons, the police department's forensic expert. He testified that his department discovered Jack's fingerprints on the file folder. In cross-examination, Bobbie asked if there were any fingerprints on the pictures themselves or the plastic wrapping they were in.

Timmons confirmed there were no fingerprints on the photographs or the plastic they were wrapped in.

"So the file folder could have been any file folder Mr. McKay had ever touched?" Bobbie asked.

"Objection," Faye strongly responded. "Leading the witness."

"I'll allow it." Judge Thompson then instructed Timmons to answer the question.

"Yes, it could have been a random folder," answered Timmons, an eighteen-year veteran of the force, clearly unhappy at having been challenged.

"No further questions." Bobbie's cross-examination of the last two witnesses had established significant doubt in the jury's mind about whether or not Jack was responsible for the download and acquisition of the pictures in the file folder. That alone, however, wouldn't be nearly enough to get a not-guilty verdict from the jury.

The DA's next witness was Gil Lattimore, the outside forensic technology expert they had asked to examine the computer, the server from McKay & Associates, and the download. Lattimore went over his experience and credentials to establish his expertise. No objection was raised by the defense.

Faye continued her questioning. "Mr. Lattimore, is there any information you can provide that could directly link the downloaded material to Mr. McKay?"

"Only two things. The password he created to access the porn site where the download came from was 'Maya6,' which I believe was a combination of his daughter's name and age. The other is the fact that the laptop computer touchpad was used by a left-handed person like Mr. McKay."

"How did you establish that the user was left handed?"

"Rather simply. The pattern of finger swipes worn into the touchpad clearly indicated continual use by the left hand. The number of people who use their dominant hand on a touchpad or mouse is overwhelming."

"Thank you, Mr. Lattimore. No more questions. Your witness, Ms. Martin."

Bobbie approached the witness. "Mr. Lattimore, did you find evidence that the touchpad on Mr. McKay's computer was only used by a left-handed person?" Bobbie asked, knowing full-well there was no way he could know that.

"No."

"Mr. Lattimore, did you find any other files on that laptop or in any backups of said laptop, which would be considered pornographic material?"

"Objection. Calls for speculation on the part of the witness." Faye was obviously hoping to let the jury speculate on that information.

The judge considered. "Ms. Villareal, unless you intend to present evidence of additional files containing pornographic materials, I'll allow it."

"We do not have any such evidence to present," Faye answered somewhat sheepishly.

"Continue, Ms. Martin," the judge said.

"Thank you, Your Honor." Bobbie repeated her question. "Mr. Lattimore, did you find any other files on that laptop or in any backups of said laptop that would be considered pornographic material?"

"No."

"Mr. Lattimore, isn't it likely anyone who knew the defendant also knew his daughter's name and age? And isn't true there are millions of left-handed people in this country?"

Faye objected. "Asking the witness to speculate."

"Sustained. Please rephrase or withdraw your question."

"Withdrawn." Bobbie knew she had made her point anyway, adding, "No more questions."

Judge Thompson stood and declared that court was adjourned for a lunch break and that the proceedings would resume at one thirty.

Seeing how the trial was unfolding, it was becoming clear to Jack just how competent Bobbie and Carl were and how complete their preparation was. It gave him renewed hope that things might actually be turning in the right direction.

As they all left the courtroom, Jack noticed Hank Reynolds furiously making notes for the lead story he and Wendy would write about the day's proceedings.

Jack said, "Hi" and Hank told him he wanted to get the morning happenings down on paper so he could focus on the events of the afternoon. Jack also saw Wendy outside the courthouse trying to interview the lawyers for the two sides. He could sense she was more than a little excited to be sharing a byline with her paper's editor on such an important front-page article.

The defense team went across the street to Mama's Café, a sandwich shop frequented by people on lunch break from the courthouse.

"Bobbie, I thought you did an amazing job rebutting the evidence the prosecution presented," said Carl.

"I hope the jury sees it that way as well."

"What happens now?" Jack asked.

"They will call their next witness, which I believe is their last. Then they will likely rest their case and we'll be up to bat."

"Who are you going to call first?" Carl asked Bobbie.

"Good question. What order do you think would be best?"

"I'd start with our expert from KnowIT since we just ended with the testimony surrounding the laptop. Then, I'd introduce the sworn statement from the janitorial service owner after which I'd call Peter Evans. I suspect that's all we'll have time for this afternoon."

"Perfect, I agree. Carl, you call Phil Thomas to the stand and get him to corroborate the numerous possibilities that other people had a hand in the download. I'll follow with the introduction of Eric Irons' statement and then start in with the McKay staff. Everyone agreed?"

Everyone nodded in agreement. Their focus returned to the food and a little small talk for the next few minutes. Once they were all finished, Jack paid the check and the group headed back to the courthouse.

Jack walked back to the courtroom alone and was soon joined at the defense table by Bobbie and Carl when the trial reconvened at one thirty. The judge first ruled on the motion regarding introduction of the report detailing the pornographic material found on Jack's computer and in the file folder found in his drawer.

"Regarding the motion on the admissibility of the exhibit which contains the seized material in question and whether or not the jury will see that material, I'm ruling that the material will not be admitted and therefore the jury will not be allowed to review it. Ms. Villareal, please call your next witness."

Faye was extremely disappointed in the ruling but, realizing that battle was over, called her next witness, Victor Forsch, the owner of Grant Street Video. After he was sworn in, Faye began her questioning.

"Mr. Forsch, you are the owner and proprietor of Grant Street Video. Is that correct?"

"Yes."

"What is the nature of your business at Grant Street Video?" The question obviously made Forsch uneasy.

"We sell adult videos and magazines among other things," he said vaguely.

"What other things?"

"Sex toys, pipes, and other paraphernalia. Nothing illegal."

"You say 'nothing illegal.' Does that mean you do not trade in child pornography?"

"We absolutely do not. We'd be busted in a minute, and I run a legit operation."

"Do you know the defendant, Mr. McKay?"

"Don't say I really know him. He did visit my store one day a few months ago."

"Is he present in the courtroom? And if he is, please point him out."

"That's him," Forsch said, pointing directly at Jack.

"Let the record show that Mr. Forsch has accurately identified the defendant. When Mr. McKay visited your store, did you speak to him and, if yes, can you tell us about your conversation?"

"Yeah, we spoke. He asked me if we had any stuff with naked kids."

"What did you tell him?"

"I told him we didn't have such things in my store and that he needed to leave."

"Did he leave promptly and peacefully?"

"Yep."

"One more question. Why did you come forward to testify?"

"I saw the guy's picture on TV and recognized him. Legitimate stores like mine have a tough enough time keeping our licenses. I wanted the public to know that we don't get involved in illegal stuff. Plus, he's a scumbag and needs to pay for it."

"Objection!" said Bobbie. "Improper characterization."

"Sustained. The clerk will strike that last comment from the record and the jury will disregard it as well. Continue."

"No further questions, Your Honor. Your witness," Faye said, feeling her point had been made.

Before Bobbie rose to ask her first question, Miles handed her a handwritten note attached to a larger piece of paper. She smiled, put the papers down on the table, and began her questioning.

"Mr. Forsch, have you ever been arrested?" Bobbie asked.

Faye immediately interrupted. "Objection. Relevance?"

"Where are you going with this, Ms. Martin?" Judge Thompson asked before ruling.

"The witness has stated that his establishment follows the letter of the law, and should that not be the case, it goes to his reliability as a truthful witness."

"Okay, I'll give you some latitude here, but make your point and then let's move on. The witness will answer the question."

He squirmed a little. "Yes, I've been arrested."

"When?"

"Two years ago."

"What were you charged with?"

"Possession of an illegal substance."

"Your Honor, I have here an arrest report stating that Mr. Forsch was arrested at his video store in possession of one hundred and twenty grams of marijuana." The report was entered into evidence without objection. "Mr. Forsch, what happened after your arrest?"

"I was released on bail and the case was thrown out after the police department failed to produce the evidence at the trial."

"Interesting. One more question." Bobbie peeked at the note one more time. "Who owns the building where your store is located?"

"Mid-Town Real Properties."

"Do you know who owns Mid-Town Real Properties?"

"Not really."

"We are in possession of a copy of the incorporation documentation, which we would like to place into evidence. It lists Randall Davies as the owner of Mid-Town Real Properties. Do you know him?" Bobbie picked up the document and waved it in the direction of the jury.

Faye reacted quickly. "Objection. Relevance?"

"We intend to show that Randall Davies is involved in the conspiracy to convict my client for a crime to which he had no involvement whatsoever."

Rumbling sounded in the gallery. Reporters texting their news organizations. The judge called for order.

"Overruled. The witness will answer the question," Judge Thompson said.

"Do you know Randall Davies?" Bobbie asked.

"Don't know him," Forsch said.

Bobbie decided to wait on connecting Forsch to Frank Ryder.

"No further questions at this time, Your Honor. We reserve the right to recall this witness at a later time."

"Granted."

The latest revelation prompted the prosecution to ask for a ten-minute recess to regroup. The judge granted the request.

As the team huddled at the defense table, Bobbie turned to Miles. "Thanks for the note. Do you have the incorporation documentation?"

"Yes," Miles said, and handed her the papers.

Understating the obvious, Carl remarked, "Now the trial begins in earnest."

CHAPTER 43

During the recess, Faye conferred with Ted Erickson and David Harris to discuss how they would respond given the direction the defense was about to undertake.

Ted spoke first. "I think we should rest our case and then see what they bring. It seems they're trying a misdirect, which we should be able to rebut. Faye, I will get back to the office to see if we have anything on the disappearing marijuana."

"Okay, then. I'll rest our case. I agree the defense is likely grasping at straws."

"Faye, be sure to watch for facts not in evidence. They'll likely try to sneak some tidbits into the questions and the testimony of their witnesses."

"Got it."

After the brief recess, the courtroom was called to order and the trial continued with Judge Thompson asking Faye if she had any additional witnesses to call.

"We do not, Your Honor. The prosecution rests."

Up to that point in the proceedings, Jack felt like merely an observer. It seemed as if he was in the audience of a play and that play was about some fictional character. It was very real now, as evidenced by the knot in his stomach and the sweat forming on his brow. He had calmly made many important presentations in his life, but this was different. It was for his life!

"Attorney for the defense, please proceed with the case for the defense."

The judge's words brought Jack back into the reality that this was, in fact, about him and the outcome would certainly affect the rest of his life.

"Thank you, Your Honor. The defense calls Phil Thomas to the stand."

After being sworn in, Carl opened the questioning. "Mr. Thomas, what is your profession and for whom do you work?"

"I am the owner of KnowIT. We specialize in web-based information technology."

"What have you seen of the technology used by McKay & Associates and, in particular, the contents of Jack McKay's laptop computer?"

"I have done an inspection of the servers at McKay & Associates which include backups of the information on Mr. McKay's laptop."

"What did you find?"

"I found just one download that was accomplished on March thirteenth of this year. The backups of Mr. McKay's hard drive showed no other files containing anything I would classify as something resembling pornography."

Jack sensed Faye wanted to object to this "matter of opinion" testimony but realized she had already conceded that her expert had not found any more such material on the computer.

"Did you find anything else that might be considered unusual or outside of normal procedure?" Carl asked.

"Yes. Two things. First, the only backups done prior to and after March thirteenth were initiated automatically by the programming inherent in the system."

"Please explain."

"When the laptop is connected to the server, either by a cable or WiFi, regularly scheduled backups, usually in off hours, are automatically initiated. The one on March thirteenth was manually initiated."

"So what you're saying is someone would have wanted to place those files into the backup on the company servers."

"Correct."

"So the person who downloaded that illegal material would have wanted to be sure that a trail showing their illegal actions was uploaded to the server."

"Objection, leading the witness," Faye said.

"Overruled," said the judge. "The witness may answer."

"Possibly," Thomas offered.

Carl went on. "What was the other unusual 'thing'?"

"Well—and this was only usual because it was an office computer—there were several visits to the typical adult porn sites over the previous several months."

Carl clearly hadn't anticipated that revelation. "Were any of these visits to what would be considered illegal websites sites?"

"No."

Carl had no choice but move on. "Your witness."

Faye rose and approached Mr. Thomas. "Did you see anything in your analysis of the laptop or the server which showed explicitly that the defendant was not responsible for downloading the pornographic material he is charged with doing?"

"I did not."

"No more questions for this witness."

Phil Thomas stepped down and Bobbie took over the defense. She turned to the judge and explained that Mr. Eric Irons, the owner of the janitorial service used by McKay & Associates, had been subpoenaed to testify and was unable to attend the trial as he was attending to a family matter.

"So we'll move on," the judge responded.

"If it pleases the court," said Bobbie, "we have a sworn statement provided by Mr. Irons which details the testimony he would have provided."

"Objection," said Faye. "The introduction of that statement into evidence negates our right to cross-examine the witness, Your Honor."

"Let me see the statement," the judge responded.

Bobbie dutifully handed the statement to the judge, who read it over and handed it to the clerk. She then turned to Faye.

"Ms. Villareal, the witness list contained Mr. Irons's name, did it not?" the judge said.

"Yes, Your Honor."

"Did you interview him?"

"Yes."

"Was there anything in that interview that contradicts this statement?" the judge asked while handing Faye the statement.

After reading it, Faye said, "No, Your Honor."

"Then I'll allow it. The clerk will please read the statement so the jury can hear it."

The clerk read the rather short statement: "On the night of March thirteenth, our janitorial service received a call from someone at McKay & Associates cancelling the service for that evening."

As the clerk read on, Jack saw Alderman Mathew's face turn ashen, which could only mean he was to be Davies's eyes and ears in the courtroom. The statement revealed that no reason for the cancellation was given and that service was to resume, as normal, after the date. While Mr. Irons had not been summoned to testify, Mathews was clearly unnerved that a written statement had come into the hands of the defense. Jack tried to imagine the wrath Davies would have for the failure of one of his cronies.

Judge Thompson nodded to Bobbie. "Ms. Martin, please call your next witness."

"The defense calls Mr. Peter Evans to the stand."

Peter walked down the center aisle, avoiding eye contact with Jack as he took his seat on the witness stand. He was sworn in, stated his name, place of residence, and position as Executive VP at McKay & Associates. Bobbie then began her questioning.

"Mr. Evans, how long have you been with the firm?"

"Twelve years."

"How would you describe your relationship with the defendant, Jack McKay?"

"It's a very cordial, close working relationship."

"Have there been any conflicts during your tenure there?"

"There are disagreements, of course, but no discord if that's what you mean."

"What about Jack's decision to represent Lindsay Revelle in the upcoming election? You would have normally been hired to run William Davies's campaign, wouldn't you?"

Peter hesitated for a moment before answering. "I disagreed with the decision, yes. But only because I felt that severing our ties with the Party would negatively impact our bottom line."

"When you joined the firm, who recommended you to Mr. McKay?"

"Randall Davies." Obviously uneasy, Peter shifted his gaze away from Jack.

"At that point in time, what was your relationship with Mr. Davies?"

"He was my boss at the Merchants Bank of Lakeville. I was the marketing director, and Randall was the bank's president."

"I'm curious, did Mr. Davies tell you why he wanted you to leave his bank and go to work for Mr. McKay?"

Peter was growing more uncomfortable by the minute. "Randall said it was a great opportunity for me and that we'd still be working together, just in a different capacity."

"Have you worked directly with Mr. Davies while at McKay & Associates?"

"Not directly. That's been Jack's client relationship."

"What about on a non-client basis?"

"Not sure what you're driving at." It was easy to tell from Peter's tone that he did not appreciate the inference.

"Have you at any time reported happenings at McKay & Associates or done the bidding of Mr. Davies while at McKay & Associates."

"No!"

"Remember, Mr. Evans, you're under oath. Perjury is a crime."

"Objection," Faye said. "Counsel is badgering the witness."

"Sustained." Judge Thompson gave Bobbie a disapproving stare. "Ms. Martin, please stick to your questions."

Bobbie continued. "Mr. Evans, phone records I have here from your office show that three calls were placed from your extension to Mr. Davies's office. They all occurred on the day after Mr. McKay informed Mr. Davies that he would be representing Lindsay Revelle's campaign, not William Davies's. Care to enlighten us about what was said in those conversations?"

Peter clear his throat. "Yes . . . I called three times, but as I recall only got through once. I pleaded with Randall to continue using our firm to represent his candidates and the businesses of his friends."

"What did Mr. Davies say?"

"He said he'd think about it."

"Did Mr. Davies ever come back to you and ask for any help in exchange for continuing the business relationship?"

"No."

"Changing subjects, do you and Mr. McKay have an agreement in writing or otherwise specifying what would happen if he left the firm?"

"Sure, we have a succession plan that says if he should leave, I would take over the business and a pre-determined buyout formula would kick in."

"In basic terms, how would that formula be calculated?"

"An independent valuation would be provided by a qualified third party."

"What would be the effect on the firm's value if Mr. McKay left the firm as a result of being found guilty in the matter before the court?"

"It would go down, of course."

"And if the value of the firm did go down, what would happen to the buyout formula?"

"The cost to me for the buyout would go down."

"A little or a lot?"

"Probably a lot."

Jack could see the pain on Peter's face.

"Sorry," said Bobbie, "but I have one more question. If that succession plan buyout were to be initiated, do you have the funding? If yes, where would the funds come from?"

"I have a home equity line of credit which would cover the down payment. The rest would come from anticipated profits."

"I apologize. Turns out I have a couple more questions. Who is the line of credit with, and what is the maximum amount you can borrow under that line of credit?"

"The line of credit is with the Merchants Bank of Lakeville. It's for a maximum of $400,000."

"Mr. Evans, I have here the appraisal for your home that was filed along with the loan documents. It shows the value of your home as $400,000. So you have a home equity loan for the total value of the home. Isn't that unusual?"

"I suppose it is, but I simply asked for the maximum amount

they would approve. They offered $400,000, and I agreed knowing I would only use the portion necessary for the buyout, which fluctuates based on the firm's valuation."

"Do you have any additional funding options if the buyout should exceed your line of credit?"

"Not really."

"So if Mr. McKay was found guilty, you'd likely take over the firm and do so at a bargain rate."

"Objection, supposition," Faye said.

"Sustained."

Bobbie waited a moment before continuing in order to let Peter's testimony sink in with the members of the jury. "Thank you, Mr. Evans. I have no further questions. Your witness."

Faye rose and began her questioning. "Mr. Evans, did you ever see any indication that Mr. McKay had any interest in pornography of any kind or exhibit any unusual behavior or interest in anything of a sexual nature?"

"Not really."

"Explain what you mean by 'not really,' please."

"Well, he often took clients out to strip clubs for entertainment."

Jack wondered where this line of questioning was headed.

"Was that an unusual practice for a business like yours?"

"I thought so."

Peter's response really surprised him.

"No more questions, Your Honor."

Bobbie rose and addressed the judge. "Redirect, Your Honor?"

With a wave of her hand, Judge Thompson allowed Bobbie to proceed with her questioning.

"Mr. Evans, did you attend any of these strip club client entertainments?"

"Yes."

"Did Mr. McKay ever behave in a manner which would not be considered gentlemanly?"

"No."

"One more question, Mr. Evans. When did you take out your home equity loan?"

"I took it out when Jack invited me to be a partner. It was required in order to show I had the means necessary to do so should the occasion arise."

"So this was not a recent event, but one that Mr. McKay's attorneys required years ago."

"Asked and answered," Faye said in objection.

The judge shrugged. "I'll allow the witness to answer."

"That's correct. Years ago." Peter seemed genuinely relieved to be able to provide the answer.

"No further questions. But we reserve the right to recall this witness."

Peter was excused from the stand and walked past the defense table again without making eye contact with Jack.

Judge Thompson checked the clock and turned to Bobbie. "Ms. Martin, we have time for one more witness before we adjourn for the day. Are you ready with one more?"

"Yes, Your Honor. The defense calls Carol Meyers to the stand."

Obviously discomforted by having to testify, Carol walked slowly as the bailiff escorted her into the courtroom. After she took the stand and was sworn in, Bobbie began the questioning.

"Ms. Meyers, what is your position at McKay & Associates?"

"I am the director of the Marketing Communications Department."

"Where would that place you in the hierarchy of the firm?"

"Number three, I guess."

"If Mr. McKay were forced to leave the firm, would you then be number two?"

"I suppose so."

"How did you land your job at McKay & Associates?"

"A family friend recommended me."

"Who was that family friend?"

"Randall Davies."

Her answer broke the silence in the gallery. The judge banged the gavel once and quiet was restored.

"What is your working relationship with Peter Evans?"

"We work together on various projects and related matters within the firm, like personnel assignments."

"Closely?"

"Sure."

"Do you see each other outside of work?"

"We've gone out for drinks after work a few times," Carol said.

Not letting up, Bobbie asked, "Have you dated?"

"Not exactly." Carol was no longer speaking matter of factly.

"Explain what you mean by 'not exactly,' please."

Carol hesitated for a moment and then answered quietly, "He stayed over at my place once."

Jack almost fell out of his chair. How had he not known about this. There was also another outburst in the gallery. A second rap of the gavel from the judge ended it.

"So if I understand all of this correctly, you and Peter Evans had a close working relationship, slept together, both were recommended to the firm by Randall Davies, who was subsequently spurned by Mr. McKay, and the two of you would ultimately end up running the firm if Mr. McKay were forced to resign from the firm. Do I have that correct?"

"Yes, but it wasn't like that."

"Did you and Mr. Evans ever conspire to force Mr. McKay out of the firm by incriminating him in a crime he didn't commit?"

"Objection—"

"Overruled. The witness will answer the question," the judge stated.

"No, it wasn't like that at all. Peter would never do such a thing," Carol said.

"Ms. Meyers, remember you're under oath, did you take part in a conspiracy to incriminate Jack McKay?"

No answer.

"I repeat, did you, alone or with help from anyone else, conspire to falsely implicate Jack McKay in a crime he didn't commit with the sole purpose being to have him removed from his position at the firm?"

Suddenly, Carol broke down, and through a sudden storm of tears, almost sounding relieved, she blurted out, "It should be Peter's company. He's the one who runs it and makes it go."

"I'll say it again, did you, alone or with help from anyone else, conspire to falsely implicate Jack McKay in a crime he didn't commit?

"I did what I did to help Peter get what is rightfully his. I love you, Peter!" she screamed.

The gallery went up for grabs. The judged pounded the gavel relentlessly calling for order. Bobbie turned to Jack and gave him a wink. He gave her a grateful smile and a wink back. Jack wondered if Peter had heard her screaming confession from the hallway where he was standing. He could and was visibly shaken, his face buried in his hands.

Finally, as the crowd quieted, the judge asked the bailiff to escort the jury back to the jury room. She then turned to Carol and in a soft tone said, "Ms. Meyers, if you are about to confess to something, I must recommend that you seek counsel before saying anything that might incriminate you. I can either appoint one for you here and now, or I can adjourn the proceedings to give you time to consult with an attorney of your choosing."

Jack could see that Carol suddenly realized the gravity of the trouble she was in as a result of her outburst. She consented to have the judge appoint an attorney for her. The judge sent her bailiff out in the corridor to see who might be in the vicinity and available. In the meantime, both sides were deciding on what to do next.

Bobbie turned to Carl. "Go see DA Erickson and find out if they're willing to have the restraining order lifted so Jack can see his daughter again. I'll go and see if we can get this whole case dismissed."

She then turned to Miles. Please go to Mickey's to see if he needs anything. Oh, and please take Molly for a walk."

"Happy to!" And he was off.

While the courtroom awaited the bailiff's return, Bobbie approached the bench with Faye close behind.

"Your Honor, in light of what we've just heard, the defense moves for dismissal of the case against Mr. McKay."

Without hesitation, Judge Thompson leaned over and said to the two of them, "We're not there yet. Once we get counsel selected for Ms. Meyers, I'm going to adjourn for the day and call for resumption of the trial tomorrow morning at ten a.m. I'll hear your motion and the arguments for and against then."

Faye chimed in, "One more thing, Your Honor, I believe Ms. Meyers should be taken into custody and bound over for the resumption of the trial."

"I'll cover that when her attorney is appointed. Remember, Ms. Villareal, she has not as yet been charged with a crime."

"She'd also be a lot safer behind bars at this point," Bobbie said to herself.

As the two attorneys returned to their tables, Ted and Carl approached them.

"Faye, I think we can safely move to have the restraining order lifted."

"I agree."

Bobbie, Carl, and the two DAs then approached the bench and made their joint motion to the judge. She granted the motion and Jack was now free to see Maya.

When Jack heard the news, he was almost unable to contain himself. "Thank you both!" His impulse was to immediately rush to Maya with the news.

Bobbie held up her hand as a signal to stop. "Not so fast, Jack. The judge has added two conditions to lifting the order. First, you are to be accompanied by an officer of the court, in this case that would be Carl. Secondly, Maya's mother must be present at all times when you are together with Maya."

"OK, but why?"

"Because the matter before the court remains unsettled. Hopefully we'll get everything dismissed tomorrow morning, but for now at least, these are the rules."

"So be it. Carl, are we good to go."

"Good to go, Jack."

Jack gave Bobbie a huge hug and then, in a flash, he and Carl were out the door.

The bailiff returned to the courtroom with Terry Chase, an experienced trial attorney who had been headed to the door of the courthouse after finishing a trial. He agreed to go to Judge Thompson's court and, at least for the moment, be appointed to represent Carol Meyers. In the brief proceedings that followed,

Attorney Chase asked for time to confer with his new client, who was soon released since she had not yet been formally charged with a crime. The current matter before the court would resume in the morning.

CHAPTER 44

As soon as the judge concluded the court's business for the day, Bobbie headed off to the parking lot. On the way, she turned her cell phone back on and noticed she had a missed call from Miles, which had come in a few minutes before. There was no voicemail. She hopped into her car. As she set off for Mickey's house, she called Miles.

"I see I missed a call from you. What's up?"

"Are you on the freeway?" Miles asked in a muffled voice.

"Not yet, why?"

"Just pull over and we'll talk."

She nervously pulled off the road, knowing the talk would not be about anything good.

"Okay. I'm parked. What's happened?"

"Bobbie . . . Mickey passed away. I'm so sorry. When I got back to the house, I found him unconscious. I called the paramedics and . . . well, there was nothing they could do. He was gone."

"I, I don't . . ." She couldn't finish the sentence.

"There is nothing you or anyone could have done. Unfortunately, this was inevitable. We all knew his time was short and so did he."

Bobbie composed herself. "I know. It's just that we had just started to rebuild our relationship and he was so happy and now . . ." Again, she was unable to finish her thought.

"I know, but these past few weeks were the happiest he'd had since your mom died. You gave him peace in his last days." Miles was doing everything he could to soothe her pain.

"Thanks, I'll be there in a few minutes. If you speak to Jack, tell him to have his time with Maya. There is nothing he needs to do here for the moment." Bobbie took a few extra moments to gather herself and then headed to the house to face the inescapable reality of her loss.

***

The phone rang in Jack's car as he was approaching Shorewood. Jack saw it was Miles and answered.

"Hi, Miles. Was Mickey excited to hear about the turn of events at the trial?"

"Jack, Mickey died."

"What?" Jack shouted as he nearly swerved off the road.

"When I got to his house, he was unconscious on the couch. Molly was whimpering and kept pawing at his leg as if trying to wake him up. I called the paramedics, and they were there in seconds, it seemed. There was nothing they could do."

"Does Bobbie know?"

"Yeah, I called her first. She'll be here any minute. She told me to tell you, in no uncertain terms, to have your visit with Maya and then to call her. OK?"

"I understand. Please give her a hug for me and one from Carl."

"I will, Jack. You give Maya a hug for me as well. See you later tonight."

Jack pulled into the Freemans' driveway. He put on his best fake smile and knocked on the door. Maya opened the door and Jack's fake smile became a real one.

"Daddy!" Maya screamed.

Hugs and kisses followed. Even Sandy gave him a brief hug. The Freemans were all smiles knowing just how happy Jack's visit was making Maya. Jack introduced Carl to everyone as they all moved from the doorway to the living room.

Maya's eyes lit up and she literally danced as she spoke. "Daddy, I want to show you my room."

"Wonderful, can Mommy and Carl come too?" Jack asked, knowing they would have to join him and Maya.

"Okay, let's go."

The entourage headed up the stairs to Maya's room. It had once been Sandy's room and featured an unusual blend of both the mother and daughter's childhoods. Maya introduced Jack to her new dolls and stuffed animals. She also showed him pictures she had drawn of the family. In all of them, she had included Sandy, Jack, and herself. Jack knew his little girl would need more than a mere semblance of that family going forward.

"Anybody hungry?" Sam asked the group.

"I am, Grandpa. Can we go to Big Bill's Burgers?" she pleaded. It was Maya's new favorite place.

"Sounds like a plan," Sam agreed.

So it was off to the restaurant which was just a few blocks away. Maya rode with Jack and didn't stop talking even after they arrived. It was as if she wanted to be sure to tell Jack everything that had happened while they had been separated. He loved hearing the stories, but mostly loved just hearing her happy voice.

At the restaurant, the conversation was lighthearted with Maya taking center stage. She only paused long enough to finish off a hot fudge sundae. After they finished eating, they headed back to the Freemans'. More hugs and kisses before Jack and Carl would drive back to Lakeville to face the sad scene at Mickey's.

As he was walking out the door, Sandy stopped Jack.

"You know Maya's birthday is Saturday. She has a kid party and then I was hoping you and I could take her out to dinner."

"I'll be there, of course." Jack decided not to spoil the happy reunion by sharing news of Mickey's passing.

Sandy smiled and turned away. As he and Carl walked toward the car, Jack thought how wonderful it was that he and Sandy could now be civil to one another. He now felt confident that coparenting would work out.

Once on the road, Jack called Bobbie, but it went straight to voicemail. He then tried Miles, who answered.

"Hi, Jack. How is Maya doing?"

"We had a great time together. It almost made me forget about what had happened to Mickey. Is Bobbie with you?"

"She's in her room resting."

"I tried calling her, but it went right to voicemail. I assume she turned her phone off."

"She did. How soon will you be back?"

"About an hour. I'm going to drop Carl off at his car in the courthouse parking lot first and then I'll be back."

"Sounds good. See you soon."

Carl, who had been silent since they left Shorewood, decided to speak. "You kept it together really well considering the news you got about Mickey before we arrived."

"I've always been able to compartmentalize the things that have happened in my life. Sometimes it's a good thing, like in this case."

"When is it not a good thing?"

"When it costs you a marriage."

Silence took over again until they arrived back in Lakeville.

When Jack got to the house, it was quiet and mostly dark except for one light that was on in the living room. He opened the door and Molly came to meet him, only without the usual squeal and tail wagging. How uncanny, he thought, that dogs grieved so much like humans.

Miles was watching the news when he walked in.

"Anything about the trial make the evening newscast?"

"I just turned it on, and they were already on to the weather."

"Where's Bobbie?"

"She's still upstairs. She told me it would be okay if you came to her room to talk."

"Thanks."

Jack climbed the stairs not knowing exactly what to say. He was seldom at a loss for words, but this was one of those times. Fortunately, Bobbie spoke first.

"I can't believe this happened so soon. Today of all days!"

"Regrettably, we don't have control of such things. Mickey had his ups and downs, but the last few weeks were the ultimate ups for him. He died happy. We should all be so lucky."

"I know but we were just . . ." Unable to finish the sentence, she started to cry. Jack took her in his arms and hugged her tenderly until her sobbing subsided.

"Have you thought at all about what comes next?"

"The funeral home will pick him up from the hospital morgue tomorrow. I guess I'll have to go there sometime during the day to discuss the arrangements."

She went on to explain how Mickey had specified that he only wanted a gravesite ceremony and that he be buried in his plot next to his wife, Dolores. Jack thought they should have some kind of a wake. Mickey had a lot of friends who'd like to pay their respects in some way. Bobbie agreed to have a small gathering at the house the evening after the burial.

"Jack, I really appreciate you staying here tonight. I just couldn't be alone." She buried her head in her hands.

"I feel the same way," Jack lamented.

CHAPTER 45

The following morning, Jack was in the bathroom shaving when Bobbie knocked on the door.

"Come in, I'm decent," he said.

"So I've been told." Bobbie's sarcastic sense of humor had, at least for the moment, returned.

"What's our plan for today?" he asked.

"We go to court and get this mess resolved."

"Can't Carl handle it? You have enough to deal with right now."

"Getting your case dismissed will be the best medicine I can think of."

After Jack got dressed, he and Bobbie headed to the courthouse to meet Carl. Miles stayed behind to take care of Molly. She likely would be taking care of him too, as they both dealt with missing Mickey.

When they arrived at the courthouse, Carl and Faye were conferring outside of the courtroom.

"Hi," said Carl. "Ms. Villareal has some good news for you."

"Yes, I do," said Faye. "Carol Meyers has decided to plead guilty to participating in the conspiracy that led to Mr. McKay being wrongly prosecuted for a crime he didn't commit. Her guilty plea included a cooperation deal with us, which will substantially reduce any penalty she would face, and which will assist us in punishing the other individuals responsible. Mr. McKay, we're sorry that you had to go through this, and we hope whatever damage was done will not cause you any further distress."

Jack was about to speak, but Bobbie put up her hand and responded first.

"Does this mean you're going before the judge to recommend dropping all charges against my client?"

"Yes."

Jack was ecstatic.

"Good. Let's proceed."

They all entered the crowded courtroom together. Before they took their seats at the defendant's table, Bobbie pulled Jack aside.

"I stopped you from saying anything to the DA because I wasn't sure what you were going to say. We've won and anything else, particularly anything said in anger, is irrelevant."

Surprised at that, Jack responded, "I was just going to say thank you."

"Good. You can still do that after we're done here."

The judge asked the attorneys to approach the bench. She asked Faye if the prosecution wanted to proceed with the case against Jack. Faye said no and went on to explain the plea deal which had been struck with Carol Meyers. She then made a motion to dismiss all charges against Jack. The judge accepted the motion and ruled the case dismissed. The jury was discharged, and the trial was over.

Noticeable in the gallery were Hank and Wendy. The *Lakeville Examiner* now had a huge story on their hands. It was likely more of their staff would join in on it as the story would evolve into a series of exposés on the wrong doings of the people behind this case and other cases of misdeeds, which would likely grow from it.

As Jack and the attorneys walked out of the courtroom, Jack thanked Faye for her apology. Carl shook hands with Bobbie and Jack and told them he'd see them at the get-together at Mickey's house after the burial on Sunday.

Jack went with Bobbie to the funeral home directly from the courthouse. Once there, she was to discuss the arrangements for

Mickey's internment. Jack waited in the reception area while Bobbie went alone into the funeral director's office. She emerged twenty minutes later with her eyes reddened from the emotion of the discussion. The casket and the burial would be simple. Mickey's pastor, the retired prison chaplain who Mickey had befriended in jail years before, would say a few words. They'd all recite the 23rd Psalm. Mickey would be laid to rest on Sunday morning and that would be it.

"He would've wanted it just that way," Jack said, doing his best to be comforting.

"I know. It's just hard. So final."

"It always is, unfortunately. There is really no good way to say goodbye to someone who's not there to hear it. Mickey loved you, and you had the chance to show him you loved him back. That's the best sendoff you could have given him."

"You're right, I guess. It just going to take me a while to come to grips with all that's happened," Bobbie lamented.

Jack fought back tears of his own. It all came crashing down on him that he won, that his reputation would be restored, and his best friend Mickey wasn't here to see it.

Word of all that had just transpired at the courthouse reached Randall Davies immediately. He knew all roads would lead back to him and the Party and likely uncover a treasure trove of wrongdoing. His first thought was to destroy anything he possessed that could be incriminating. There was so much, he'd have to have assistance. Even though he was boiling mad at Frank Ryder, he needed his help. So he picked up the phone.

"The whole thing with McKay just blew up in our faces. Get over here. We have some work to do to cover our tracks."

"On my way." Randall was furious with Frank, but he also knew that the anger was secondary to his need to get rid of evidence linking Randall and his associates to this and so many other crimes.

Following instructions, Frank made his way to Randall's office arriving less than an hour later. They set about collecting all the files that contained any possible evidence of wrongdoing. Then they combed through Randall's computer to delete any files or emails that might be used against him. Being old school, Randall hated technology so there wasn't a huge amount to get rid of on the computer. After about three hours, Frank left with several boxes of files to destroy. Randall called his attorney and gave him a heads-up as to what was coming. The attorney advised him to stay calm and continue doing business as usual.

Easy for him to say, Randall thought.

Over matzo ball soup and a shared pastrami sandwich, Jack asked Bobbie what she was going to do with Mickey's house, Molly, and all the stuff Mickey had accumulated.

"I haven't totally committed to this yet, but I'm thinking of offering Miles the opportunity to move into the house provided he would also adopt Molly. I can't let the house go just yet. Plus it eases the burden of rushing to go through the decades of stuff my parents accumulated."

"I overheard him once talking to Mickey about his apartment. He mentioned that his rent is about $1,400 a month. Likely he'd be more inclined to accept your offer if you'd take that same amount as rent for the house."

"That would be fine with me. Plenty to cover the taxes and some maintenance. Maybe he'd even kick in for the utilities. If I decide to go that route, I'm sure we can come to an agreement."

"I'm sure too."

They finished their lunch and headed back to the house. Along the way, Bobbie told Jack she had decided to, in fact, make the housing offer to Miles. Just as they entered the house, Lindsay Revelle was calling Jack.

"Jack, I just heard about your case being resolved. I'm so happy for you, man."

"Thanks. It's been a very trying time, but now it's over. Seems to me the news accounts of what actually happened should give you a boost at the polls."

"That would be great, if it happens, but right now I'm just glad justice prevailed. Speaking of the election, we're having an election night rally back at La Follette Hall and I'd really like you to be there."

"I wouldn't miss it for anything."

"You're welcome to bring a guest."

"Thanks, maybe I will." Jack immediately thought he'd like Bobbie to be that guest. She had been through a lot and could certainly use the lift the victory celebration could bring. Besides, he really enjoyed the thought of them being there together.

"When you get to the hall there will be a table with badges for special guests. There will be two badges waiting for you. Please come backstage before the polls close at eight. The election is likely to be called shortly thereafter and I'd like to say hi before I have to speak to the crowd. Robin wants to chat with you as well."

"Thanks so much. I'll definitely be there for what I know will be a victory celebration."

"Hope you're right. See you Tuesday night. Bye, Jack."

Jack immediately made up his mind and decided to go into the living room to ask Bobbie. She was thrilled to be included in what was likely to be a great election night event. In return, she told him she had made the offer to Miles.

"Now I need your help, Bobbie."

"Again, Jack?" she teased.

"This is serious business. Maya's seventh birthday is Saturday and I need to show up with an extra special gift."

"How about a puppy?"

"A puppy would be perfect, but I'm not sure Sandy or her parents would approve."

"Doesn't hurt to ask."

"I'll get right on that," he said.

Surprisingly, Sandy agreed on one condition. "The dog needs to be a rescue. It seems only fitting given you and I have been rescued ourselves recently."

"I can't argue with that," Jack said.

Randall was holed up in his office having just given Frank some files of an incriminating nature to dispose of before the authorities could get their hands on them. Ironically, when Wendy arrived at Randall Davies's office building hoping to secure a comment from him, she noticed a man leaving and loading some file boxes into his car. Not sure if it was related in any way, she nonetheless took a picture of him, his car, and license plate with her cell phone's camera.

She rode the elevator to the third floor and proceeded down the long hall to Randall's office. The receptionist announced her over the intercom. A couple of minutes later Randall emerged from his office.

"Mr. Davies," she asked, "do you have any comment on the allegations made in court today that you played a role in setting up the case against Jack McKay?"

"No comment," he replied, then turned and strode back into his office.

Wendy left the office without a story, but when she reached the lobby, she texted the picture to Ron Archer, the head of the research department at the *Examiner*, and asked him to see what he could find out about the man she photographed.

CHAPTER 46

Jack was up at the crack of dawn. It was Maya's birthday and he couldn't wait to see her face when they told her about her gift. After letting Molly out to relieve herself, he decided to go to the Olympus Diner for breakfast, allowing Bobbie to continue sleeping uninterrupted.

Over his poached eggs and breakfast sausage patties, he started assessing his options going forward. Obviously, he had a company to run, but did he want to continue running it? He was hoping this was the beginning of new a relationship with Bobbie. Where would that lead? Maya needed a full-time dad or at least as full-time as his being divorced would allow. There was so much to consider.

His concentration was interrupted by a familiar voice. It was Hank Reynolds from the *Examiner*.

"Hi there, Jack. Congratulations. So nice to see you out and about."

"Thanks, Hank. Care to join me?" Jack said, knowing he would.

"Love to. You must feel like the weight of the world has been lifted from your shoulders."

"And then some. I assume you guys will be busy following up on the story that came out of my case being dismissed."

"Absolutely. It could shake up the entire political landscape of the region. What we've uncovered so far is that Carol Meyers had originally been recruited by Randall Davies to spy on you. Once he had his claws into her, and given her feelings for Peter Evans, escalating her activities into framing you was inevitable."

"This should keep your staff occupied for quite a while, I assume."

"No question about it. May I check in with you along the way?"

"Sure, always happy to help. Particularly under these circumstances."

"As a member of the campaign staff, any thoughts on Tuesday's election?"

"I haven't been directly involved with the campaign for some time. I do, however, hope Lindsay wins. He'll be a great Congressman if he does."

"I'd be very surprised if he doesn't win."

They finished breakfast with talk of the Packers' victory the previous week and the coming of another brutal Wisconsin winter. As they walked to their cars, Hank turned to Jack and asked, "I'd like to publish something about Mickey Martin's passing, other than just an ordinary obituary. You knew him better than anyone. Care to weigh in?"

Jack considered. Mickey certainly deserved a tribute. "I'd like that. Give me a couple of days and I'll send you my thoughts."

Jack's early start got him to the Freemans at nine thirty. Diane greeted him at the door and told him Sandy and Maya were getting dressed and would be down shortly. Sam offered him coffee which he declined. He was already over-caffeinated.

A moment later, Maya came bounding down the stairs. "Hi, Daddy! I'm seven today!"

"Yes you are! And we have a present for you that's perfect for you being seven."

"What? What?"

Sandy, who had followed Maya down the stairs, took over the surprise.

"We thought it was time you had your own puppy."

"Oh my god! Oh my god!" Maya was running around the room

repeating that phrase. Stopping for a moment, she asked, "Where is it?"

Jack smiled. "That's the best part. You and Mommy and I are going to the Humane Society where you get to pick out your own."

Maya was so excited she was almost breathless. Sandy got Maya's coat and the three of them hopped into the car and headed downtown.

When they arrived, there were several other families in line to look over prospective pets. When their turn came, they walked down the corridor to the area where the adoptable dogs were housed. Maya went up to each of the cages and greeted the dogs inside. Halfway down the aisle, she fell in love with Lester. He appeared to be a mix of poodle and cocker spaniel with a few other possibilities thrown in. His light brown curly hair and bright eyes made for an adorable combination. The volunteer who accompanied them opened the cage and Maya wrapped her arms around her new birthday present. They were a perfect match.

Sandy and Jack filled out some paperwork and then helped Maya carry Lester to the car. She talked non-stop to her new best friend all the way home. When they arrived, Diane and Sam were waiting anxiously. They had been to the pet store to buy all the necessities: a leash, bowls, food, a couple of gates to keep Lester out of trouble, the whole nine yards.

"You are the best birthday present ever!" Maya told Lester. Lester responded by licking her face.

The fun continued with the party that afternoon. Sandy and her mom had decorated the rec room in the basement with balloons and pictures of puppies. Nine of Maya's neighborhood and school chums arrived at one-o'clock to celebrate with cake and Kool-Aid. Lester joined in by scarfing up any cake bits that hit the floor.

The party ended at three. Everyone, including Lester, was exhausted. Jack gave Maya another hug before leaving. She whispered in his ear, "Thank you, Daddy. I love Lester and I love you."

Jack was without words. He could only smile.

On the drive home, Jack decided it was time to speak to Peter. It would not be an easy call as there were open wounds on both sides. Peter answered the call on the first ring.

"Hi, Jack. How are you doing?" Thankfully, Jack did not detect any malice in his voice.

"Doing well. You?"

"The same."

"Listen, Peter, we have a lot to discuss and I'd like it to be face-to-face. Any chance you could meet me at the office in an hour?"

"I can. Before we meet, I just want you to know I had no idea about what Carol was doing."

"I believe that, Peter. It's also why we need to get together and work out some things about the firm. It's not about trust issues, I assure you."

"That's a relief. See you in an hour."

Jack stopped by the house on the way to his office to pick up his laptop, which had been returned by the DA's office. Miles was there and said Bobbie was off doing errands. He also told Jack that he and Bobbie had come to an agreement about the house and since he rented his current apartment on a month-to-month basis, he'd be moving in within a couple of weeks. Miles was obviously touched by her generosity and kindness. Molly seemed to be pretty much back to her old self. Maybe she sensed Miles was there to stay.

Jack grabbed his computer and a few papers then headed off to his office. He pulled into the parking lot, as he had hundreds of times, but this time it felt different. Like he was a stranger. The same feeling he had had when he went back to the house he, Sandy, and Maya had once shared.

He walked through the front door and headed down the hall to his office. As he passed Peter's office, he waved and proceeded to his office. Everything was exactly as he had left it, but it felt strange. Something in his subconscious was weighing in on what he would say to Peter.

Shortly after he sat down at his desk, Peter appeared in his doorway.

"Ready for me?" he asked.

"Absolutely. C'mon in."

As Peter approached the desk, Jack got up and then the two men shook hands. Not merely a "hello" handshake, but a sincere "how are you" handshake. They then moved to Jack's small conference table in the corner by the window.

"Peter, let's start off by addressing the elephant in the room. I want you to know that I, in no way, blame you for what happened. In addition, I want to apologize for the grilling you took on the witness stand. My attorney was only doing what she had to do to keep me from going to jail for a crime I didn't commit."

"I know, Jack. I'm just glad you were exonerated." Peter sat down, obviously at ease now.

"Obviously there's a big void left by Carol's untimely departure. Any ideas?"

"I think Rachel is ready to move into that chair. I also think it's time to elevate a very deserving Donna into the role of Director of Operations. What do you think?"

"I think both moves are excellent calls, but ultimately it's your decision."

"My decision, why?" Peter looked at Jack quizzically.

Jack took a deep breath and put his hand on Peter's shoulder.

"Because, Peter, I've decided it's time for you take over running the company. In fact, if you're willing, I'd like us to activate our buy-out agreement."

"I'm very surprised. Why?"

"Simple. This whole incident has made me realize how much I need to make changes in my life. First, I have a daughter who needs her dad on a regular basis. Also, I realized as the trial was going on, I could be away from the business and it would function just fine without me. My ego took a little bruising with that revelation, but I'm good with it now. Lastly, I want to explore other avenues where I can use the skills I have to do good things. Don't get me wrong, we've done some good things for our clients, but I want to do things that give back to the community as a whole without a profit motive or political agenda. Do you know what I mean?"

"I do. As you know, I have a home equity loan lined up to assist with the financing. That is unless some bank examiner kills it. I should have known—"

Jack interrupted. "Stop. You did nothing wrong. Randall Davies is the culprit, not you. Besides, you're not going to need your line of credit."

"I don't understand."

"Here's the deal. I want us to come up with a plan where you buy me out over time using a portion of the profits from the company. Some formula which also includes a small portion of my current compensation so I can maintain employee status for insurance, 401(k), etc. Then a manageable amount of the profits to buy out my stock over a reasonable timeframe."

"You've obviously thought this out in some detail."

"Actually I'm making it up as I go along. Are you on board?"

"I am." Peter was excited about the plan but, at the same time, sad to be losing Jack as a partner.

"What do you think will happen with the Consolidated–PetroMark deal?"

"I had a conference call with the key people on both sides. With William Davies likely out of the planning commission and Lindsay Revelle's likely election, they're abandoning the harbor depot and simply moving ahead with the joint venture."

"Wow. Great news. Maybe I should have asked you about that before proposing our deal." Jack laughed so Peter would know right away he wasn't reconsidering.

Their discussion then turned to planning for account transitions and shifting personnel around accordingly. When they finished, they shook hands again and pledged to get the ball rolling with the attorneys as soon as possible. Having that discussion behind him, Jack drove out of the parking lot feeling truly free for maybe the first time ever.

When he got back to the house, Bobbie and Miles were setting up some tables and chairs they had rented for tomorrow evening's celebration-of-life for Mickey. They had sent out numerous emails and made some calls to invite everyone they thought would want to participate.

"How can I help?"

"Put tablecloths on the tables we've put up. They're in a stack on the kitchen table."

"Yes, ma'am. Looks like you're expecting a lot of people to show up."

"Hope so," said Miles.

At the end of the evening, they sat in the living room and cracked open a fresh bottle of Irish whiskey in honor of Mickey. After finishing the entire bottle, they all fell asleep where they sat. Waking up at various times during the night, they each retreated to their respective rooms to finish their whiskey-induced slumber.

The beeping of the alarm clock at high volume woke Jack. He dragged himself to the bathroom, his head pounding from the aftermath of the whiskey. When he arrived at the door, he could hear the shower running so he decided to wait. A couple of minutes later, Bobbie emerged with her body wrapped in a bath towel and her still wet hair combed out. *She is really beautiful,* he thought.

"My turn?" he asked.

"All yours."

After he had showered, shaved, and dressed, he joined Bobbie and Miles at the kitchen table. Miles had made coffee and Bobbie was toasting an English muffin. It was unlikely any of them would want much in light of their whiskey-produced hangovers.

After breakfast they headed off to the cemetery. The funeral director was there with the grave attendants who were finishing preparing the gravesite. Mickey's casket was in the hearse parked nearby. The pastor arrived a couple of minutes later. The service and burial process took less than thirty minutes. It was very emotional for all three of them. Even Miles had to reach for his handkerchief to wipe tears from his eyes. After shaking hands with the pastor and funeral director, they got into the car and headed back to the house to prepare to receive the people who would be coming to pay their respects.

People started arriving around 6:00 p.m. As usual, the last of the over fifty mourners left as soon as all of the deli and liquid refreshments had been consumed. By ten thirty they had the dishes done and the rented tables and chairs stacked for the Monday morning pick up. After a long and trying day, Jack crashed in bed. Everything was different now that Mickey was gone.

CHAPTER 47

Tuesday was election day. The headline in the morning online edition of the *Lakeville Examiner* read, "Lindsay Revelle Expected to Win First District Congressional Election."

When Jack and Bobbie arrived at the hall, people had already started gathering in anticipation of a great victory celebration. There was a long line at the bar and a band was playing upbeat jazz music. Jack walked over to the credentials table to check in. He was handed two badges and a note asking him to proceed to a private room at the back of the hall.

As directed, he and Bobbie walked through the crowd to a doorway behind the stage. A few steps down a dimly lit hallway landed them at the entrance of the private room. Jack figured the room was likely used mostly as a dressing room for the acts who periodically performed there.

There were about a dozen people in the room when they entered. Jack recognized several of the Revelles' family members and a couple of staffers. He then saw Lindsay and Robin seated on a couch in the corner of the room. As he and Bobbie walked in their direction, the Revelles stood to greet them.

Lindsay spoke first, offering his hand. "Jack, so glad you could come."

Jack took his hand and replied, "Glad to be here, soon-to-be Congressman-elect."

"Don't jump the gun, my friend."

"Okay, but I'm sure your staff has seen all the positive signs in their exit polling."

Already the cautious politician, he replied, "Well, we're just going to wait and see what happens when the polls close." Reaching his hand out to Bobbie, Lindsay continued, "You must be Ms. Martin." Jack had given Lindsay a heads-up on his guest.

"Yes, nice to meet you. Please call me Bobbie."

"Bobbie, please accept our condolences over the loss of your father. I really admired him."

"Thank you."

"Let me introduce you to my wife, Robin."

Bobbie and Robin exchanged greetings and then Robin turned to Jack.

"Good to see you, Jack. If you have a moment, I have something I'd like to discuss with you."

"My time is yours."

They walked over to the opposite corner of the room, leaving Lindsay and Bobbie to exchange pleasantries.

Robin got right to the point. "You know about my work with the Water's Edge Trust, don't you?"

"Of course. It was a front-and-center issue in my firm's work with PetroMark."

"I know Lindsay thinks I'm jumping the gun, but here goes. The Water's Edge Trust is being folded into a much larger environmental organization with a lot more reach and substantially more clout. The group is the Conservancy Initiative Great Lakes. They pronounce their acronym, CIGL, as 'seagull.'"

"Catchy."

"Their executive director is a man named Daniel Thornton," she continued. "He's a PhD in hydrologic science. He's a brilliant researcher who will do great things guiding the scientific work, but the organization needs someone to spearhead their fundraising and lobbying efforts. You'd be perfect in that role."

"I certainly didn't see that coming. I'm not sure I'm ready to jump into anything like that just yet."

"The organization is located in downtown Milwaukee and has offices along the Milwaukee River just down the street from the University of Wisconsin-Milwaukee School of Freshwater Sciences with whom they partner. I did a little digging and found out your daughter's now living in Shorewood. You could live near her and only have a ten-minute commute to downtown."

Jack chuckled. "You should be a recruiter. You had your pitch down cold."

"Actually, I'm going to be a lobbyist. When we get to Washington, I'm planning to join an organization focused on promoting the candidacies of women and people of color. Back to the topic at hand, please have an open mind about taking this on."

"I'll give the opportunity serious consideration," he said.

"Good. I made an appointment for you to meet Daniel at his office next Wednesday at one-thirty. Do us both a favor and have the meeting." Jack could tell from the look in Robin's eyes that her request was actually more of a demand.

"Obviously, you're a very good lobbyist already," Jack said, only half joking. "The least I can do is have the meeting. Thank you for putting this together. Now we'd better get back to our dates before they run out of things to talk about."

Jack and Bobbie wished Lindsay good luck and headed back out to join the crowd. Shortly after the polls closed at eight, the results came pouring in. It would turn out to be a landslide. Confetti flew and the band played "On Wisconsin." Lindsay was now Congressman-elect Lindsay Revelle.

Jack felt a sense of pride for his friend. From the day he met Lindsay, he knew he was destined for great things. And Jack had a hand in helping him get there.

CHAPTER 48

The McKay trial was over, but Faye was already at work on the case that was to follow. She poked her head into Ted Erickson's office to fill him in on the latest developments.

"Got a minute?" She asked.

"Sure what've you got?"

Looking down at her notepad, she relayed the details of the latest development.

"I called, or should I say, I tried to call Roger Obregon at the DOJ to ask for his assistance with the investigations into the conspiracy that was uncovered at the McKay trial. I was immediately transferred to David Harris, who told me Roger had decided to take some unscheduled vacation days immediately after the trial. I sensed David was annoyed at having to deal with the fallout from the trial without Roger's assistance. Regardless, he agreed to have the DOJ supply whatever assistance they could in the ongoing investigation."

"Anything else?"

Faye thought for a moment before answering. Picking her words carefully, she answered.

"It seems obvious, based on what we uncovered at the trial, that the task force's investigation was compromised. There is no way Jack McKay could have been framed unless someone on the inside at the DOJ was helping them."

"You think it was Roger Obregon?"

"Seems likely."

"Did you share your suspicions with David?"

"No, but I think I should." Faye was looking for permission. She got it.

"Go ahead but be careful not to make a direct accusation. David's a smart guy. If he thinks it has credibility, he'll pursue it. If they have a bad apple, he'll want to get to the bottom of it."

After finishing their discussion of the call with the DOJ, Ted and Faye went before the judge to ask for search warrants so they could begin proceedings against Randall Davies, his son, and several of their associates, including Frank Ryder. Ultimately, they would seek a wide range of charges including conspiracy, money laundering, mail fraud, extortion, bank fraud, and racketeering.

The DA's were sure Frank Ryder knew they'd be coming after him for numerous crimes. Given what the DA had on the other likely defendants, they also expected he would immediately hire an attorney and seek a plea deal. It turned out to be a solid strategy.

What they didn't know was that Randall Davies was holed up in his house, feeling defenseless, and brooding about what was to come next.

Wendy was at her desk, preparing for her next article by gathering together the various bits of information the members of the investigative team had compiled, when she received a text. It was from an unknown sender. It read, "Frank Ryder has important evidence stored at Granville Store-It, in unit number 146. Suggest you get there quickly." She noticed the text was sent both to her and to Faye Villareal.

Wendy realized the text had to be from Miles Darien who was making good on his quid pro quo promise. She stopped by Hank's office to fill him in about the text. He was reviewing the front-page articles about Lindsay Revelle's being elected and the ongoing investigation of Randall Davies and his associates.

"Great work on the investigation story, Wendy."

"Thanks. It appears I have a scoop for the next installment."

After she showed him the text, he told her to immediately go out to the storage facility to get the story. Realizing that a photo of the evidence seizure would make great art for the front page, a photographer was assigned to accompany her. The two rushed out to Granville Store-It to wait for the authorities to arrive with a warrant.

Wendy and the photographer were already at the gate to the storage facility when Faye and the policemen arrived. Faye showed the warrant she had obtained to the attendant on duty who led them to the unit and unlocked it. They found, among other things, three file boxes Frank had taken from Randall's office which he was supposedly to have been destroyed. When Faye and the officers left with the evidence, Frank's bargaining chip for a plea deal left with them. When Wendy left, she had plenty to include in the next installment of her ongoing story, which would now also include a front-page-worthy photograph of the seizure.

The following morning, the *Examiner's* entire front page was devoted to the scandal. The pictures and details surrounding the evidence seizure, accompanied by the other information the team had gathered, painted an ugly picture of political corruption and other crimes allegedly committed by officials of the Party and their minions.

The second story added the latest details of the paper's investigation into the criminal investigation and political corruption surrounding the activities of Randall Davies and his cohorts. One of the revelations was how Wendy's quick thinking and reporting led to the arrest of Frank Ryder. Jack read the article and knew immediately that Ryder would sing like a bird to save his skin. Randall Davies was in deep, deep trouble.

That afternoon, Elenore Davies returned from shopping and opened the garage door with the remote on her car's visor. To her surprise, Randall's car was in its usual spot but with the headlights and taillights on. She got out of her car and, as she tried Randall's car door handle, she saw her husband slumped over the wheel, tightly gripping one last cigar in his lifeless right hand.

CHAPTER 49

As he let the hot water of the shower pour over him on Friday morning, Jack finally made his decision about seeking the job at CIGL. He'd share it at breakfast with Bobbie, who was packing to return to Madison.

When she came downstairs, Jack was toasting an English muffin and offered her one and a cup of coffee and some more to go.

She took out her thermos. "I'm heading back to Madison right after breakfast. I have an afternoon meeting with a client, and I need a little time to prep beforehand."

Jack poured the coffee for her. "Got a few minutes to talk?"

"Let me guess. You've decided to go after the job in Milwaukee."

He grinned. "I have. It's a great opportunity to take what I know how to do and apply it to doing something truly altruistic. Besides, being able to be a regular dad for Maya is a huge factor. A new beginning, so to speak."

"I fully support your decision. It's undeniably the right one."

"There is something else I'd like your take on," Jack began. "I've been thinking about all we've been pulled into, you and me. I know my life has turned upside down recently, but I've had great people by me who have helped me pull through the biggest mess of my life. You're at the top of the list. I care deeply about you and—"

Bobbie kissed him on the lips. She stepped back, leaving him dumbfounded.

"I'm sorry," she said. "That was for what you did to help me and my father. When we still had time."

Jack scratched his head. "Of course. It would be silly to pursue anything, wouldn't it? We live in different cities, eighty miles apart."

Bobbie's face showed her embarrassed agreement. "We could end up getting caught in one another's drama, and who knows what we'd start feeling."

Jack laughed. "We would have to draw up a relationship agreement."

"I know, right?"

She stirred the milk in her coffee. He drummed his fingers on the counter.

"I should go now," said Bobbie. "It's going to be a long drive. And I suppose I have a lot to think about."

"Me too," said Jack. "About the future."

"Yes, the future." She headed to the door and opened it. "I'll call you when I get there?"

"Ball's in your court then," he said.

"It is. Bye, for now."

Jack smiled as he watched her walk out the door.

ABOUT THE AUTHOR

Harry's passion for writing was really ignited at the University of Wisconsin where he studied journalism and wrote for the campus newspaper. After many years as a partner in a marketing firm, he formed a consultancy to focus totally on writing for business-related publications, creating marketing content and materials for both digital and print media. Coupling that passion for writing with his love of mysteries and thrillers, Harry completed his debut novel, *The Kingmaker's Redemption.*

"After so many years writing content for my clients, I finally decided to write something for myself. This novel has allowed me to creatively express my point of view through storytelling. I can't wait to get started on the next one."

Harry and his wife Jackie live in Milwaukee, Wisconsin.